WHAT DO YOU DO?

Rosebud Birdshaw Mapel

TALL ROCK PRESS

2020

Here's to John Prine.
A singular music maker and lifter of hearts and spirits.
Listening to his songs and watching videos of him dancing off the
stage after shows is sweet medicine these days and always.

ONE

What do you do when you've finally made peace with being alone, when you've settled into your solitary life and accepted that sleeping solo in the center of a bed built for two is your *forever* life, and then out of the blue you receive an invitation? An actual printed party invitation, delivered to your post office box, the forlorn mailbox you rarely check because nothing but bills and junk mail appear there anymore.

Well, if you're me, you let hope and imagination fly you away to a lovely little boutique, otherwise known as your sister's closet, and you pick out a pretty dress. A wispy floral frock that leaves your shoulders and collar bones bare and is unlike anything you normally wear.

You fret over how to do your hair. Up? Down? Half up and half down? A crucial decision you have to make before you can know which earrings will be right.

You borrow a pretty pair of strappy sandals from your other sister, check the tops of your toes for random hairs, and try your damnedest to do a decent job of painting your toenails a deep plum-rose. No slopping over the edges onto skin. No coloring outside the lines, which has been a challenge for you since you were an eager kid with crayons and coloring books.

You offer no resistance when visions of meeting a wonderful guy commandeer your mind and your anticipation bubbles up and threatens to spill over like froth from a champagne flute.

The occasion, according to the invitation and its sender, my best friend: our friendship anniversary. A confounding number of years had disappeared behind us since the day Eve Ellen Minton and I met. Years gone by so fast, my memory captured and kept almost nothing from some of them. Many days remain clear and bright in my mind. I can see them as vividly as if I'm living them again. I can hear the conversations I had or overheard. I can feel what I felt—my mood, my emotions. I can feel the weather. But I've lost some days so entirely, it's as if they never happened. Even some that I recorded in my journal now seem like they are from somebody else's life because I just don't remember them.

The morning Eve Ellen, or Evie, first entered the archive of memory movies in my head is one of the most vivid. We were both ten when her parents bought the fishing camp closest to my family's place from our elderly neighbor, Fred Pratt, who hadn't been back there since the year I turned eight. Early that June, before it was even officially summer, before my family decamped to the lake from our house in Saratoga Springs, Fred stumbled over a tree root, went down hard, and broke his hip. It was the accident my parents had feared every summer of my life, though they joked about it as "the pratfall just waiting to happen." I felt guilty about that, the joking, and guilty for being glad that new people, strangers, were moving into Fred's house. But it had been sad having it sit empty, and Eve Ellen looked to be just my age.

I was lying across a bed out on the sleeping porch, flopped belly down and propped half up on my elbows, studying a collection of rocks on the windowsill when I caught a glimpse of the Mintons through the trees, arriving in a mini caravan of shiny new jeep pulling a boat and faded old station wagon with a small trailer hitched to the back. Fred's furniture was going to stay where it was, where it had probably been in his house since the Second World War, but Evie's mother had brought a bunch of what she called "family hodgepodge" to make the place feel like their own. Old photos in rickety frames, wobbly trophies, bad paintings, craft projects her kids had done at school and in the Scouts, crocheted afghans that looked as if they'd been made with leftover yarn in every clashing color combination possible—a motley collection of things Mrs. Minton probably wanted out of their lovely and relatively small home in Albany.

As Evie went from the trailer to the house and the house to the trailer helping unload the hodgepodge, I crawled on my elbows to the head of the bed where a pair of birding binoculars hung from a nail in the knotty pine wall. From my cover on the sleeping porch, my bird blind, I peered through the binoculars, studied my new neighbor, and suspected she was going to make my life more interesting. She looked ready for adventure, from the top of the tattered Mets baseball cap on her head to the soles of the high-top sneakers on her feet.

My suspicions proved right. That first summer, it was Evie's idea to build a twig shelter down by the water and live in it until we had to leave the lake and go back to school. We lasted a week before we'd had enough of the mosquitos and moved back in with our families, but it was a thrilling week. When we were fourteen, I went to spend a couple of days with her in Albany and she masterminded our boldest ever escapade—we snuck away for a full day and pooled our money for train tickets to Manhattan, where we explored on our terms, rather than following our parents from museum to museum. We walked the streets and poked around in little shops. Antique and curio cubby holes packed with odd and enchanting and beautiful things. A magic store several floors above street level that Evie had heard about from a cousin. A pawn shop that disturbed me after Evie explained that its contents were the possessions of poor people who'd needed money and had exchanged their belongings for cash, though hopefully only temporarily. When we got hungry, we ate Korean barbecue from a food cart while we watched street performers and people-watched in general. It was the first time I'd ever been loose in the world, without adult supervision, and I still rate it one of the most magical, exciting, terrifying days of my life.

I was always the kid who plunged into adventures with equal measures of joy and terror. The kid who willingly jumped feet-first into the water from a high cliff, but flailed and screamed all the way down, "No! No! No!" Eve Ellen was just the opposite. She went in headfirst. Her plunges were a precise, tidy "Yes!" to my messy, uncertain "No!" Which was really, "No! But, yes!" She would size up a situation, a potential escapade, and if she decided the odds were too high in favor of it turning out badly, she would decline to participate. But if she thought there was a reasonable chance things might come out okay, she would dive in without any equivocation or hesitation, without holding back. Once she decided to go for it, for anything, she went all in.

That never changed, and it applied to the parties she threw, so the moment I saw her invitation, I knew this one would be no small affair. I hadn't seen it coming because she wanted to surprise me, and I couldn't have known or imagined all that would happen in its wake, but I knew Eve Ellen was going to make it a doozy.

There would be a feast of food, booze, music, dancing, and roving entertainment—one year it was a palm reader who roamed the crowd doing her thing in a hot pink caftan, matching turban, and jeweled eyeglasses so large they looked like they could use a pair of windshield wipers.

There would be people. Lots and lots of people. Entertaining was something Eve Ellen did very seldom, at varying intervals, after waiting until she'd accrued a pile of social debt going back anywhere from two to five years. She was an introvert by nature, more so than many people probably realized, but when she decided it was time to pay up for the holiday parties, sit-down dinners, and backyard cookouts she'd been to at friends' houses, she'd throw a big bash. She would concoct a theme or special occasion and invite anybody and everybody she'd laid eyes on since her last party to ensure she cleared her ledger. And all invitees would come. Once Eve Ellen decided it was time to put on her dancing shoes, everybody put them on. Never mind debts and accounting systems, the sincerity of her belief in celebration as a gratitude ritual, a dance done to acknowledge life's goodness and give thanks, was infectious and irresistible.

So I knew every neighbor on her street in Saratoga would join us in celebrating our friendship. As would her colleagues from Skidmore, where she taught future teachers. As would her husband Greg's coworkers at Saratoga's City Engineers Office. I knew she would summon all our friends and our families—siblings and cousins and their kids. Her daughter, Annie, was studying art history in France and couldn't come home, but even Annie's old babysitter would be at the party because she had become a beloved member of the family.

There would be single men, including at least one who was straight and under the age of eighty. More than one if Eve Ellen could manage it, and she would try because she had not made peace with my post-married status. She knew me well enough to know I hadn't, not really, no matter what I told myself, so she hadn't either. She understood that a person can have wonderful friends and family and still be lonely. She always saw through my fake-it-until-you-make-it happy act, never wanted or expected me to pretend I was okay when I wasn't, and knew exactly what to do to make me feel better. To feel less alone.

One day during my first holiday season on my own, she sidled up next to me at my sister Glyn's Christmas party and whispered an Edith Wharton line from *The Age of Innocence*. Tossing around quotes was my trick and she used it on me like an inside joke or a secret language we shared. Whispering, so no one else would hear her, she said, "Real loneliness is living among all these kind people who only ask one to pretend."

Then she asked me if I knew what worked almost as well as a shower for muffling a meltdown cry, and without waiting for an answer, she pulled me into Glyn's coat closet and shut the door.

"Coats can be pretty effective soundproofing," she said. "They don't hide tears like a shower will, but you can use them to wipe your eyes and nose. Just avoid the rain slickers. They're too slick and only smear everything around. You'll end up with trails that look like a herd of snails traipsed out of your nostrils and had a play date on your face. Trails are a dead giveaway that you've been blubbering, so no slickers."

She had me laughing with that but kept going, explaining that "A brushed cotton trench would be best, but a wool coat will work. Feel around for one in a soft cashmere because it'll be nicest to your nose."

Crammed in there in that closet, in the dark, we both laughed so loud, the whole party probably heard us.

Midway through my second solo summer, two years after my life as a wife came to an end, I was still working around the hole my husband left. I hadn't been able to fill it with any of the things I loved to do. I couldn't read, write, hike, bike, swim, garden, cook, or eat enough to fill the void.

"A garden can't be a husband," I told Eve Ellen. "I can take my coffee out there and sit beside a tomato vine while I read the

Sunday paper, but the tomatoes won't say a word when I read bits from interesting articles to them. They won't read any tidbits to me. They won't ask for my help with the crossword puzzle, then read the clues aloud and brainstorm with me until we come up with the right answer."

Eve Ellen said, "Who knew? Who knew a garden can't be a husband?"

Then she cooked up an occasion—our anniversary—put a stack of party invitations in the mail, and commenced planning and arranging. She booked a caterer, assembled a playlist of dance music, and hired a couple of costumed jesters adept at mimicry, magic, and mind-reading ruses to weave among and wow her guests with impressions, illusions, and sleights of hand and brain.

When the big day arrived, I put on my sister's dress, pulled my hair up into a loose bun, and dangled drops of green amethyst from my earlobes. I buckled my borrowed dancing sandals, practiced a few moves in front of the mirror, and wince-laughed at how much they looked like spasms. I was too self-conscious, but trusted a glass of wine when I got to the party would help, so one last spasm and laugh and I was out the door.

TWO

I am not a good drinker. Not in the sense that I have a past littered with embarrassing stories and mugshots. I don't. There are some lines I stay within, crossing them rarely and never going too far. It's more that I always feel beat up the day after I've had more than one glass of anything with an alcohol content greater than mouthwash. One is usually fine, two is asking for bruising blows to both head and body, three is going to be crippling and cost me at least a few hours of total dysfunction. Even though I'd switched to water from wine in plenty of time to drive home, I woke up the morning after Evie's anniversary bash feeling too awful to do more than move from my bed to the sofa, where I stayed until two that afternoon, huddled in my pajamas, replaying certain parts of the party in my head and Googling germane material on my phone.

Despite the hangover, I hadn't had so much to drink I couldn't remember everything, including two particular guys. Only one was even a long shot for more than friendship because only one lived on my side of the continent, but both were great fantasy fuel, and fantasies were at least *something*. They could be tailor-made entertainment, a temporary escape, or a placeholder for the real deal until it came along, if it came along. Yes, they could. So I would gladly take them over *nothing*. Yes, I would. I would take Tom and Pete.

Tom, the sunbaked, soap-scented biology teacher who made me hot in places the sun never sees. A man with eyes winged with squint lines and a grin that takes no prisoners. A local boy just enough older than I was that our paths never met or merged when we were kids, though we'd traveled parallel routes to and from and around the lake every summer of our lives. We swam, boated, and fished the same water.

And Pete. Head-spinning, unprecedented Pete, unlike anyone I'd ever known. A few years older than Tom, or so I guessed, but not too old to look good in a pair of Levi's and a t-shirt. Recently retired, but not yet eligible for senior discounts, not yet a codger. A friend of Greg's from California, who was traveling coast to coast on an epic road trip, singing in small clubs and coffee houses. More specifically, a former civil servant "doing Woody Harrelson doing Roger Miller" at open mic night shows across America, according to Pete's twenty-something son Hank, who was along on the trip. As I understood Hank's explanation, Pete was impersonating the actor impersonating the singer, playing guitar and fiddle, performing Roger Miller songs as Roger wrote them or with his own creative spin. At one show, he might do "King of the Road" as Roger penned it, then at the next venue change up the words and sing about being a "prince of the plains."

"*What???!!!*" That was my immediate thought, and later it was the first thing that sprang from my mind and landed in my journal when I went to write everything I could remember about Pete's roadshow, as described by Hank. I knew who Woody Harrelson was, but almost nothing about Roger Miller or his music, which was of the country variety and had enjoyed its peak popularity before I was born. I didn't know much about *any* music that might be called "country," and I'd already had the three glasses of wine I would drink that night, two glasses past my limit, so Hank could have been explaining the physics of flight or time, for all I grasped. Of course, I acted as if I were right with him, following everything he said.

All I actually knew: Pete, though he wasn't like anybody from my world, was as easy to talk with as if I'd been friends with *him* since I was ten. As easy as if we were old pals catching up, swapping stories about past capers, and confessing caper fumbles. My first impression, picked up as he and I sat at a table with several other people, had been that he was quiet, more of an observer and listener than a talker. And that turned out to be somewhat true, but he was also a great conversationalist and storyteller when he took a turn speaking, and he made me laugh harder than I had in a long time.

Tom, on the other hand, had said only enough to keep me blabbing, and nervous about it. I knew I was yammering on, but I was too tipsy and too rattled by my attraction to him to make myself stop, and every time I started to wind down naturally, he'd ask another question and keep me going. He kept that up for ten or fifteen minutes—until the dozens of conversations overlapping across the yard fell silent, Eve Ellen's voice rose, and everyone turned to where she was standing on a chair, clutching Greg's shoulder with one hand, holding a wine glass aloft with the other, and launching into a toast.

"I've been so lucky in life," she said, at which point Tom turned back to me again, for just a second, and grinned with his whole face.

"So lucky to have all of you for friends," she continued. "But I'm afraid you know I play favorites. You know I have two besties, even if you haven't met them yet. The one standing here beside me, making sure I don't fall and break my neck, my Greg. And the one standing straight ahead of me, on the other side of the pool, the one we're here to celebrate tonight, my Isla Frances Griffin."

As Evie said my name, and all eyes pivoted toward me, Tom turned back again and gestured with a dramatic flourish, with a sweep of his hand, as if presenting me to the crowd, like a game show prize to a TV audience.

I smiled, but whisper-growled between my clenched teeth, "Thank you, Evie. Thank you, Tom. Damn both of you."

After Eve Ellen finished with a funny summary of our history and an inventory of my virtues, which she had promised she wouldn't do and later blamed on "booze and love," and after the applause hushed, I tried to deliver a witty toast to her and came up short on both wit and praise.

I said something to the effect, "Actually, we're here to celebrate *us*, not me, but that's Eve Ellen for you, always making it about somebody else, stepping back and putting the other person forward. Let's hope it hasn't become such a habit she does it to you one day as a bus is going by. I know she would never intentionally shove you into harm's way, but habits can be hard to resist. Seriously, you know how amazing she is, so I'll say just that she could quit teaching future teachers tomorrow and teach everybody how to be a real friend—how to do real friendship, out here, offline, in this wild and wooly, wonderful and messed up world. I am beyond lucky to have her. Cheers to Eve Ellen."

Right away, I wished I'd done better because Evie deserved better, but I didn't have time to obsess about it. Tom turned around one last time, with that killer grin, lifted his glass high, then dipped his head low, into a bow for what was apparently another toast to me. It was a smooth move and could have come across as a little too charming, but I took it to mean he was a little drunk. When he brought his head up, he looked sheepish, and pointing at his empty glass, he said, "Don't disappear. I want to hear more, but I have to go give back some of the beer I took and squirreled away in my bladder."

No doubt about it, he was operating under the influence, but he wasn't too far gone to be just the right amount of charming and a more potent heat source than a midsummer sun in a cloudless sky. I needed a cold shower or a cool dip in the swimming pool.

Instead, I got a splash of Evie. She walked up as Tom was walking away to find a bathroom, her face plastered with an expression that was a combination of delight and self-satisfaction. She was already certain her teacher friend and I were a sure thing, if only I would cooperate.

She said, "He's really something, right?"

I answered, "Teacher Tim?"

"You have to get his name straight! It's Tom, as in Thomas," she hissed.

I'd purposely called him by the wrong name, knowing it would rile her. I loved riling Evie.

"Listen, missy, he's not going to be single for long. And for the record, he's a tenured professor, Dr. Stanek, and highly respected in his field."

"Yay for him," I said.

"He doesn't have a whiff of ego about it, I promise, and there's a lot more going on there. He's really interesting, Isla."

"Duly noted, Dr. Minton," I replied. Then to mess with her some more, I said, "But I gathered he's been divorced for years and happy to stay that way. Unattached and free as a bird."

I hadn't learned anything of the sort, but Evie narrowed her eyes, curled her upper lip, and snarled the way she always did when I called her on a bluff or any kind of bull, so I figured I must have landed close to something she suspected.

I wasn't about to tell her what I was really thinking and feeling. I'd make her stew for a little while. There was no harm in having some fun. Not to mention, I wanted to be sure it wasn't the wine making me feel the way I did. I can now say it wasn't, but I couldn't say that then.

The next day, despite the hangover, I remembered all too clearly how I'd laughed until I snorted with Pete and talked too much to Tom, clueless about how to turn our conversation around to him and his life. Recalling how I'd snort-laughed with the impersonator-singer was less painful than remembering how I'd yammered to the teacher, so I spent hours on the sofa, Googling on my phone, reading everything I could find about Roger Miller and listening to his music, with the volume turned low to spare my aching brain.

And despite the headache and a sour stomach, I soon found myself snapping my fingers and trying to sing along to the merrier tunes. Some of Roger's songs were melancholy, but many were cheery, with goofy lyrics about things like trying to roller skate in a buffalo herd, take a shower in a parakeet cage, and catch fish in a watermelon patch. The cheery songs were a fast-acting antidote for those that weren't happy, so I kept working my way through all of them until I got to the sad "Husbands and Wives." I listened to that one, then decided it was time to pull myself together and salvage some of my day.

Gingerly, to avoid jarring my head, I got up and made my way to the clawfoot tub squatting in what had once been an open-air side porch, where my grandfather gutted and cleaned his catch, and fed the fish parts he didn't want to my grandmother's cat. The porch was enclosed and converted to a bathroom when the kitchen was expanded and absorbed the space that had been the toilet closet, back when the camp had neither bathtub nor shower and a swim in the lake sufficed for bathing. With windows lining the top half of three walls, the "new" bathroom still felt open to the outdoors, which I loved, but I didn't enjoy the way the circular shower curtain tended to suck in and cling to my legs, and I really wasn't up for it that day, so I pushed the curtain aside and took a bath—a hot one, hoping it would boil away any alcohol lingering in my veins.

Soaping up, I thought about Tom and how good he'd smelled. How powerfully I'd been drawn to him, beguiled by my hormones or his pheromones or both. Then to escape another onslaught of embarrassment about how much I'd talked when I was with him, I started singing. I made up a song that stuck in my brain and kept coming back to me for days, amusing me at first and then annoying the hell out of me when it wouldn't stop. The torture went on for days until I unwittingly performed the magic trick that made it quit—I whined about it in my journal and wrote out the song's dopey words.

Dang it all
Yeah, Monkey too
Every beast in this miserable crew
They make such a racket, I can't think a thought
I can't even recall that fish I allegedly caught
At the aquarium
In the city
With my bare hands
Oh, it's such a pity
'Cause it seems that's one fish tale I'd like to tell, here in jail

Oh-oh oh-oh oh oh oh
Every day here is just too long
So listen well, my friend, to the moral of this song
Take a net next time! Take a net!
I mean, don't go fishing where it's just plain wrong
No, don't go fishing where it's just plain wrong

Dang that judge
And the jury too
They sent me back to this stinking zoo
Judge said I had to do some time, pay a price

So next time I might use my head, I might think twice
Or at least once
Before fishing
In his city
Or even wishing
To do the dumb-ass stuff I'm inclined to do, but ought not to

Oh-oh oh-oh oh oh oh
Every day here is just too long
So listen well, my friend, to the moral of this song
Take a net next time! Take a net!
I mean, don't go fishing where it's just plain wrong
No, don't go fishing where it's just plain wrong

After the boiling bath and then lukewarm soak, I felt better, other than the stupid song circling in my head, and I went out to my garden to pick some herbs for an omelet, for my late breakfast and lunch, and early dinner. I was in the middle of the picking, snipping sprigs of thyme, when my phone vibrated in my back pocket and tickled my butt. It was Evie. When I saw her name on the screen, I waited until the last moment to answer, and prepared myself to hold back anything I wasn't ready to reveal. Finally, on what I knew would be the final ring, I trusted myself to take the call and say nothing more than I wanted to say.

I said, "Speak softly and mind your manners, sister."

She replied, "That's the way you greet me the day after our anniversary, after a wonderful evening celebrating *us*? What crawled up your rear end?"

Before I could answer, she went on, "Attitude adjustment, Isla. We're going to graze leftovers and play cards. Come over."

"I don't think so," I said. "I'm still recovering."

"Recover with us, come on. Please. To thank me for last night. I want Pete and Hank to have a good time, but I'm too tired to be fun and to host by myself. If you and I each do half on the fun front, it'll be much easier for both of us."

"Easier for *you*. Easiest for me would be to stay home and go to bed early. And you aren't hosting alone. You've got Greg."

By then, I knew I would go. I did still feel bruised from drinking too much, and I couldn't give into Eve Ellen too easily, as a matter of principle and to make sure I didn't appear too eager to see her house guest again, but I did want to see Pete. Over the course of the day, as I thought about him, I realized just how much I had relaxed while we were talking and laughing together. I realized how wary and wadded up in a self-protective ball I'd been for a long time, and how I had let that go when I was with him. I was curious about why he'd had that effect on me, and I was thinking about it again when Eve Ellen made another plea for me to join them.

"Greg wants you to come too," she said. "Please, please, please. I'll drive up there and get you."

"No," I told her. "I want to have my car handy, so I can leave the second I'm ready to go, without arguing and having to drag you to the door."

THREE

I used to wonder whether things could have gone another way for my marriage, or if it was always going to end as it did. Whether I was fated to find myself starting over, trying to create a new life at an age when I had thought I would be in the middle of the one I'd made with my *forever* husband, Scott. In the first year after my divorce, if my journal entries from then are any indication, I thought about little other than how much I'd taken for granted, never thought to consider or reconsider, or chose to ignore, and how it might have made a difference if I'd done things differently.

I'd always known I wanted to get married and have a family, and just assumed I would, but it was only after the divorce that I could admit the house Scott and I built was never a place I could see kids growing up, running around, being kids. Instead of a family home, it felt like a staged model we'd created as a marketing tool for Scott, to establish an image he could use to build his professional identity.

Having a home worthy of the magazine photo spreads and interviews my architect husband sought wasn't something that ever interested me, but it was easy to ignore my reservations about our house and go along with Scott's vision because I knew how important it was to him on a personal level, as well as professionally, and I'd never had any set ideas of my own about the sort of house I wanted to have one day. I'd grown up in a homey Saratoga Victorian and my family's funky but comfy fishing camp, and I took it for granted that my adult life would be equally comfortable.

Scott grew up in a moldy house that was a steam oven in summer, a freezing meat locker in winter, and home to his hoarder parents' out-of-control collections—hubcaps found on the road and hung from the ceiling when there wasn't any more room on the walls, dead crockpots and other small appliances his father "rescued" from trashcans and meant to repair, chest-high piles of magazines his mother said would be worth something someday. The place was bad, but it was the least dilapidated of the dozen bungalows at the bungalow colony Scott's father operated before he lost the permits he needed to stay in business. He'd billed his resort as an "affordable paradise" and "paradise within reach," but it hadn't been anything close to heaven on earth for a long time. When it finally closed to paying guests, Scott's parents couldn't afford to keep it and their house in Schenectady too, so they opted to take ten-year-old Scott, their only child, to live year-round at the deserted resort. When Scott left for college, he was determined he'd never again live anywhere that couldn't be made to look nice with a little work and creativity. That included his dorm room, for which he paid extra so he wouldn't have to share with a roommate.

Sometimes, when he had me sit with him during interviews, when writers would come to the house and talk with him before writing articles about his developing career, and when we'd pose for the photographs that would accompany those stories, I felt like an actor in a play watching my own performance from the wings, or from a seat out in the audience, but I believed it was the interview process that made me feel that way, not our life, which I never questioned.

From the start of our relationship, I believed Scott and I were fated to be together and would be for the rest of our lives. I thought the evidence was undeniable. What were the chances, I reasoned, two kids who shared all the same interests and came from adjoining counties on one side of the country would land on the opposite side, on the same college campus, and meet for the first time in a class with just sixteen students? Two kids whose few differences were also ideally matched—complementary rather than conflicting, so much so they almost never had even a minor argument.

In all the years Scott and I were a couple, our worst clash came and passed quickly when we were newlyweds living in Brooklyn. We were talking about his job after work one day, having our usual drink before I started making dinner, and I asked him if he thought he'd wanted to be an architect so he could build something better than what he'd had when he was growing up. Both symbolically and literally.

Instantly angry, he said, "You think I'm that pathetic?"

Scrambling to repair the damage, I replied, "No! I just think everybody is doing some version of that. We all try to create a present and future that feel better than our past in some way. Better because they make up for things that had been bad or we just hadn't totally liked."

In a poisonous tone, he asked, "So what is it you're making up for, Isla? What?"

Stung, I stared at him and he stared at me, with his question hanging between us. Then I saw his face shift, and I thought he was going to apologize, so I started to relax. And I got stung again.

"Come on, Isla, what is it? Oh, wait—do you feel guilty about your fairytale childhood, so you want to save me from the crappy life I had as a kid? Is that what we're doing? You're trying to make up for having had it so good?"

All I could think to say was, "I'm sorry. I didn't mean to offend you."

His response: He threw the rest of his drink into the sink, set the glass down with a bang, and proceeded to leave the kitchen.

Not sure what to do, I said, "I think it's a good night to have takeout delivered. Go ahead and order whatever you want to eat. I'm going to go for a walk."

He stopped while I was talking, but kept his back to me. When I finished, he went into the bathroom and shut the door.

I'd turned angry too, about how contemptuous he'd sounded, as if I was pathetically clueless because my childhood had been great, with nice homes and untroubled parents—my high school principal father and art teacher mother. But I was even more frightened than I was mad. The ruthlessness in his voice scared me. And I was upset about hurting him. I knew he wouldn't have reacted as he did unless I'd touched on something painful. The few times he'd talked to me about the house he'd lived in as a kid, he'd made a joke out of it. I realized he probably did that to avoid the unpleasant truth, but I hadn't understood how raw he still felt about his childhood.

When I got back from the walk, he was making dinner and had one of our favorite shows, *The Wire*, cued and ready to go. Watching while we ate was something we liked to do on work nights, but doing the cooking was his way of apologizing and changing the subject. All through that meal and program, all I could focus on was how the characters and their stories depicted what I'd tried to say. Rigid with tension, I hoped Scott wasn't making the same connection.

The Wire was about the residents of a horrific housing project trying to escape its misery by dealing drugs or doing drugs or other means, lawful or unlawful. Not exactly architecture, but their own avenues out of their hell. Scott and I usually started talking about each episode as soon as the closing credits began, but we didn't talk that night and we never touched the subject of his childhood home again. When the show was over, I said I was going to bed, he followed a few minutes later, and we had our first ever makeup sex. Initiated by Scott, it left me with a confusing stew of emotions that I didn't want to think about, much less examine. I just wanted to put the whole thing behind us and move on. I was so young, so inexperienced.

After I was a little older and we were farther into our marriage, if you'd pressed me to think about whether I could know fate, or even if there is such a thing, I may have conceded that I couldn't know, but I would have added that I knew my husband loved me, I loved him, and we were so bonded, nothing was ever going to come between us. We were partners for life.

Scott and I met our first year at the University of Oregon, both of us drawn across the country by Oregon's natural beauty, which we'd discovered in photographs and films and wanted to see. We were outdoorsy. Loved hiking and camping, and swimming in creeks and lakes. We'd grown up within thirty miles of one another in upstate New York and loved the Adirondacks, but we were infatuated with the idea that the mountains in the West were the youngest in North America, and we believed the Pacific Northwest was a frontier less fully explored than most other places in the lower forty-eight states. We wanted to be frontier explorers.

Scott also wanted to study architecture at the university and run in its fabled track program. Both of which he did on a full-ride scholarship that covered everything but the extra he paid for his dorm room, using the money he'd earned working summer jobs at resorts that made his parents' place look even worse. After graduation, with letters of recommendation from two of his professors, he got a job at an architecture firm back in New York, in Manhattan. I got a job teaching at one of the city's best public schools, and we rented a basement apartment in Brooklyn before it was the hip borough. Together we planned our future. We got married and decided we wanted to be back on our native turf upstate within five years, where Scott would start his own practice, I'd get a new teaching job, we'd build a house, and make babies when the time was right.

It turned out to be just over seven years before he opened his Saratoga office, and the baby-making never worked out. We both had fertility issues. Defective eggs for me, our biggest problem. Scant, sluggish sperm for Scott, which wasn't ideal, but not the deal-breaker. We talked about fostering kids, with the hope that it might lead to adoption, but ultimately decided we'd had enough heartbreak trying to become parents, including the time we'd come close to having a son, within days, or so we thought, of bringing home a baby boy, after months of talking with a pregnant young woman on the phone, supporting her financially and emotionally, traveling to meet her, flying her to the Alabama beachfront hotel she chose for our meeting and for five days of getting to know one another. She said neutral territory would be best. That was in the middle of her second trimester. Then, close to the end of her third, shortly before her due date, she disappeared. The phone number we had for her was disconnected. Emails to her bounced back with an "undeliverable" message. Our attorney said she'd changed her mind and didn't want any more contact, so she could prepare for her son's arrival. When we learned she'd done the same thing with a previous pregnancy, we were still too heartbroken to feel much anger. We were mad, but couldn't be enraged, and there wasn't anything we could do anyway. She'd always had the right to pull the plug on the adoption, as our attorney unnecessarily reminded us. It's not like we had ever, for even a moment, forgotten or failed to fear that possibility.

Most traumatic of all, I got pregnant naturally, after we'd given up on making it happen with donor eggs, given up on adoption, and decided against fostering. We let ourselves believe the pregnancy could go full term, until it ended in a miscarriage that we should have known would come. Rather than a possibility, losing that baby was a certainty, but we let ourselves forget and we failed to fear. We'd been told my eggs couldn't produce a viable embryo, but we buried that devastating reality and believed we were going to be parents. We postponed making a doctor's appointment, telling ourselves we were just waiting until after the madness of the holidays was over, and we calculated my due date based on our desire to believe we'd conceived on a weekend getaway to a romantic Vermont inn.

Then our berry-sized baby, unviable, was expelled from my body into a toilet at a Saratoga movie theater. After we quit crying that night, we decided we'd make a different kind of life for ourselves. One that would be full and rich and good in other ways. We'd work hard to excel at our jobs and we'd play hard. We'd have a life of travel to other countries and day-trips back to the city, where we'd splurge on expensive Manhattan restaurants, attend concerts and plays, visit museums and galleries. I would write books about gardening and food, and Scott would work on qualifying for the Boston marathon.

We did make a good life, or so I'd thought. Scott's Saratoga practice grew and he snagged some high-profile projects. He ran well in marathons and made it to Boston. I polished a manuscript I'd already written, and I managed to get a literary agent with an auspicious name, given my interests—Lillian Bean. Agent Bean managed to score a publishing deal for me. The book didn't sell well, but it received encouraging reviews from the few readers that did buy it, prompting me to attempt a new project.

I was midway into the first draft of my second book, making slow but certain progress when Scott came home from work one day and told me he wanted a divorce.

"I've gotten involved with someone from my running group and I want to be with her," he said, without looking at me, without taking his eyes off the wine cork he was nervously tapping on the table between us.

I was trying to catch my balance and breathe when he added, "It's not too late for me to be a father, and I want that more than I thought. I'm sorry."

It felt like the room was suddenly spinning and airless, and I couldn't hear anything he said next, if he said anything more. The shock and pain were smothering, deafening, blinding.

Somehow, I made my way to the bathroom, shut the door, and sat on the cold marble floor, with my legs drawn to my chest, my arms wrapped around them, and my forehead pressed to my knees. I cried some, but not much. I was too stunned to put any energy into it, so my tears stopped before they really got going. After a while, I realized Scott was sitting on the other side of the door, just inches from me. I heard him sniffle and knew he was crying.

My ex-husband wasn't a bad man. I wanted to believe that, and I usually succeeded, after I got past the period a therapist, if I'd had one, might have called the anger stage of my grief. The stage when I was certain Scott was Satan's crowning achievement in the narcissism department. When I wanted to drive a garden stake through his heart, then changed my mind and decided a rusty railroad spike would be better because it would more reliably cause a lethal infection that would kill him eventually even if it turned out his chest cavity was empty and he couldn't be killed immediately by way of cardiac impalement.

It's true that he wanted what he wanted, and sometimes wasn't quick to consider how pursuing or having it, whatever *it* was, would impact anybody else, but I'd always believed he was just trying to get what he thought he had to have to feel okay, to make his life feel right, and he never meant to hurt anyone. When he told me he wanted a divorce, he sounded genuinely miserable about hurting me. I believe he was. My sister Dale disagrees. At the time, she told me, "His conscience has become as pockmarked as pumice stone and it's rubbing on his pecker's fragile skin. That's the misery you heard in his voice. It's the rub between what he wants to believe about himself, the kind of man he wants to think he is, and what he's been doing with his jogging ho."

What I didn't know that night: My husband's running pal was pregnant. It was several months before I learned he had twins on the way. I'm glad I didn't know. I don't think I would have been able to get up off the floor.

After we'd been sitting there on opposite sides of the door for a while, without talking, I broke the silence and asked, "Are you alright?" When I told Dale about that the next day, her eyes nearly shot out of her head.

She said, "*You* asked *him* if he was alright? He just ripped out all your vital organs and tossed them to the floor, and you asked him how *he* was doing?"

I can see why it looked like I'd gone into martyr mode, put myself aside to spare Scott and take care of him, but what I was really doing was buying myself some time. I wasn't ready to discuss next steps. Not yet. And I didn't want to talk about me because that would make me feel worse. So I asked about him. I'm no stranger to strategic deflection. I'm not above using questions to keep somebody's attention aimed elsewhere, which is maybe why I'd guessed Teacher Tom had been doing it with me at the anniversary party.

Scott's answer: "Screw how I feel. When you're ready to talk, we will. Until then, I'll keep my mouth shut and try to stay out of your way."

I think we sat there silently for another hour. Then I ran a bath and stayed in it until the water was cold. I don't know when Scott got up and left, but when I opened the bathroom door, he was gone. The bedroom door leading to the hall and the rest of the house was shut, and I left it that way. I crawled into our bed and laid there sleepless all night, going back and forth between feeling I was outside my body, removed from the security of its familiar cocoon, and then back in it, caged with ravenous pain that would consume me if I didn't escape. My heart raced and pounded, and adrenaline flooded through me. Again and again, I went into a panic attack and felt like I was about to be swallowed into an abyss that would be the end of everything. When I'd finally calm down and start drifting off to sleep, another attack would begin.

The next morning, Scott was sitting at the kitchen island, eating cereal, and reading something on his phone when I went downstairs. I knew I looked awful and I was glad to see he did too.

Well, in fairness to myself, "relieved" is more accurate than "glad." I didn't want to think he could blow up our world, then sleep soundly and feel fine the next morning, but I wasn't happy that he'd had a rough night.

FOUR

Divorce, it turns out, can be arranged more easily than adoption and wrapped up in less time than it can take to get pregnant with purchased eggs, if you're *ever* able to conceive that way.

Dismantling your marriage can be especially fast work when your financial affairs are uncomplicated. Ours were not that. Scott's architecture practice, which we owned jointly, had provided the bulk of our income once it got going and new projects started coming at a pretty consistent pace. After he started making money, my teaching job went from being our sole source of support to providing extra for trips and treats, and for saving toward retirement. We tried to bank half of my take-home pay every month to supplement the teacher's pension I would draw when I retired. Half of my pay, sounds good, but we often missed that mark and we were far behind where we should have been. We had nowhere near enough saved to see us through a serious emergency, much less make sure we'd have what we needed when we were old and falling apart, limb by limb and organ by organ.

Our savings were paper-thin because of how much we'd spent trying to have a baby. Because we did not live frugally. Because of our beautiful home. Our house, conceived by Scott as a showcase for his architectural mastery, was built without a single sacrifice to limit expenses—the countertops had to be stunning slabs of natural Calacatta Borghini marble, and we had stunning mortgage and credit card debt to go with them. Monthly payments so large, I'd never be able to handle them alone. Scott would have been able to cover the mortgage and credit cards if his income held steady, but he couldn't buy me out of either the practice or the house, much less both. Not without robbing a bank.

Further complicating our money matters, I had taken a break from teaching to concentrate on book number two—and to avoid being surrounded by small children every day while I tried to get used to the idea that I would never be a mother. Going back to school after my miscarriage had been tough. Every time one of my kindergarteners patted me on the arm to get my attention, or took my hand while telling me some big news from home, or scooted close and leaned against me as we sat on the floor for circle time stories and discussion, an electric current of grief coursed through my body. I couldn't wait for summer break. When the break was over, I couldn't go back. So I took a year off. I'd had Scott's blessing, but I alone own my decision to sit out that school year. Bottom line: I was unemployed. No job. No income.

We had a lot to figure out and work through. Early on in that process, as we were disentangling and separating our lives, I read an article about how midlife divorces often wreak financial ruin that's never reversed, especially for women. I'd seen how true that was for Eve Ellen's mother after Evie's father left their family when we were in high school. Some days, I'd think about that and I'd be afraid I would never fully recover, that I'd be struggling for the rest of my life. I'd see myself old and alone, sitting at my kitchen table with a pile of bills, worrying about having enough money to cover them. I'd have to remind myself about how fortunate I was, and that I was going to be okay. I'd moved to my family's camp and found a teaching job within driving distance. I had an income again and a place to live. The house at the lake, originally my maternal grandparents' fishing retreat, was passed on to me and my two sisters by our mother. It was still where we gathered as a family. It's where my sisters, Glyn and Dale, rendezvoused with their husbands and kids every chance they got, so my nieces and nephews could experience some of what their mothers and I had when we were young. But Dale immediately suggested I live there, Glyn agreed that was a great idea, and they joined forces to get the place ready. Enlisting their husbands to help, they extended the sleeping porch and finished the attic, so when they came to visit, which they stressed they would never do without an unsolicited invitation, they could stay without crowding me too much. Eve Ellen and Greg helped with the construction too, and also replaced the caulk around all the drafty windows and stockpiled enough firewood to see me through two winters. I moved to the camp and joined the crew before the work was done, which meant I saw all of them every weekend for a while, which meant my transition was less difficult than it might have been. Having them there in those first weeks was like having the proverbial wagons circle around me and guard me from the wolves of despair and other dangers lurking in the dark.

My incredible little sisters, my best friend, and their husbands came to my rescue and gave me a safe place to regroup, which is so much more than many people have when disaster strikes. And just fourteen months to the day after Scott told me he wanted to be with somebody else—in a fraction of the time we'd spent trying to have a child—our financial and legal disentanglement was seemingly complete. Other than the empty hole he left in my life, I knew I was one of the world's lucky people. I was living at the lake rent-free. Scott and I had sold our house for enough to nearly clear our credit cards, and he'd figured out a way to buy me out of the practice. Or rather, another architect had joined him in business and was buying me out in quarterly installments, after a decent down payment. With that income, I was able to take care of my share of the remaining credit card debt and start saving again, to plump up my half of what Scott and I had banked over the years. My account didn't grow dramatically overnight, but the quarterly checks had started to fatten it up.

I wasn't in a position to buy another house, and wouldn't be for a while, not without wiping out my savings and leaving zero cushion for unexpected expenses—a dead refrigerator, a busted water pipe, a broken bone and the hospital co-pay that would come with it—but I thought I might be able to rent something perfectly decent, if not perfect by Scott's standards. I floated that idea by my sisters and their reaction silenced me for a while, but it didn't kill the dreaming I was just starting to do.

Exploding in unison, they practically shouted, "Why? Why would you even think about moving?"

Dale added, "You're living the dream, Isla. You're living it here. If you move, your first stop should be a shrink's couch."

We were at the lake, sitting on the dock, dangling our feet in the water, and drinking iced tea, which was dressed up with Irish whiskey because Dale had pulled a bottle out of her bag and said, "Look! I found this brand-ass-spanking-new Bushmills in my car on the drive up. Let's make this tea worth talking about." Then when Glyn and I looked at her with arched eyebrows that said, "It's only noon, what's wrong with you?" she added, "You know it has to be a gift from the gods, that's the only explanation. We don't want to piss them off by refusing their gift, do we?" And Glyn, always our voice of reason, replied, "Good point. Get that bottle open." The spiked tea made what was already an idyllic day feel even more blissful, so I could see why my sisters' would think what they thought, but they didn't change my mind. I wanted my future to begin and I wanted it to look different than my present. I didn't want my family to see me as somebody they had to take care of, a problem they had to solve, and I didn't want the solution they'd created for me at the camp to be anything more than temporary. My thinking and clarity hadn't gotten much farther than that, so I dropped the subject and didn't try to explain to Glyn and Dale why I wanted to move. I didn't tell them, or anybody, about how I would take drives to neighborhoods or areas where I thought I could afford a decent rental and still save some of my paycheck every month. How I would try to see myself in those places and I'd do the math. I'd imagine finding a little cottage and furnishing it sparely, so it felt airy and peaceful. I'd picture myself putting in a new garden behind or beside or in front of my little house, anywhere sunny that a vegetable bed, or two, would fit.

Hopefully, I wouldn't be alone for the rest of my life, but if I was, I wanted it to be a tasty life I created. I didn't try to explain that to my sisters, and I didn't bring up leaving the lake again until I was past the dreaming stage.

FIVE

In Eve Ellen and Greg's driveway, I pulled up behind a car that could only be Pete's—an immaculately restored station wagon from, I estimated, the 1950s or 60s. Glossy red and white, with California license plates in frames that said, "Music makes my world go around," it looked like a cartoon car to me, something the Jetsons would drive if they didn't live in space and jet around in a space vehicle. Crisp lines and sharp corners made it look as if it had been designed for aerodynamic flight, and picturing Pete and Hank driving it between California and New York, across the wide-open spaces of the Midwest, made me laugh as I nosed up to the gleaming bumper.

"Hey ho, anybody home? I think the Jetsons left a car in your driveway," I called out, after letting myself into the house.

"Not so loud, please," Eve Ellen called back. "We have headaches in here."

She didn't sound like she was suffering, and when I reached the kitchen, she and the three guys looked like they could do the party all over again. Pete stood up, like an old school gentleman.

Greg said, "Forgive me for not budging, but it's too late for me to learn new niceties." Then he looked over at Hank for backup. Hank lifted his hands, palms up, and shrugged his shoulders as if to say, "What can we do? We are what we are."

Pete whacked his son on the chest with the back of his hand.

"Hey, careful with your picking paw, guitar man," Hank said, as he rubbed the spot his dad's knuckles had touched so lightly, you could have called the whack a love tap. "Be easy on the hands, you have a show tomorrow."

Eve Ellen crowed, "Yeehaw! I'm so looking forward to it!"

"Me too," Greg grumbled, "but right now I'm hungry, so let the grazing begin."

As Greg got up and started setting the table, Evie started emptying the fridge, pulling out platters of crab cakes and sliced prime rib, cold corn on the cob and myriad other side dishes. So much food it covered the kitchen's big island. It was my job to make everything fit on the island, and it wasn't easy.

"This isn't leftovers," I said, "it's another party. Did anybody eat last night?"

"Like locusts," Greg replied. Then he chimed, "Ding, ding, ding goes the dinner bell. Let's dig in."

I wasn't sure my stomach was ready, and I was nervous about finding out, but once we'd filled our plates and sat down at the table, I forgot about that. We started talking about the party, about the jesters' antics, the conversations we'd had, and people we'd met as we drifted around Evie and Greg's sprawling backyard. Greg had bunched some tables and chairs around the perimeter of the lawn, but many people stayed on their feet and kept moving, going from one acquaintance to another to catch up.

Our fresh memories sparked old ones about past parties, which sparked memories about other things. Over dinner, and then umpteen hands of Hearts, I got to learn more about Pete. He and Greg reminisced about being in the Navy, stationed in San Diego, where they met. They told stories about how they'd flaunt the rules when they were on duty, how they'd body surf in the ocean on their days off, and drink down in Tijuana, where they could afford to eat lobster and gulp margaritas until their eyeballs floated in their heads.

As they talked, they bounced off each other, taking turns doing the storytelling. When they finished a funny story about their last night partying together, at the end of Greg's active duty, I wanted to casually ask Pete a few questions and try to fill out some of what I'd heard about him from Eve Ellen. I knew from Evie that he had stayed in San Diego after he left the Navy, married his surfer girlfriend, had two daughters and then Hank, took early retirement to care for his wife while she was battling breast cancer and then lost her.

I started by asking Pete if he'd joined the Navy, like Greg had, to help pay for college, or for "more noble, patriotic reasons."

"No college for me," he said, laughing. Then he explained that he'd always wanted to work on airplanes and helicopters, tinker with their engines, and understand how they worked, so he joined up to get tuition-free training and experience.

"After six years," he said, "I left the Navy, but stayed on at the base, on Coronado Island, and kept working for Uncle Sam, maintaining his helicopters."

"Did you become a pilot too?" I asked.

"The military brass never saw fit to put me at the controls of anything that was going to leave the ground, but I did take private lessons and got my license," he replied.

"Do you still fly?"

"No, not for years."

I practically yelped, "Why?" As if there couldn't possibly be any good reason he'd stop doing something so cool, something he must have loved.

He smiled, but I could see sadness in his eyes when he said, "My wife didn't fly."

I felt awful and didn't know what to say. It was probably just a second or two, but felt longer before Greg came to the rescue.

"Lainie was strictly land and sea," Greg said. "She was famous for punching a shark after it took a bite out of her surfboard. She popped it on the nose so hard it decided to go elsewhere for lunch. And I once saw her charge across yards of blistering-hot sand and into a riptide to save a guy nobody else had noticed was drowning. But she didn't do planes or any mode of air travel. She didn't want any distance between her and planet Earth."

Pete picked up from there. He said, "So I became an avid road tripper. We drove to Texas almost every year to see my family, and the years we didn't do that, we went down into Mexico in search of undiscovered beach towns."

Without directly mentioning his wife or her death, he explained, "Once I became an aimless retiree with time to fill, I thought about flying again, but decided I'd rather try some things

I'd thought about doing but hadn't gotten around to when fatherhood officially ended my youth and curtailed my free time."

As he said that last part, he flashed a wry smile and nodded his head in Hank's direction.

Hank said, "And among those other things was taking his Woody-Roger act on the road."

Pete lifted his hand as if he were going to whack his son again, but then just wagged a warning finger at him.

"Speaking of the Woody-Roger show," Eve Ellen interjected, "what time tomorrow?"

"First," Pete said, "I'm not doing Woody. I'm doing me paying heartfelt homage to Roger. And hopefully giving a few people a little something to smile about. I've taken love and joy on the road to spread them where I might."

With that, he faux-smacked the back of Hank's head, and Hank bobbled like a dashboard figurine.

"Second, Miss Eve Ellen," Pete continued, "that's a very good question—about showtime tomorrow. I'll check with my crew and get back to you." Then, turning to Hank, he asked, "What time do we go on tomorrow night?"

"There's no *we* here," Hank replied. "It's all you, Pops."

Pete made a flicking motion in his son's direction, as if to flick him away, then answered Evie's question.

"Sign up is at seven and the show starts at seven-thirty. My ten minutes at the mic are whenever I get a spot on the list, if I get one. This is the legendary Caffe Lena, after all, where Bob Dylan played back before he became a legend. I might be dreaming the impossible dream."

"You're going to get a spot," Eve Ellen said. "We can walk there from here in five minutes. Let's go early and have dinner someplace nearby, so we don't dawdle around this table and can make sure you're the first in line."

"Sounds good to me," Pete said.

"How about you, Isla Frances?" she asked, using both my first and middle names, as my mother always had when we were among non-family and she wanted me to do something but didn't want to give me a direct order, lest she look harsh.

"Sounds great," I said, as I kicked Eve Ellen's leg under the table for her double foul. And kicked her again, lest she think she'd gotten off easy.

Foul number one: Evie knows I don't like "Frances," my legacy from my father's mother, who was happy once upon a time, according to my own mother, but in my experience could be pleasant and judgment-free only on days the wind blew magic fairy dust in her direction. Nana Frances, or Granny Franny, as my sisters and I called her when we were trying to get her to lighten up, was a woman who freely shared her thoughts about anything she considered a flaw in anyone passing through her line of vision. If she thought somebody was packing an extra pound or two, she'd say, "He's not missing any meals" or "She's certainly well-fed." When Glyn was twelve or thirteen and dealing with the usual adolescent angst, in no need of any extra, Granny Franny told her, "That curly hair of yours is unfortunate, but there are worse things. You just need to work at taming it down."

I wanted to grab a handful of her starched bob and yank so hard she'd bite her tongue. I kept my hands to myself, but I said, "Don't listen to her, Glynnie, she's gone senile. You won the Triple Crown—you have a glorious mane I'd take in a hot second, a brain so brilliant I could only wish I had one half as good, and a great heart, unlike some members of our family."

My mom, who was her mother-in-law's biggest defender, thought I went too far with the heart part. She apparently had no problem with my "senile" jab, but said, "That's enough, Isla. You should have stopped with Glyn's wonderful brain. The rest was excessive."

I told her, "My Triple Crown metaphor wouldn't work with just *two* things. As a life-long thoroughbred racing enthusiast, you should know that."

She laughed before she could catch herself. Granny Franny fumed. I stayed huffy but started to feel guilty too. Our usual family dynamic.

Foul number two by dear Evie: She put me on the spot in front of Pete, leaving me with no way to wiggle out of her plan for the following night. I didn't want to wiggle out, but that was beside the point.

When I knew I had just enough steam left to make the drive home, I waved off Greg, who was about to deal another hand of cards, and I said, "It's going to look like I'm a sore loser and leaving because I've lost every round, but I'm ready for bed."

Pete said, "I have the low score, Isla, and I'm not ashamed to say I'm ready to hit the sack too, so I can cry into my pillow about my poor performance."

Hank said, "It's your performance tomorrow that matters, but I wish we'd been playing for money tonight."

I laughed, said my goodbyes, and headed for the door. As I was going, I heard Pete say, "Gloating is lowly business, son. Even if you don't care what Isla thinks about you, how about you don't make her think I've raised a cretin."

I thought, "Cretin. Good word."

SIX

"Don't think I've forgotten about Tom," Eve Ellen said, as she walked me out to my car.

My mind shouted, "Danger! Danger!" I knew Evie was up to something. I didn't know what she was planning, but I knew she had something in the works.

"What are you doing, Evie?" I asked her. "What have you already done?"

"I'm going to ask him to join us for dinner and Pete's show tomorrow."

I stopped, and I barked, "Evie!"

She put an arm around my shoulders and said, "Trust me, Isla. It'll be much more natural to get you two together again now, with Pete and Hank there. It's going to be a group outing, rather than a setup. Everything's going to be fine."

I have no doubt she meant that, believed it, wanted it to be true. And I did loosen up a little. But it didn't last.

I was outside watering the next morning when my phone rang. It was Tom. He'd just heard from Eve Ellen, with her invitation to join us for dinner and Pete's show, and he'd asked her for my phone number, so he could ask me if I wanted to drive down together. He told me he was staying at his place on the lake all week and could swing by to pick me up, then bring me back.

"You'll have a designated driver to get you home safely," he said. "So you can drink with abandon."

The gears in my head flew into action, but not fast enough to come up with a response before he noticed my hesitation and added, "Unless you need to have your tonight."

Choosing the safest words I could come up with under pressure, I told him "No drinking for me, but I'd love a lift."

Then, of course, I was a wreck.

I tried to distract myself with chores, but my damn gears raced so fast I could almost hear them spinning and smell them smoking. I feared another round of Tom's questions and worried about my inability to stop talking when I was under his spell. I told myself to calm the hell down, but my mind careened on until I slumped onto the sofa and fell asleep.

Luckily, when I woke up, I didn't have time to pick up where I'd left off with my nervous breakdown. I had to shower and dress. I had twenty-six minutes, says my journal entry from that night. No time to second-guess the white t-shirt and jeans I put on. The jeans I called my "pity party pants" because I'd embroidered one leg from thigh to calf over the course of my first winter alone at the lake, when I was at the height of feeling sorry for myself and angry at Scott. I couldn't concentrate on reading that winter, and the only videos that weren't too jarring were Bob Ross's hypnotic painting tutorials, so I would put on one of those for background sound and work on covering the left leg of the pants with a crazy jungle—tangled vines hanging heavy with things that grow in gardens and things that do not. Along with ripe red tomatoes and purple morning glories, I stitched forks and spoons with pale gray thread close to the color of scuffed sterling silver. Dangling like pea pods, half-hidden amongst verdant green leaves and curling tendrils, the silverware was my attempt to amuse and cheer myself. And it worked, to a certain degree. The vines were all I meant to put on the pants, but I after I finished the forks and spoons, I kept going and gave the garden a bunch of Black-eyed Susans, two blackbirds, a monarch butterfly, and two dragonflies.

When I heard the crunch of car wheels on my gravel driveway announce Tom's arrival, I was spritzing my hair with orange blossom perfume. One more squirt and I was ready to go. And I actually felt good. Sleep and the fragrance of any citrus flower will do that for me. I suffered a quick prick of anxiety when Tom knocked on the door, but just a little one.

"Hey there," I said, through the screen door. Then, as I pushed the door open, "How are you? Ready to hear some music?"

Blinking several times, after a quick but unmistakable glance at my body, Tom said, "I'm great. Looking forward to this. A guy doing Woody Harrelson doing Roger Miller has to be something to see, right?"

I felt another prick of anxiety and wished I'd worn something less form-fitting, but I put on a bright smile, stepped out onto the porch, and replied, "I think we're about to find out."

"Great to see you," Tom said, leaning forward to kiss me on the cheek. Then, maybe joking or maybe not, he quickly added, "Wait, was that bad, a Me Too no-no? Should I take it back?"

Call me a bad feminist, regressive, weak or whatever, but I wasn't bothered by the kiss and thought he was funny, whether he intended to be or not, so I laughed, and said, "No. Not a no-no. Let's go-go." Then I desperately hoped the cute humor worked better than it sounded to me once it was out of my mouth and I couldn't reel it back in.

In the car, Tom started up with the questions again, but I was able to ask some too. Enough to get the general outline of his biography and a few interesting details, including the fascinating fact that he'd been a Benedictine monk and spent six years in a monastery. An actual monk. He came from a devout Catholic clan, but his father, far from pleased with his son's religious calling, was devastated that Tom wouldn't pass on the Stanek name to a new generation. Tom felt bad for his dad, but certain the monk's life was his destiny, until he realized it wasn't. When he left the monastery, he took the clothes he was wearing, a small box of books, and a knack for beekeeping.

I was so fascinated, I plowed ahead, even as I feared I was getting too personal. I asked, "What made you realize it wasn't for you after all?"

"Well," he started, then stopped.

Mortified, thinking I'd made the same mistake with Tom that I'd made with Pete when I asked him about flying and blundered too close to the painful subject of his wife, I said, "I'm sorry if that was inappropriate. Too personal."

"You're fine. It's a fair question," he replied, sounding friendly, but also guarded.

"Thank you, but I take it back anyway," I said. "Rewind."

"The truth," he said, as a grin spread across his face, "or part of the truth is that I didn't feel any longing to add to my family line, but I didn't want to give up the deed that sometimes leads to kids. There were other reasons I left, but I'd be lying if I didn't confess that a big part of my decision was the celibacy. Permanently cut off from women just didn't feel like the way I was supposed to live my life. It seemed like being half alive."

I hadn't told him about my attempts and failure to have a baby, and hoped he hadn't noticed my wince when he said "family line." To be safe, I forced a fast, wide-eyed smile. One that I meant to come across as fake shock masking sly understanding about not wanting to give up sex. I was trying to be amusing, but Tom responded with a smile that surprised me with its wistfulness. I didn't know what to make of it, or how to rearrange my face in response, so I turned to look at the road and said, "Oh, life. It's something, isn't it?"

I had told him some of my divorce story when we were at Evie's party, but he pulled more out of me on the drive to Saratoga, and I learned that he'd been married for ten years, produced two Stanek sons, much to his father's joy, and had a good relationship with his ex-wife.

"How about you and your husband," he asked. "Is there any friendship left?"

"Not really," I said. "We wouldn't stab each other with our forks if we found ourselves seated at the same table at a wedding reception, but we're not pals. No friending for us, real or virtual."

He nodded, but didn't say anything or ask another question. That threw me, and rattled my nerves, given that it broke the pattern I'd gotten used to with him. So, naturally, I started talking again to fill the silence. I told him about how I'd read that some people who've been through something traumatic together form a tight bond and become very close, while others go the opposite direction and avoid all contact with one another to avoid remembering their experience. I blabbed on and on about how I'd read that many Vietnam vets, after they came home, tried to forget the horrors of combat by having nothing to do with guys who had been their closest friends during the war, guys they'd thought of as brothers and whose safety they'd put before their own. I said, "Maybe my husband and I have a minor case of that."

It would have been a bad analogy even if Tom had known what Scott and I had been through trying to have kids, but without knowing about that, he must have thought I was cracked.

"Maybe," was all he said. And again, no follow up questions.

So onward I went, burning down any dignity I may have had left. I told him, "I have a tendency toward over-the-top analogies and bad metaphors. I'm queen when it comes to those, just ask my editor. Or my family. My husband and I don't have any ill will toward one another. I got past my homicidal hate. I was a very angry ex during that dark phase, but it didn't last long and I'm proud to report I was over it before I went as far as acquiring the stake or spike I was going to drive through his heart. Now, I think we both sincerely wish the best for one another in our new lives, which are very different. He's passed his last name on to twin daughters and is dealing with sleep deprivation and bodily emissions from points north and south, or so I've heard from other people, and I'm focused on perfecting my enchilada recipe. So we don't have much spare time or common ground anymore. Otherwise, if not for the parenting and enchiladas, we might be the best of old buddies."

Damn me! I'm beyond hopeless. Silently, I snapped at myself, "Grow up, calm down, and get a grip. You're not fifteen."

Tom finally spoke again and said, "Poop, pee, spit up, and tortillas wrapped around some sort of meat or cheese. Thank you for that. It's quite a combo plate. Now if I could just power-wash my mind."

"You forgot snot," I told him. "Poop, pee, spit up, and snot. And my enchilada filling tends toward squash and things I grow in my garden. Vegetarian, though I tend toward omnivore feeding in my eating habits."

SEVEN

Eve Ellen and the guys were already seated when Tom and I arrived at the restaurant. Pete elbowed Hank and together they stood up. Greg stayed in his chair and made a show of lazily waving his napkin in our direction, welcoming us with the enthusiasm of a kid forced to greet boring old relatives.

"Glad to see you too, Greg," I said as I blew him a kiss.

Taking a seat next to Evie, I scanned the table, and it suddenly struck me that Pete, Hank, and Tom were still strangers to me. I'd spent a fair amount of the last forty-eight hours with them, or thinking about them, but I didn't know them.

Another way to put that: The fresh hope and frothing anticipation that filled my head the moment I opened Evie's party invitation evaporated in an instant. Poof. Gone. For that evening anyway, I was back in my right mind, relating to Pete and Tom as any sane person would relate to new acquaintances, rather than seeing them as, say, two reasons I might want to assess the situation in my lingerie drawer and replace any sad panties and shabby bras I should have retired already. The sanity didn't last, but it gave me a brief break.

Thanks to Tom's penchant for interrogation, and Pete's tendency to treat conversations like verbal potlucks, encouraging and enjoying contributions from everybody, I gleaned a fair amount from our dinner table talk. But I took it all in without trying to compute what it might mean to my love quest, my mission to find a new partner.

I was formally introduced to Pete's guitar and fiddle, which were named Dog and Cat. They were there with him in the restaurant, in battered cases, standing up in a chair pulled close to the table, the only place they'd be out of the waitstaff's way. I didn't get the story on their names, but learned that Pete got both instruments when he was a boy, and he'd learned to play the fiddle first, from an uncle in Texas, then taught himself to play guitar because he thought it was "more rock and roll." He said, "Music and flying machines were always my twin loves."

I learned that Tom, like many guys before and after him, had tried to master bass guitar when he was a kid, to impress girls, but found his hands were "like baseball mitts" and he had "tin cups for ears." Before the bass, he'd been only slightly more successful with accordion lessons, taking them to please his father, who played in a polka band and transformed from "a reserved accountant to a jolly squeeze box jockey" when he performed at dances. Tom hadn't inherited his father's music genes, and couldn't play or sing, though he could do a tolerable job with the daily chanting when he was in the monastery. Well enough that none of his Benedictine brothers had used their turn at kitchen duty to poison his food. "Probably," he said, "because they liked it when I took my turn at the stove. My specialty was cod with a white wine sauce. They loved that, but I also made a mean corn chowder they practically licked from their bowls. I think it made them more forgiving with me."

About Hank, I learned he was a grill master. According to his father, he made the humble hamburger a life-changing experience and smoked a great beef brisket. He could also play almost any musical instrument and often played with Pete at home, and with friends, but he wouldn't perform in clubs or any public venue for any amount of money, applause, or premium tequila.

I even discovered that Greg, who was far from a stranger to me, had been known for his way with a harmonica when he was in the military, and I heard about the "speaker-phone jams" he and Pete used to do. "They started," Greg said, "when I called Pete one night about seven or eight years ago. He picked up and said, 'Hello,' and I began blowing my harp, playing some song we used to do when we were Navy swabs. Without missing a beat, he joined in and sang the lyrics, but when we finished the song, he said, 'Who is this?' I didn't want to give him the laugh he was looking for, so I launched into another tune, and he joined in again. Then we did two more songs before we exchanged one word of regular conversation."

Later, I learned from Evie that once Greg found out Pete's wife had cancer, he'd call and give Pete an outlet when he wanted to talk about Lainie, and an escape when he wanted to talk or think about anything else. When he wanted an escape, he and Greg would sometimes play music together on video calls, in what they called, "The FaceTime Sessions." Pete provided guitar and vocals, Greg played his harmonica. Then Lainie died and the music sessions stopped.

I'd vaguely registered that Greg and Evie had flown to California for a funeral right after I learned about Scott's babies, but I hadn't asked about more than who had died, so I knew only that it was the Navy pal's wife. I'd heard about Pete over the years, but I hadn't met him. I knew he and Greg tried to meet up at a music festival in Texas every year, and he'd gotten Greg and Evie to go to Mexico with him and his family a couple of times, but he'd remained an abstraction to me. The idea of a friend, rather than a real person. Sitting across from him in the restaurant, near the end of our meal, I started piecing together what I'd gathered about him, before and since Eve Ellen's party, and I probably looked lost in thought.

"Yoohoo, Isla Frances," Evie said. "Time to go get Pete his spot on that list."

As she predicted, Pete did get to play at Caffe Lena. We didn't get there in time to put him first in line, but we arrived early enough, and he signed up for his ten minutes. Until it was his turn, we all sat together and watched the people who performed before him, starting with a young woman on guitar, who did two songs, shifting between singing the lyrics and speaking them. I was still trying to settle into her style, trying to figure out how to go with it, when she finished her set. She was followed by a guy who made his mandolin sing on an extended instrumental number that sounded to me like a beautiful hillbilly opera, with slow and moody parts, lively and climactic passages, and a big dramatic ending. Then right before Pete, there was a young woman who sang so hypnotically, I couldn't say whether she strummed a single chord on the guitar she was holding. Her songs sounded like old folk ballads but could have been original compositions, for all I knew. Whatever they were, I thought it was going to be rough trying to follow her. I looked over at Pete and he was smiling, and shaking his head, as if to say, "I can't be expected to follow that! No way!" But I couldn't tell whether he was truly worried because he also looked delighted by the music. His eyes were lit up and a smile stretched across his face.

When he took the stage for his own set, long and lean Pete adjusted the microphone, raising it to accommodate the fact that he was much taller than the woman with the hypnotic voice. As the mic went up and up, the adjustment became a comical contrast between him and the young woman, and she was once again the center of attention, though she was no longer anywhere in sight. The audience laughed and Pete shook his head. When he had the mic where he wanted it, he looked up and out at the crowd, rubbed his chin, and said, "Dang me. She was good. Really good." And the audience laughed even harder, acknowledging the challenge he faced and sympathizing with him.

"Well, here we go, with all I got," he said, as he started picking out a line on the guitar.

Within a few notes, I somehow remembered "Dang Me" was the name of a Roger Miller song I'd listened to the morning after Evie's party, when I was hungover and sacked out on the sofa, and I knew it was the song Pete was going to play. I felt clever for being a step ahead of the audience, or thinking I was a step ahead.

Pausing on the guitar, Pete said, "The entire entirety of what I'm about to do is dedicated to my son. He's come nearly three thousand miles with me so I could be on this stage tonight."

Then he went back to the song, starting with the chorus, which started with "Dang me" sung twice, and he drew another round of laughs. When he got to the song's first verse and sang about living like a fool, the audience howled and nearly lifted the roof.

I thought Pete sang well, and I liked that his voice sounded lived-in and natural, with no performance frills or affectations, but his comedic timing and delivery were perfection personified. I'd watched only a few brief video clips of Roger, and had mostly listened to his songs without seeing him perform them, so I couldn't say whether Pete was mimicking Roger's physical mannerisms, but he was hilarious. Not slapstick funny or farcical—more subtle than that. Wry, but not mocking or ironic. Somehow, he was both hilariously droll and sincerely sweet.

I tried to see what Hank meant about Woody Harrelson, and thought Woody and Pete might look a tiny bit alike if you gave Woody a full head of hair and crossed your eyes when you looked at him. But even then, you'd have to really work your imagination. I decided I could more easily detect something Woody in Pete's laid-back nature and what was left of his slow Texas drawl, which came through even when he was revved up.

From the videos I'd watched, I'd say Roger Miller spun at a higher speed than both Woody and Pete, but Pete could get going too, and he did rev up that night. He finished "Dang Me" with a ripping stream of countrified scat singing—a rush of nonsense syllables and goofy vocal effects. From there, he went right into a speedy version of Roger's "Chug-a-Lug," with modified lyrics. Replacing "mason jar" of "homemade wine" with a "fat joint" of "homegrown weed," and changing "chug-a-lug" to "huff-n-puff," he barreled through the verses and into famously weed-loving Woody territory. I thought, "Ah, that's it. There's the Woody." But Hank, after laughing along with everybody in the room, leaned over and whispered in my ear, "He's never done it that way. As a weed song. He's messing with me."

For his last number, which he didn't introduce, Pete quickly swapped his guitar for the fiddle and did an instrumental that was also fast and humorous, but poignant too. The best way I can describe it would be to say imagine a movie in which two people say goodbye, one drives away in a car with the other running alongside at first, laughing and waving, then when the car moves ahead and the running guy has to run faster but just can't keep up, the amusement on his face fades to something moving and tender. The humor is still there, but also heartache.

At the end of his fiddle song, which came suddenly, before its energy and speed faded, Pete called out, "Here's to Roger Miller! Thank you very much!" And he practically sprinted off the stage, fiddle and bow in one hand, and his guitar in the other, while the audience applauded and again nearly blew the roof off the room. Hank, Eve Ellen, Tom, and I were the last to quit clapping. Greg cackled and slapped his leg. I think we were all amazed by Pete's performance. And it stayed with us for the rest of the evening. It stayed with me, anyway. We watched everybody who played after Pete, but his turn at the mic was still reverberating in my head when we bid our goodbyes and headed home.

"What a night," I said to Tom, as we walked to his car.

To myself, I said, "What an intriguing guy Pete is," and I made a mental note to circle back later and come up with the right word to replace "intriguing."

What was Pete? Weird? Cool? Fearless? Demented? I mean, who besides a weird, or possibly cool eccentric, a fearless kid, or a demented person decides to drive across the country, hoping, with no guarantees, to snag a few minutes on stages here and there to play two or three songs for audiences that may or may not find worth in their goofy wit and poignant emotion? Who does a trip like that in an ancient car? Yes, Pete's station wagon had been restored, but it was so old and heavily modified to operate as a hybrid electric vehicle, if anything went wrong, getting replacement parts would likely involve more than a run to a standard auto supply store. It could take days to get what Pete needed to make repairs. Who risks that? Who dreams up something like the Woody-Roger road trip and goes for it?

EIGHT

The drive back to the lake brought no new embarrassment. Tom didn't grill me and our conversation, an easy back and forth, stuck to music. We talked about our past and current favorites, concerts we'd been to and loved. I learned that he listened to avant-garde jazz more than anything else, but also had a thing for Bach. He learned that I had listened to classic rock and roll until I picked up my parents' love of Big Band music and Swing Era jazz, which had been their parents' beloved music. I told him I liked to listen to Ella Fitzgerald when I cooked, and pulled out my phone to play an Ella song for him, at his request, then Googled a song he wanted me to hear.

I didn't tell him that cooking to my parents' Ella records was something I'd started after my divorce, to feel less alone while I made dinner. I also didn't tell him his favorite kind of jazz was my least favorite because it left me feeling a little cold. It was cerebral music and appealed to your head, versus aiming somewhere farther south, below your shoulders. It was cool, and I liked mine steamy. Or danceable.

Maybe because the night was warm, Tom's car was comfortable, and I got sleepier with every mile, I'd calmed down so much it didn't occur to me to wonder or worry about whether he would want to kiss me goodnight or come inside for more than a kiss. It didn't cross my mind until I was climbing the porch steps, with him on my heels, following me to the door. Then I had a minor flurry of fraught thoughts. Will he go for my lips instead of

45

my cheek this time? How's my breath? Do I want to kiss him? Do I want to ask him inside?

I'd forgotten to turn on the porch light before we left, so it was dark, and I had to fumble to find my keys and fumble some more to get the door unlocked. While I rooted in my bag, then groped for the keyhole, Tom held the screen door open for me, but when I finally stepped into the house, he made no move to follow. I flipped on the porch light and he flipped up his hand, in a wave that didn't wave. It looked more like he was about to take an oath of honesty before testifying in court. He said he'd had a great time, thanked me, and shut the screen door between us.

There would be no kiss, and I realized I was glad about that. I was glad to let go of the worrying and relax.

All in all, it was an easy end to the evening. I said goodbye, floated off to wash my face and brush my teeth, then got into bed and fell asleep within minutes.

The next thing I knew, it was morning and my phone was ringing—the landline that had been on the kitchen wall and had had the same phone number since I was a kid. Nobody called it anymore, not since cell reception at the camp improved to fairly reliable, but it was jangling away. I practically ran to the kitchen, simultaneously hoping I wasn't running for nothing, to catch a call to the wrong number, and hoping I was indeed running for a faulty dial, because why would anybody ring so early except to deliver bad news?

It was Eve Ellen. Ringing to tell me Tom had called her. He'd just found my cell phone in his car, but he was half-way back to Saratoga to pick up some things, and from there he had to go to Albany to catch a flight to Florida, so he asked her if he could drop my phone at her place.

"He said to say he was sorry he didn't find it in time to take it to you," Evie told me, "but I have a great plan. How about I bring it up there? How about I come with the guys? We could all go for a swim and hang out for a while."

I thought, "Oh no, here we go again." But I was excited. Nervously, dizzily excited. What was happening to my quiet life? To my cloistered existence? After school had let out for the summer, I regularly went days without seeing a soul. I may as well have been the only person living on the lake. Evie's parents sold their camp when they divorced and the people that bought it still owned it but rarely appeared anymore. The house, barely visible through the trees, which had grown denser over the years, was the only human habitat in sight. My next closest neighbors were on the other side of the Minton's camp, and I couldn't see their place from mine.

Evie said, "We'll bring food, so you won't have to do a thing."

I said, "No, don't do that. I'll make something. Or we can put Hank on the barbecue. I have chicken I can take out to thaw now. If he wants to do burgers or brisket, you'll have to stop at a store for the beef and buns."

"Yay! Beef, buns, and we'll be on our way to you by noon."

"Oh boy," I gasped, as I hung up the phone.

But once again, all was well and my worry was for nothing. Hank grilled burgers and I pulled together some sides—a carrot and red cabbage coleslaw, a lettuce and tomato salad, and a pot of baked beans, which were a hit, even though I took a shortcut involving a can opener. If you add bacon, a little brown sugar, and a few caramelized onions to a can of anything, it's going to make people happy.

We played horseshoes, swam, switched from iced tea to beer, built a fire in the fire pit when dusk started creeping up, though it was still hot, and we made popcorn in my long-handled popper pan to go with the beer. Then we made honest-to-god s'mores because that's what you do with a campfire.

"The only thing missing is some music," I said. "If only *someone* had thought to bring a guitar and fiddle."

Pete turned to Hank and said, "I'm docking your pay."

Hank said, "If you paid me, I might have thought to load up Dog and Cat. But what about that harp in your pocket? How about you play us something on that?"

"For classic campfire music it has to be a guitar," Pete replied.

"That is *so* not true," Hank said.

"Come on, Pete," I pleaded. Then I started chanting, "Music. Music. Music." Eve Ellen and Hank joined me.

Greg smiled like we were all nuts, and Pete asked him, "You have something to play?"

"Nope. Left mine at home," Greg answered.

So Pete played alone, taking our requests, which varied hugely, but never stumped him. Not that we didn't try to stump him. When I asked him to play "Moon River," he pretended he didn't remember it.

"I think you may have got me with that one," he said.

"I know you know it," I persisted. "Audrey Hepburn? Breakfast at Tiffany's?"

"It sounds like it might be in Hank's area of expertise, what with his love of bygone TV shows and movies, but sing a few lines and maybe it'll come to me," Pete said.

"Nice try, but no."

"Just sing a few bars to jolt my memory."

Instead, I hummed the start, then said, "Now play for your supper!" And he played such an achingly lovely "Moon River," it was obvious he knew it well.

After the fire burned down to ashes and Pete said he had no more breath, we all went up to the house, and I served a late-night spread of grilled cheese and tomato sandwiches, with a virtual garden of my homemade pickled preserves—baby cucumbers, garlicky green beans, smoky red peppers, spicy cauliflower, and tangy beet relish. I debated bringing out my emergency bag of potato chips, but hospitality won and they went into a big bowl and onto the table too. Dessert was slices of cold cantaloupe, given that I'd consumed every bite of ice cream and every cookie in the house earlier in the week and vowed to resist restocking.

Even with the makeshift dinner, I think the day was as good as days ever come. When everyone left—after Hank said he'd load the dishwasher, and Eve Ellen announced there wasn't one and said she was going to do the dishes the old-fashioned way, and after all three guys helped dry and put everything away, with me sitting at the table and directing them to the right cupboards and drawers, like a traffic cop in a kitchen full of clowns—it was back to bed for me. I'd need as much sleep as I could still get in the hours left before morning because, in a moment of unthinking enthusiasm, I'd volunteered to take Pete and Hank on a tour of some of Saratoga's claims to fame the following day. Eve Ellen and Greg had a wedding to attend, so I said I'd be at their place to pick up their house guests at nine.

NINE

It felt like five minutes after I'd crawled into bed that I was again pulled from sleep by an early morning call. Even earlier this time, though it hadn't really been just minutes since my head hit the pillow.

My cell phone starting buzzing and squirming on the nightstand. The ringer was turned off for the night, but the vibrate mode is usually enough to wake me up. When I saw the name on the screen, my stomach lurched. It was Scott. I hadn't heard from him since the sale of my half of the practice was worked out. He and I didn't exchange holiday cards, birthday wishes, photos of our breakfast, or anything else. We didn't check in on one another's health and happiness.

I knew his call that morning wasn't going to be good. I knew that as surely as I know floors are flat and wheels are round, so I closed my eyes and took a deep breath before answering.

"Hey there," I said, trying to sound only mildly surprised. It wouldn't have been natural for me to not be surprised, so I didn't pretend I wasn't, but I also wanted to sound like I'd moved on and I was fine.

"Hey, Isla," he said, practically whispering. Not a sneaky whisper, but rather one that's about being so shell-shocked or drained you can't produce any volume.

I rolled over onto my back and asked, "What's up?"

"I have some bad news," he answered.

"Okay?" I said, trying to sound unworried, but bracing myself.

"Craig was arrested last night."

Craig was the architect who had joined Scott in business and was buying me out.

"Arrested?" I replied.

"Yeah. The short version is he embezzled money from his old firm. A lot. Not the petty cash."

Trying to hold onto a filament of hope that there wouldn't be any fallout for me, but knowing that Scott wouldn't be calling if there wasn't, I waited for whatever was coming next.

"Isla, I'm pretty certain the money he gave you for the down payment was stolen. I don't know if you'll have to give it back, but for sure there won't be any more quarterly payments. If he was covering those with anything other than what he was earning, if he was using the stolen money, I don't know if you'll have to return what he's paid you so far, but there won't be any more coming."

I took another deep breath and made a mental note to keep my tone calm and in control, then asked a string of questions.

"If he was just arrested last night, it's too soon to know if he's really guilty of anything, right? What's he saying? Is he denying he did anything wrong?"

"I haven't been able to talk to him. His lawyer called me and said he doesn't know much yet but can't believe Craig has knowingly done anything wrong. He's the same lawyer Craig used when he bought into the practice, so he's not a criminal defense attorney."

"Okay," I said again, calmly, trying to make it sound like, "Okay, let's take a breath and figure this out." But in my head I was screaming, "No! Why is this happening?"

Neither of us said anything for a few moments. Scott sat on his side of the phone line and I sat on mine. I'd pushed back the sheets and was sitting up, cross-legged, on the bed. Eventually, I asked, "What's next? What do we do?" When I got to "we" my stomach did a somersault. Then Scott abruptly ended the call.

He said, "We wait. I'll let you know when I hear something, but I've got to go now. The girls have a checkup this morning."

When I heard "the girls," it was more than my belly that reacted. It felt as if my whole being staggered and nearly lost its footing.

After we hung up, I stayed there on the bed for a few minutes and thought about how Scott had mentioned his daughters in such a casual way, it suggested I was familiar with his new family, with his babies and the wife I'd never met and had never discussed with him since the day he told me he wanted a divorce so he could be with her. So he could take another shot at having kids.

I could feel myself sliding into old poisoned thoughts about my ex-husband's potential narcissism, his claim to the crown rightfully due to Satan's biggest narcissist. I went as far as saying to myself, "Of course the whole world is familiar with his girls. We're all tuned into his life, listening for every breath he takes, following every move he makes, because he's special."

I could almost taste the bitter poison in my mouth when another thought occurred to me and my anger gave way to anxiety—if I had to return the money I'd received from Craig, I'd be in trouble. I didn't have all of it anymore. I'd been good about socking away some of it, but a chunk went to the credit card debt.

Then the phone, which was still in my hand, vibrated again, with a text from Evie.

Thank you for today! Have fun with P and H! Love you!

TEN

I was minutes away from Evie's house when my cell started up yet again. The ringer was back on, with the volume cranked to the maximum level, where I'd put it before getting in the shower, and the car filled with the jangle of an old-fashioned phone, like my landline at the camp, but harsher. I looked over at the passenger seat, where my cell was face-down so I couldn't see who was calling. Aloud, I said, "Really? Now what?"

For a moment, I thought about letting the call go to voicemail. But a combination of fear, curiosity, and guilt got to me before the ringing stopped, and I pressed the pick-up button on my steering wheel.

It was Tom making sure I'd gotten my phone back, and apologizing for not being able to bring it to me himself. To assure him that wasn't a problem, I said it had worked out great because I got to have another fun day and more music from Pete. Too late, it occurred to me how that sounded, and I added, "Eve Ellen and Greg brought him and Hank to the lake yesterday."

Not a smooth move. Oops.

"Sounds fun," Tom said. "And what are you up to today?"

I'm really not in the habit of lying, but I was tempted to say, "Just out running errands." Instead, I said, "Playing tour guide for the Californians, taking them to see some of our local sights while Greg and Eve Ellen are at a wedding. What about you?"

We chatted for about five minutes. He told me he'd gone to Florida to take care of some things for his parents, who were up in their years. Ninety-one for his father, ninety-two for his mother. He asked me about my garden and I gave him a quick rundown of which plants were thriving and which were giving me grief. I told him about some repairs I'd made to my greenhouse, and did my best to be sunny and engaging, figuring it would be good practice for the day ahead.

Then just in time, Tom had to hang up and go clothes shopping for his father, "the incredible shrinking man," and try to find something the old guy wouldn't deem too flashy, which meant something that was, according to Tom, "Beige or gray, with no flare, ornamentation, or branding. No alligator or polo pony or logo of any kind on the chest."

I wished him luck, hung up, and pulled into Eve Ellen's driveway. A millisecond later, a thought, or more like a conversation between Isla and Isla, ran through my head and left me with another reason to be distracted all day. I asked, "Am I growing more attracted to Pete, who lives on the other side of the continent, and less interested in Tom, who is essentially my neighbor and really the only realistic option between the two guys? Am I that dumb?" And I replied, "Don't be stupid. Love the one you're with, Isla. The one close enough to see without going through airport security and spending money you don't have."

Tom was the local, I reminded myself. We grew up playing in the same lake and exploring different patches of the same woods. The places and paths of our lives were nearly a perfect match. And at least some of our interests were too. He was a beekeeper, for God's sake. No monk pun intended. Bees and gardens go together more naturally and necessarily than bacon and eggs.

Pete could have been from Mars, rather than California, given how different our worlds were. By his own admission, the only thing he'd ever tried to grow was an avocado tree from a pit he'd half-submerged in a glass of water on his kitchen counter. When that experiment failed, he'd hung up his gardening gloves for good.

"Okay, enough of that, Isla," I said, as I knocked on Evie's door and then let myself in.

I can't say I completely forgot about Scott and Craig, or Pete versus Tom, while I was playing tour guide that day, but I can say my thoughts about both situations were few and fleeting. Most of the credit for that goes to Pete and Hank, who were just so damn fun and easy to be with, but our packed itinerary helped. I'd planned it and wanted to pull it off perfectly.

Saratoga's auto museum had been my first thought. It was an obvious choice for a guy who put years into restoring and modifying an old car, but Greg wanted to take Pete and Hank to the museum. The Saratoga Race Course was out too because Evie had big plans for all of us to spend a day there later in the week. So I went with an American history theme, as suggested by Greg when we talked about it at my place the night before.

Pete said, "I wasn't going to ask, but I'd love that, and the Hankster could use the education."

To which Greg said, "Hank's plenty educated. He just prefers vintage TV shows to books about the old white dudes who've been Mr. President. Even when he's not stoned, he'd rather watch *Hogan's Heroes* than read the biographies you're working your way through like a beaver gnawing on a tree. Which Commander in Chief are you on now?"

Before Pete could answer, Hank said, "He's a fast reader and already up to the black dude who came after all those white dudes. Since when have you seen me stoned?"

Greg studied his watch, then replied, "Since now."

"I'm not stoned. I ate one CBD gummy bear to level the playing field and give you guys a chance against my younger and more agile mind."

Greg shot back, "That's what you're doing? Well, let's see how it works for you tomorrow when these two start nerding out on the history trail."

So I planned a full day of hopscotching from one historic site to another. After picking up a picnic lunch to take with us, I drove out to Saratoga Battlefield, where the Revolutionary War's tide turned against the British and in favor of the American troops. We did the road tour and stopped at each wayside panel. I'd read them all before but got out of the car with Pete and Hank. While they read and took in the views, I tried to focus on the landscape's beauty, rather than thinking about the bloody warfare once waged on the ground beneath our feet. Like Pete, I have a thing for America's story, but my very visual imagination can be a problem.

After the battlefield and visitor center, we drove to the monument built to commemorate the Saratoga victory. We spiraled up the stairs to the top of the 155-foot obelisk, enjoyed the views of the surrounding countryside, which was peaceful and green, then went back down and out onto the trail into Victory Woods, where the British troops—and also a contingent of American men, woman, and children who were loyal to the British crown—made their last camp and endured conditions so horrible, nobody would want to visualize them.

Next, we ate our lunch in the car as I drove up to the top of Mount McGregor, where tuberculosis patients and military veterans once sought healing in the mountain air. Where former Union general and United States President Ulysses S. Grant lived his last weeks in a borrowed cottage and raced to complete his memoirs, hoping their sale would provide for his family after he was gone, and writing the final page just three days before he died.

On the drive to the cottage, I couldn't help congratulating myself on how it was a perfect match to Pete's interests. He'd said he thought Grant had written one of the best memoirs ever produced by a president. If I hadn't been so pleased with myself, I might have remembered Granny Franny's oft-repeated, "Pride goeth before the fall."

From the heights of Mount McGregor, we drove back down into Saratoga Springs—Spa City—for a walk through Saratoga Spa State Park, starting at the Roosevelt bathhouse. We didn't indulge in mineral baths, but we checked out as much of the grand building's interior as we could without treatment appointments, and roamed around the exterior, taking in the beautiful architecture and setting. Envisioned by President Franklin Roosevelt, the spa was built during the Great Depression, as one of the job-making projects of the Works Progress Administration. Roosevelt believed Saratoga's natural mineral waters had helped with his polio, and he thought other people would benefit from them as well, so he included the bathhouse project in his New Deal.

"But presidential history aside," I told Pete and Hank, "you can't come to Saratoga and not check out the springs. They've been bringing cure seekers here since the beginning of time, since long before the first Europeans seeking land and new territory crossed the Atlantic and started staking claims. And the Roosevelt

Baths & Spa is just one of the places you can 'take the waters,' as we say. Before I'm done with you, anything that ails you will be cured. It'll be history."

Given that it was already late afternoon when we arrived at the park, I had to be selective about what I showed the guys, but we were able to walk some of my favorite stretches of trail and visit several springs, including the Geyser Island Spouter, which shoots up from the ground through a mound of hardened mineral deposits—an island of rock. As we were starting out, I explained that each of the springs is different, with its own unique taste and healing powers. I said, "You'd want to drink from different ones, depending on what's wrong with you—gout, dyspepsia, anemia, eczema, arthritis, rheumatism, sinus issues, liver or kidney conditions, et cetera. You name it, healing happens here."

At one point, we were walking along a trail and Pete stopped, turned his head from side to side, and took in the beauty in every direction with a look of pure pleasure on his face. When I walked in the park by myself, I always paused in that same place. There wasn't any water in sight, but it was so pretty and peaceful, away from the popular spots everyone wants to see, I liked to just stand for a moment and take it in. When Pete did the same thing, it reminded me of how easily he and I had clicked the night we met, and I made a mental note to come back to that idea later, for a thorough mulling.

For our final destination, we left Spa Park and backtracked a little to take one last sip of curative water at High Rock Spring downtown, in High Rock Park, and then have dinner across the street at the Olde Bryan Inn. With my tour guide performance almost over, I went for a strong finish. I told Pete and Hank how the earliest portions of the Olde Bryan dated to 1773 and a log cabin that served people who came to take the cure, and how the first white man to seek healing at High Rock is believed to have been a sick French officer carried there by native Haudenosaunee people in the 1750s, from Fort Carillon, the military post that later became Fort Ticonderoga and passed from French to British and then American control.

Over cold beers and roast beef sandwiches, I went total nerd and brought up how the Haudenosaunee Confederacy of native nations—the Mohawk, Onondaga, Seneca, Oneida, Cayuga, and

Tuscarora—influenced the United States' Constitution with their own Great Law of Peace.

Pete said, "And today the six Haudenosaunee nations continue to keep their peace while the people of the United States are less united and at uglier odds with one another than we've been in generations."

Then, obviously trying to counter what he'd just said with something lighter, he added, "But I like to think what we're going through now will prove to be growing pains."

From there, we were on a roll. We nerded out together, as Hank pointed out, and closed the loop I'd planned for the day, making a full circle back to America's founding, where I'd started "Isla's Grand Saratoga History Tour." When we finished, as we were leaving the inn and walking out to my car, Pete backtracked to FDR, Franklin Delano Roosevelt, and brought up how his New Deal projects included recording and preserving traditional American music. And I congratulated myself again for how well my tour had been suited to Pete's interests, and how much Hank had seemed to enjoy it too.

Only later, when I was driving home alone, did it occur to me that the visit to Grant's cottage and all my talk about Saratoga's healing springs and taking the waters—the cure—might have brought up painful memories for Pete and Hank. In an instant, I fell headlong and hard into the depths of shame and embarrassment. I wondered if Pete had thought about his wife when we were up on McGregor. I worried about Hank. Neither of them had shown any sign that the cottage made them uncomfortable, but how could it not? I remembered how Pete stood looking at two leather chairs pushed together, facing one another, in the room that functioned as both Grant's bedroom and workspace. Unable to lie down because of the cancer ravaging his throat, Grant slept sitting up in one of the chairs, with his legs extended onto the other. In that same spot, he worked on his memoirs when bad weather or bugs drove him in from the porch, where he liked to write when he could get out there. When I noticed that Pete appeared to be spellbound by the chairs, I assumed he was thinking about the book Grant had written in them. I didn't think about Lainie's cancer, not then, and not even when we stood looking at an actual bed and listened to a docent explain that it had been brought in when Grant was very close to dying so he could finally lie down, as he wished to do at the end.

How could Pete and Hank not think about Lainie as they heard how Grant died in that bed, surrounded by his family? For the rest of the drive home, and until I finally fell asleep, I thought of nothing but my thoughtlessness, and what I should do about it. Apologize? Say nothing? Would bringing it up only make matters worse?

ELEVEN

The next couple of days felt like the proverbial quiet after a storm. The social hurricane was over and I didn't see or speak with anybody. The only human voice I heard was my own as I muttered about "Isla's Grand Saratoga Tour of Death." I'd decided I shouldn't say anything to Pete and Hank, but that didn't stop me from talking to myself. I cursed my idiocy. "Damn you, Isla. Damn, damn, damn you. Death and disease all day!"

I got the usual texts from Eve Ellen and my sisters—photos of food they were about to eat, links to news articles they'd just read, funny videos they wanted me to watch. But we didn't talk. I thought about calling them to ask what I should do about Pete and Hank, but decided to avoid the additional humiliation that would come with broadcasting what I'd done. Surely, I wasn't such an idiot I couldn't figure it out on my own.

"Grow up, calm down, and get a grip, Isla," I barked for the umpteenth time.

Then I had a good cry. Like a cracked reservoir dam that finally blows and lets loose a torrential flood, I wept because I felt bad about what I'd put Pete and Hank through, and because I felt sorry for myself and guilty about feeling that way when so much of my life had been wonderful and I was still more fortunate than many people would ever be. I mean, truffle salt was a staple in my kitchen even then. I used it sparingly, my budget being what it was, but it was never not in stock at my house. At my rent-free, lake-front home where, in winter, my bed sported a down-filled duvet. I slept under an organic cotton comforter filled with the finest, softest parts of a goose's undercoat. Goose underwear, plucked from the bodies of I don't know how many geese, for the fluffiest warmth money can buy.

I cried because I missed my mother and father. And because, despite knowing how fortunate I was, I couldn't help feeling life had been unfair in dealing me nothing but winning cards for nearly forty years—not counting the losing hands of in vitro fertilization and adoption—before suddenly slamming me with one major loss after another in thirty-six brutal months, starting with my parents' deaths in a car accident, followed by the deaths of my two grandmothers, the only grandparents I'd known. Then the miscarriage and the end of my marriage. In one rough run, much of what had been my life and all hope for what I'd thought my life could still be—the future I'd have with Scott—disappeared.

I'd never even lost a pet as a kid because my father was allergic to anything with fur or feathers, and my sisters and I weren't fond of fish in tanks that had to be cleaned. I was entirely unfamiliar with grief and unprepared when I experienced it for the first time when my mom and dad died. When I came to know grief as something more than a word in books, a word worth at least nine points in Scrabble. After my grandmothers died that same year, I tried to believe it was a good thing they'd all gone so close together, that I was done with death for a while. But then I feared I was tempting fate with that thought, and, to reverse the curse, I warned myself another loss could come at any time, there would be more deaths and other sorts of losses, and they would come more frequently as I got older because that was the nature of life. I should have stopped there, but I foolishly thought about how losing my parents and grandmothers left me better prepared for future losses. Foolish, foolish me. I was not ready to lose the baby and then my husband.

I cried because I was trying to fend off a swarm of feelings about Scott, and because I didn't want to believe he was the shit that Dale said he was, but I couldn't help going there myself sometimes. I didn't want to think that I'd never really known him and he'd never really loved me. But right or wrong, true or not, I'd always believed that, while lots of different sorts of attractions and transactions are called love, they're actually something else. They might coexist with love, within a relationship between two people, and they might be great, but they're their own things, and there's just one thing that's love, and it's more than attraction, and it isn't a transaction and never ends like one, like a completed exchange, or an exchange you quit making because it doesn't interest you anymore or no longer meets your terms and conditions. There's no such thing as *conditional* love, and if you've ever truly loved someone, you don't stop loving them. Even if you find you have to leave them, you still love them, so you handle it decently, honorably, because love is always decent and honorable.

You don't picnic on cannoli and ravioli, eat ice cream, and act as if nothing has changed until the moment you announce you're leaving to be with someone else.

You don't come home from work one day, rip out their heart and lungs, and walk away.

I had a big, wet weep because I didn't want to believe I was wrong about love. And because I envied Scott for his babies and his partner. And because I believed I should be farther along toward understanding what happened in our relationship and what my part had been in getting us to where we ended up. Once, when I said something about that to Dale, she said, "Yeah, it takes two to tango or waltz or whatever, but sometimes one of the dancers is a fucking turd on legs and all fault belongs to him. Scott owns this."

I know she was trying to help, and she really does see all blame as Scott's, but clinging to that thought wasn't going to get me anywhere good. At best, it would keep me in a dark place and I'd never move forward. Even if it were true that Scott was a heartless narcissist, it could only be good for me to understand how and why I'd lived with that. And why I'd blindly, obliviously believed I had an invincible marriage even as my husband eyed the exit. Maybe I couldn't know certain parts of the full picture, things only Scott could know, but I wanted to understand who I was for all those years and I wanted to move ahead with my eyes open. If I'd pawned any part of myself, I wanted to get it back.

After I thought I'd sobbed myself dry, soaking half a box of tissue with grief, guilt, and self-pity, I tried to make myself laugh about how my life had become something straight out of a country song, one of Roger's Miller's sad ones. That threatened to start another wave of weeping and wallowing, so I went for a swim, then dove into more productive therapy. I finally started going through the things that had come with me after the divorce. Most of that stuff was stored in a barn at Dale's place, packed up and hauled there by a numb robot that looked like me but wasn't me, and I'd been meaning to bring batches of boxes to the camp and do a purge. I'd brought an initial batch, but it was still stacked along a wall in my bedroom. Three tall columns, five boxes high, loomed over one side of my bed. It was past time I went through them and started lightening my load. I didn't need two sets of dishes, in addition to the china I'd inherited from my Granny Franny. I didn't need a dozen Moroccan tea glasses, ten vases, four cake stands, three citrus zesters, six water bottles. My goal was to get through enough of my stored stuff to stock a worthwhile barn sale before the weather turned cold and whittle my belongings to what I liked to think of as an elegantly efficient minimum. No excess, nothing ridiculous, which meant my fluted parfait dishes were headed to a new home. When I moved to a new place myself, I didn't want to take anything that should have been sent somewhere else by then.

Box number one: the contents of my ridiculous utensil drawers. I had so many of the same tools, it's like they'd bred in the dark when the drawers were shut. The potato peelers coupled and begat more peelers. The spatulas spawned a dynasty. No fertility issues for them.

By late afternoon the next day, I'd been through thirteen boxes and had two left. To stay cool, I'd been working in my swimsuit on the porch, stopping to jump in the water when I got hot, then toweling off and going back to work in my wet tankini. I'd just started on box fourteen, after a quick dip, when I heard a car on the gravel drive at the side of the house. By the time the car came into view, I was inside, pulling a tank dress over my head. A good thing because I could see through a window that it was Tom. He was making his way up the stairs with two jars of honey balanced on a book.

With his hands full, he called out through the screen door, "Knock, knock."

My immediate thought was a screeching, "No!" Fortunately, I pulled off a better response.

"Hey there," I said. "You're back from Florida. Quick trip."

"Yeah, I thought I'd need to be there longer, but I got a lot done pretty fast."

Then, looking at the two separate piles of boxes I'd made on the porch, a small one for the things I was keeping and a much bigger one for the stuff going to the barn sale, he said, "It looks like you're getting a lot done here too."

Leap-frogging over his comment about my purge progress, I said, "You come bearing gifts. What's the occasion?" But I was thinking, "What do I need to do to meet the minimum level of hospitality required? How do I handle this uninvited visit without blowing it too badly or making it last any longer than I can avoid?"

That wasn't very gracious, I know, but after a couple of days alone, I was back in my solo camper mode and forgetting how to be socially acceptable. I was also excruciatingly aware of the wet circles blooming over my boobs from the sopping swimsuit beneath my dress, and I was torn about whether I should cross my arms over them or act as if I didn't know or care that they were screaming, "Look at my breasts!"

Tom did glance at them, but got his eyes back to my face fast and said, "They're not gifts. They're an excuse to come see you. I could say I wanted to apologize for anything out of line I may have said when I was in my cups at Eve Ellen's party, but I could have done that when we went to see Pete, and I wasn't all that drunk anyway. Sober enough to remember that I had a great time talking with you that night and Pete's night too."

He'd handed the honey and the book to me and I used them as an excuse to look down, away from him, as I said, "You didn't say anything out of bounds, not that I'll hold against you. Is this honey from your hives?"

By the time he finished telling me that, yes, the honey was from his bees and the book was about preserving vegetables and fruit with honey, I was conflicted. I was still frazzled about his surprise appearance, but succumbing to his charms. If he stayed much longer, I'd need to jump into the lake again. Not only did he have a garden and beehives, he also canned what he grew. It almost felt like the gods were playing a prank on me. Like Tom was too good to be true. That thought made me laugh out loud, but I pulled myself together when he reacted with a puzzled look.

"I love that you're a canner," I said. "I don't know why that amuses me, but it does. Sorry."

Still looking puzzled, he said, "Glad to entertain you. How about I keep it up over dinner sometime?"

So we made a date for the first night we'd both be free, which happened to be a week away, and he left. As swiftly as I'd been yanked from silence, I was yanked right back into it. I could hear water lapping at the dock's legs and a bird somewhere, but the house was again dead quiet.

TWELVE

Getting rid of possessions from my previous life, winnowing my material load, really was effective therapy. After getting through the first fifteen boxes, I was on a roll and kept going for a third day. I took some of the sorted things, all I could cram into my car, back to Dale's barn, and borrowed her truck so I could haul a bigger load of fresh boxes up to the camp and finish taking the original batch back to the barn in just one round trip.

As long as I kept moving and working, I hardly thought about my ex-husband, the money I might need to give back, and the Saratoga Tour of Death. I can't say I didn't think about Pete and Hank, but I didn't obsess about my blunder. I hoped they were having a wonderful time with Greg and Evie, but I didn't replay my day with them and stew over it. Thankfully, I was in the purge therapy zone and feeling lighter and better with every box I finished.

Seeing things I'd acquired while I was married to Scott could have brought up thoughts about him and our divorce, but I had visions of a house in my future and I pictured its rooms furnished with what I was keeping from the whole of my life. My buttercup yellow stand mixer, a wedding gift, sitting out on a kitchen counter. One of my mother's oil paintings hanging in a light-filled living room. My grandfather's unusual oak filing cabinet, perched on tall legs, repurposed as a side table and topped with a bouquet of fresh roses in my grandmother's sterling silver water pitcher. Scott had kept the art we'd bought together, and many of our larger pieces of furniture, all of which had been part of his vision for the modern-meets-historic farmhouse he'd designed for us. When we divvied up the contents of our carefully appointed home, I kept everything from my office, the kitchen, my favorite guest bedroom, and a closet full of the exquisite linens that were a weakness for me—sheets, towels, tablecloths, napkins. Plus a few random pieces of furniture and hodgepodge from both my married and pre-married lives.

I loved imagining my yellow mixer on the kitchen counter where I could see its happy color every day. Scott had insisted it live in our pantry, out of sight when not in use because it messed with the look he wanted. As much as its color cheered me, I did understand how it might not work for everybody, so I was able to convince myself I was fine with the pantry arrangement. I actually did like the pantry, and having the mixer in there meant it greeted me as soon as I opened the door and flipped on the light. I enjoyed that. If Scott had insisted on hiding it in a cupboard, I would have gone to the mat to resist. He knew that and thus his compromise. In fact, he'd probably included the pantry in his plans when he designed the house so he could shepherd onto its shelves everything I'd normally have out on the counters.

I did and I do share Scott's preference for clutter-free rooms, but only up to a point. I like having things around me that remind me of my parents and grandparents, and I like efficiency. In my next house, in the cottage of my dreams, both my mixer and my toaster will live on the counter where I can use them without a hassle. At the camp, we've had the same Sunbeam two-slicer sitting next to the sink for as long as I can remember. While you wait for your toast to reach the right shade of gold, you can look out the window to the lake and enjoy the view. Without moving from that spot, you can take a knife from the flatware drawer and butter your toast while it's still warm. Standing there one day, waiting for my toasted bread to pop up, and watching a pair of ducks on the water, I actually said out loud, "I will never again live in a house without a toaster permanently planted in a place that makes sense. I will never again haul my toaster in and out of a pantry, or give up and just use it in there, in a six-by-ten-foot space where the aroma will be trapped and can't fill the kitchen." Then I laughed because I thought I sounded like Scarlett O'Hara in *Gone with the Wind* when she said, "As God is my witness, I'll never be hungry again!"

As I plowed through one box after another, I was mercifully free of worry. I did think about my future, but only in terms of positive possibilities, the good things I hoped would happen. I thought about the love life I wanted. The romance. When I opened a box that was labeled "Kitchen Linens" but proved to be bedding, I pictured the antique iron bed I'd kept from the guest bedroom. I imagined it in a new house and fantasized about lying in it with a new partner. Lying between my extravagant Italian sheets. I gladly recalled that Scott had never slept on them, or in the bed, though I had on a handful of nights when his snoring was too loud.

When I opened a box of fluffy towels worthy of the best spa in Saratoga, I imagined being in a bathtub with a new love. I may be turning into a socially inept hermit, I thought, but my hormones hadn't shut off or dried up. Quite the contrary. Some days, they were so active I could paw the ground like a cartoon bull getting ready to charge. That image came to me one high-hormone day when I was alone in an elevator with a delivery guy who wore his uniform very well. He had no idea the danger he was in. I was on my way to Glyn's office for lunch, and when she saw me she asked if I was sunburned because my face was so flushed.

Since the divorce, I'd been on four dates with one guy and had zero sex. Which means I'd had "relations" with two guys in my life—my high school boyfriend, Brian, and Scott. Brian and I humped like March hares every chance we got, but our chances were few. We were already half-way through our senior year when we gifted each other with our virginity on Valentine's Day, and the months that followed gifted us with infrequent opportunities to sneak up to his bedroom or anywhere private. We had demanding classes and homework right up to graduation week, being geeks at heart, if not by reputation, and our part-time jobs went full-time after we graduated. We both worked all summer, and then it was time to leave for college, thousands of miles apart. We were sad to say goodbye but excited about going away to school, and without coming right out and saying so, we broke up and freed one another to see other people. For me, that started and stopped with Scott.

Post-divorce, it took me a while to even think about dating again, or whatever dating is called now. It was a while before I was far enough past the grief, and then I worried about whether I would even know how to date anymore. I hadn't done a lot of it before Brian, in high school, so I couldn't fall back on memory, and the world had changed anyway. I'd changed. I was either approaching the threshold of middle age, or a few years through the door, according to Google, which changed its mind from one minute to the next, depending on how I asked, "When does middle age begin?" In any case, some of my body parts were, well, different. Or no longer located precisely where they'd once been. Would that be a turn off to a guy, even one whose own parts had changed? I didn't know. I knew I shouldn't care, I should be "body positive," but I couldn't help wondering about it.

A year after the split with Scott, I decided I didn't want to be like two of my school colleagues who had been single for more than a decade before marrying their second husbands. It was another six months before I could bring myself to act on that decision. When I finally took a big breath and went for it, one guy was enough to make me decide I wasn't quite ready after all. Dale had been badgering me to try online shopping for love, so I did, and I met an Albany chiropractor on a matchmaking site. He and I agreed to meet for coffee and that went fine, no red flags, so I accepted when he asked if I wanted to go on a snowshoe hike. That went well too. Light on talk when we were on the trail, heavy on laughs during a snowball fight he started. I gave him points for playfulness and for being outdoorsy. Back at the lodge, where we'd arranged to rendezvous and park that morning, we had soup and talked about other hikes we'd done, and ones we would like to do, exotic trails in other countries. I told him Italy's Cinque Terre was on my bucket list but didn't say it was something Scott and I had hoped to do together. It was a good sign, I thought, that I could bring it up without feeling sad. And an excellent sign that the chiropractor's bucket list included hiking Austria's Cheese Road, or KäseStrasse Bregenzerwald, to taste cheeses at the dairies that produced them. He described it as a breathtaking trek through forests, meadows, and pastures. I hadn't heard of it before, but added it to my list, and put it near the top—travel, hiking, nature, and food were a jackpot combination, as far I was concerned.

When we said goodbye out in the parking lot, standing beside my car, and again there hadn't been any red flags, I said yes to dinner at a fancy French restaurant the following weekend. That date, our third, was a talkfest of topics ranging from politics to our favorite popcorn toppings, and we finished the night with a kiss so heated, I still cringe to think about how we were in very a public place. It was a real "Get a room!" moment. He'd walked me to my car, and, in a jokey French accent, asked, "A goodnight kiss for dessert?" I jokingly puckered up and he planted a quick one on my closed mouth, then pulled back, laughed, and returned for a real smacker. He held my head between his hands, with his fingers up in my hair caressing my scalp, and moved his mouth on and *in* mine for a very long time. It was so intense, it left me feeling a weird mix of turned on and put off. Though not so put off I didn't want to see him again.

In fact, when he texted a few days later, I not only said yes to seeing him, I decided to be bold and jump off the cliff headfirst, Eve Ellen-style. He said he'd like to come up and have a look at the lake "in its winter glory," and asked if he could take me to dinner someplace I really liked, with "lake views and a roaring hearth." I suggested that I cook dinner at my house and told him I had a great stone fireplace and would make it roar. Getting ready for that evening, I thought the chiropractor and I might end up on the rug in front of the fire, so I made sure there was plenty of extra firewood stacked on the hearth, and I put on my best bra and panties.

But then, as we made our way through the cheese course I'd assembled with a little fiscal guilt and lots of foodie joy, he said, "Isla, I don't want you to feel I haven't been honest with you from the start, or that I've wasted your time, so I'd like for us to talk about what we hope we might have with one another."

Something about the way he laid down his knife and fork to give his full attention to what he was saying made me nervous, so it took conscious effort to keep my voice nonchalant when I replied, "Okay."

"I'm glad you're comfortable with talking," he said, which made me even more nervous. Then he went on to tell me his marriage may have survived if he and his wife had been able to discuss what they were feeling and thinking, and what they wanted and needed. He said he hadn't ruled out getting married again, but he'd figured out that he wouldn't be happy in a relationship that excluded sex with other people. He said he needed something other than "traditional monogamy." He asked me, "Have you ever thought about open marriage?" Then, after a pause, "Or swinging?"

Over his shoulder, I could see the flames in the fireplace were hungry for a fresh log. Silently, I told them they could starve. I plastered a smile on my face and said, "You know, to this day I enjoy the swing that's been hanging from a tree outside since I was a kid, but I can't say I've ever given any thought to open marriage. Let me get back to you on that, and, in the meantime, let's try the apple tart I made for dessert before you have to get on the road. Albany's a fair piece from here."

I said "fair piece," an expression I'd never heard come out of anyone other than maybe a character in a cowboy movie. It certainly hadn't ever come out of my mouth until that moment, when I morphed into a woman from the Old West crossed with an apple tart-making Julia Child from the 1950s or 60s.

My response was purely spontaneous, a panicked knee jerk, but as I conferred with my journal about it that night, I decided it worked. It would get the job done. I was sure I couldn't have been clearer if I'd told Mr. Free Love, "Open marriage? I'd rather rub maple syrup all over my naked body and lie down on an ant pile. I'm not up for anything less than air-tight monogamy, so get away from me with that swinger business." So I was sure I wouldn't hear from him again. Two days later he texted me.

Him: *Any thoughts yet?*

Me: *Hi there, I've decided we're not a match, but I wish you all the best.*

Six more solo months passed before I was ready to have another go at dating. When I got there, Evie decided it was time to throw our party.

I'd come away from the four dates with the swinging chiropractor thinking I should think about what I wanted in my next partner and relationship, but I wasn't quick to follow through with the quality time and attention it would take to reach conclusions. Perhaps because when I tried, I couldn't help thinking about Scott and what I'd thought I had with him. Rather than go there, I stuck to vague fantasies about meeting a great guy and didn't try to get specific about him. A week before Eve Ellen's party, if you'd made me describe this fantasy fellow, I might have painted a picture of somebody a lot like Tom. Fast-forward to a few days after the bash, and as much as Tom made me hot, it was Pete that my mind went back to most often. Maybe that was about being excited by the prospect of an adventure into unknown territory—while Pete was as easy to be with as an old friend, he was also like a distant land that was new to me.

Whatever it was that caused me to think about Pete didn't matter, I reminded myself. I needed to get over it because he was going to be gone soon, back to California, and I wasn't looking for long-distance love. That much, I did know.

THIRTEEN

After a blur of nonstop days ferrying loads to and from Dale's barn and sorting my things into categories—keep, sell, donate, trash—I finished just in time for race day. Off I went to the track with Eve Ellen, Greg, Pete, and Hank. Evie had been adamant that we go early enough to get seats on a tram tour of the stables that morning and then have breakfast trackside, so I left my place extra early and had time for a cup of coffee with the guys while Evie finished getting dressed. A cup of coffee and some new stories. Since I'd last seen them, Greg had gone with Pete and Hank on the final eastbound leg of their trip and the three of them told me about it. Their first stop was Boston, where they went sightseeing, hit another open mic, and camped on an island in Boston Harbor.

"I want to go camping there!" I said, sounding like a kid left out of a game.

"You would have loved the whole trek, from start to finish," Greg said. "It was right up your back-to-nature alley. Rock-hard ground for a bed and shared public bathrooms, when there was a bathroom at all."

He grumbled but had clearly enjoyed himself. From Boston, they went north to Orono, Maine, where Pete did three Roger songs at a brewery and they camped for another night, before pushing on to Lubec, Maine, where they crossed the bridge to Campobello Island to visit Franklin Roosevelt's Canadian retreat and camp for two nights at Herring Cove.

I blurted, "You live in California, practically the other side of the planet, and you made it to Herring Cove before me! I've always wanted to camp there!"

From Campobello, they crossed the bridge back into Lubec and made the quick drive to Quoddy Head State Park, the easternmost tip of the continental United States.

"I haven't been there either," I said.

"Isn't it just like all of us to never get around to seeing the sights close to home?" Pete replied. "It's so cockeyed that we'll travel to the far side of the world for vacation, but not the cool places right up the road. Or relatively right up the road."

When Eve Ellen walked in, ready to go, Greg was grumbling about the marathon drive home from Quoddy Head. She let him finish his thought, then said, "No more complaining. Today, we're going to celebrate our good fortune—without losing a fortune on slow ponies, remember that part of the plan—before Pete and Hank leave and we don't get them back out here for another quarter-century."

"It hasn't been that long," Pete replied. "Not a day more than twenty-four years."

For a second, I wondered where I'd been the last time he came to town, and why I hadn't met him then, but I quickly went back to thinking about how he seemed to be a fellow lover of nature and camping and good words—"cockeyed" is one of my favorites, right up there with "cockamamie."

In retrospect, thinking about both of those words now, I could apply them to the plan Pete got me to agree to that day. Between races, the five of us agonized over our token bets and made up crazy racehorse names, competing with one another to come up with the wildest name—originally my mother's game and then something I found handy in social situations. And the three guys told more road stories, as nuggets came back to them. After another one about Campobello, I said, "I should have been there!" I must have looked like an envious and pouty kid because Hank started insisting I join him and Pete for the first few days of their westbound drive back to California. I really hadn't been angling for an invitation, but Evie and Greg jumped in to back up Hank, citing both valid and ludicrous reasons I should go.

Eve Ellen warned, "You need to shake things up. You haven't been anywhere other than Albany in two years and your world has shrunk so much, pretty soon even coming into Saratoga will be foreign travel for you. You'll have to carry your passport."

Greg claimed, "You're starting to look a little crazy around the eyes and the birds at the lake are worried about you. They're talking and we hear it all the way down here."

Then Pete said, "Pay no mind to those two loons but consider coming with us two crazies. I'm not ready for this Saratoga party to end, and having you along would give us a few more days. We can put you on a plane or bus back here as soon as you're ready."

I decided right then that I would go and I felt instantly happy about it.

But Pete added, "You can extend your tour of historic death and disease—I mean, your American history tour. You can take it beyond Saratoga."

Just as instantly, I felt like I could die. Or I did die for a moment, killed by embarrassment. I didn't see a white light or a montage of my life flash before my eyes, but it was as if somebody flipped all the switches in my breaker box and life-force ceased to flow through me. I swear, I stopped breathing and my heart was surely at a dead standstill. Then Pete and the rest of our cruel little crowd howled with laughter and with a harsh jolt, I was resuscitated.

All I could say was, "I hope every one of you chokes on your own venomous spit."

They laughed even harder.

The next day, packing for the trip, I was a nutcase combination of excited and terrified. My life really had become too secluded. Until the anniversary party, I hadn't seen anybody since the school year ended. Anybody other than my family, Evie, and Greg. And there were extended stretches between my visits with them. Other than Evie, they weren't teachers and didn't have the summer off.

Even my volunteer job rarely involved face-to-face human contact—I wrote a monthly blog and an annual fundraising letter for a small nonprofit, and I communicated with the organization's staff via phone and email. Mostly email.

So the occasional visits with my small inner circle, and the few words I exchanged with the cashier when I went to the grocery store, were the sum total of my in-person interaction with other human beings. During the school year, there was never enough time to see other friends in Saratoga, the ones I was awarded in the divorce, and I'd gotten bad about tending those relationships during school breaks, bad about inviting people up to the lake, other than my sisters, Eve Ellen, and their families. At first, that was because I was too raw, then it became habit. I fantasized about having a different life, but I fell into a routine of gardening, swimming, reading, and working on my second book, which I'd started over in order to go in a new direction. I decided to jump on the "organize, simplify, make over" bandwagon and do a guidebook for renovating your food life. A makeover manual covering everything from purging and reorganizing your kitchen cupboards and drawers to shopping for groceries and putting in a garden, or even just a pot of salad greens, if that's all you could do within the limits of your space and time.

When I decided to go with Pete and Hank, for a fraction of a second I felt guilty about taking a break from working on the book, but then I realized Eve Ellen was right about the shakeup I needed, and I knew I was ready for one, so I put the book out of my mind, asked my sisters to water my garden, and packed my bags.

I packed a duffel with clothes, and another one with my camping gear, after first checking to make sure my tent hadn't sprouted mold while it was stored and my inflatable sleeping pad hadn't sprung any air leaks. While I worked on that, I thought about the rut I'd gotten into and wondered whether it might have started before the divorce. I wondered if I'd become boring, on top of having bad eggs in my ovaries.

Had I sent Scott looking for fun, as well as a baby?

"No," I said out loud, as I rolled up a purple t-shirt and put it in the bag. "I didn't send him anywhere."

Then I silently started an inventory of all the times I'd planned or spontaneously suggested outings to Scott, determined to live up to my end of our agreement to make a good life after we accepted that kids weren't going to happen for us. I started making a mental list of everything I could remember, from a bike camping trip to the surprise reunion I organized for Scott's fortieth birthday, gathering his best buddies from his high school track team and their partners for a weekend at the lake. I'd rented luxe sleeping tents and had them tucked among the trees behind the house, and I had a big round table set up on the lawn out front. I wanted it big enough to have a lazy Susan in the center so everyone could help themselves to the food without getting up, and round so we could all see each other. Scott raved about how that table made every meal last for hours because everybody enjoyed sitting at it so much. I know he loved everything about those two days. He loved the track and field events I planned, the badminton tournament, the trophies I'd made for the winners.

As I rolled and tucked clothes into my duffel, I thought about the spur-of-the-moment dashes to the city I'd instigated. We would grab coffee for the road and race down to our old stomping grounds in Brooklyn and Manhattan. We'd go to our favorite Italian deli, which hadn't changed since Scott and I were just out of college. We'd buy a picnic lunch of savory cannoli and ravioli, caponata and panzanella, and take it to a shady patch of lawn in Central Park. Then we'd go to a series of ice cream shops, one right after the other, and taste test one of the classics—strawberry, chocolate, or vanilla—or an assortment of flavors we'd never tried. Browned butter with candied bacon. Fig with goat cheese. Rhubarb. Black walnut. Meyer lemon. We'd walk or take the subway from one shop and one shared cup of ice cream or gelato to another until we thought we'd be sick if we didn't quit. Back in our car, on the three-hour drive home, we'd debate which flavor had been the best and assign ratings to all of them.

Yes, I had a bum body that couldn't make a baby, but I wasn't boring back then. If anything, I thought, I might have tried too hard to make our life fun and full. That might have gotten old for Scott. Maybe it felt strained. But I was sincere. I didn't fake anything. He can't claim the same. The last of our city trips to picnic in the park and taste ice cream was just two days before he dropped the divorce bomb. I gave top marks to a gelato flavored with basil and lavender. He gushed over a pistachio-cardamom combo and never once let on that he was going to leave me.

He went along with every adventure I cooked up, acted like he enjoyed them, and didn't let one sign slip that he was involved with his running friend. He came home from work every day and kissed me as he always had. We only occasionally did more than that daily peck, but I was fine with less frequent sex after all the failed attempts at baby-making, and I assumed he was fine with it too. It didn't occur to me that it wasn't a temporary thing, a recovery retreat, or that he was getting his fill elsewhere.

Every night, we went through our usual ritual. Before I made dinner, we had a drink and told one another about our day, what had gone well and what hadn't. We discussed or bemoaned the latest news out of Washington and around the world. Once I started cooking, and while we ate, we observed a "no negative subjects over food" rule. If we needed a dinner table topic and nothing else came to us, we went with our standby—we talked about the vacation fantasies we hadn't yet fulfilled. Hiking the Cinque Terre in Italy. Eating our way from Hanoi to Ho Chi Minh City in Vietnam. Going on a wildlife photo safari in Botswana. He participated in those conversations as if he didn't know there would be no more vacations for us.

Eventually, before I finished packing to go with Pete and Hank, I caught myself and quit the program running in my head. I quit listing the fun that I'd orchestrated, and the ways I'd been innocent and Scott had not.

"Oh, Isla," I lectured, "let go, wish him well, and concentrate on your own future. Your present. Enjoy Pete for a few more days. Have a great time with him and Hank while you can. Then do a blowout barn sale, lighten your load, and create your next life. Finish your book."

FOURTEEN

Damn me! Just as I was drifting off to sleep, after struggling to wind down because of how excited I was about hitting the road, I realized I wouldn't be back in time for the dinner date with Tom. I thought I should call him, rather than text, but eleven-o'clock was too late to call, and I'd be leaving too early in the morning to do it then, so I had no choice—I texted him and hoped his phone wouldn't buzz and wake him up if he was already asleep. I wrote that I was sorry about canceling and told him about the trip, and about forgetting our date when I agreed to go with Pete and Hank. I probably said more than I needed to or should have, but by the time that occurred to me, it was too late to take the text back. Tom replied immediately.

Happy trails. We can reschedule.

Based on nothing more than my imagination, I feared there might be some snark or resentment behind his few words, and I lost another hour of sleep worrying about it and feeling bad. I had to start over with the winding down.

When my alarm went off and woke me up, I wasn't exactly fresh and fully recharged, but I was still glad I'd decided to go and determined to take a break from worrying.

I told myself, "Stay relaxed, go with the flow, and have fun. Laugh until you snort and don't be prissy or neurotic about it."

Before I'd gone to bed the night before, I'd put my duffle bags and camp chair in my car, laid out my clothes, and filled a thermos with coffee, so all I had to do was shower and go. Pete and Hank were ready and waiting at Evie's when I got there. They loaded my things into and on top of their cartoon car, made room on the back seat for me, and away we went.

Our first stop: the town of Woodstock. The famous festival didn't happen there, despite the name, but it was once home to Dylan and The Band, and Pete wanted to check it out. In addition to traveling the country to do some singing himself, his trip was a pilgrimage to sites significant to music, with bonus stops at a few places not about music, but of interest to him for other reasons. Presidential history, for instance.

At a café off Woodstock's village green, we had breakfast, then walked around town for a while, saw a lot of tie-dye, and bought some handmade chocolate before driving on to Hyde Park, where we spent some time at Franklin Roosevelt's presidential library and estate.

From Hyde Park, it was a short drive to the campground where Pete had reserved a site. As we pulled in, Hank asked, "Are we going to sleep under the stars here, cowboy-style, since this is a one-nighter?"

Pete said, "The tents take five minutes. Let's get them up and then do dinner."

I feared he said that for me, so I asked, "What do you usually do when you're going to be someplace for just one night?"

Hank swung his door open and said, "I was being lazy. Let's do this."

He sounded sincere, rather than chastised, but something made me certain they wouldn't bother with a tent if I hadn't been there, so I said I'd love to sleep under the stars, and I'd always loved it when I camped, and I missed it. Which was true. I hadn't been camping since the last time I went with Scott. I knew it was going to be a different experience with Pete and Hank because we were going to use our campsites like motel rooms, just places to stay between our destinations, but I was looking forward to it anyway.

In the end, the weather forecast, which warned there might be a light rain coming, settled the matter. We put up the tents. Then we set out our camp chairs and made sandwiches from the cooler Pete had restocked in Saratoga. It was so warm that night, we didn't build a fire, but we sat around the fire ring anyway.

While we ate, we exchanged stories about things like the first album we'd bought when we were kids, the first concert we went to, what we thought about Dylan being awarded the Nobel Prize in Literature. We played the desert island game, naming the things we'd want if we were stranded and could have just one kind of food, one kind of music, or a single book until we were rescued. Which might not happen for years, or ever, so our one thing would have to be something that would satisfy us for the rest of our stranded lives.

We talked about the original Woodstock music and peace fest. None of us were old enough to have been there—Hank and I weren't born yet—but Pete joked that he would have gone if the universe hadn't skipped a beat.

"I would have been first in line for a ticket if a gravity glitch or hiccup hadn't distorted the space-time continuum and bumped my birth forward into the future, and made it too late for me to be old enough," he said. "I got a raw deal. Instead of going to one of the events of the century that summer, I was probably learning to ride a bike without training wheels and eat apples without the baby teeth I was starting to lose. My only solace is that Joni Mitchell got an even rawer deal. She was supposed to perform and made it as far as the airport and then got held back by her agent."

I said, "Gravity glitch? You sound like you're tripping. Did you do some LSD to get into the Woodstock vibe?" I was just joking too—and trying to sound like I knew what I was talking about. Psychedelic drugs were the only time I said "No" to an adventure, and meant "No," when Evie said "Yes." I figured my mind was loopy enough. Evie figured hers could use a little more loopiness.

I wasn't serious about Pete tripping, but I understood what he meant about being born later than he should have been. I've sometimes thought I would have felt more at home in my grandparents' generation, back when they danced to live Big Band music until World War II took so many men, musicians included, away to Europe and the Pacific. I could see myself living back then when they grew victory gardens to supplement their war-time rations, cooked everything from scratch, and gathered around radios after dinner because televisions weren't yet standard in every home.

But putting on some more of my faux hippie cool, I pressed Pete, "You dosed yourself with acid, didn't you?"

He laughed and said, "I'm high on music."

"If you're a would-be Woodstocker," I asked him, "why are you traveling the country doing Roger Miller?"

"Because he makes me smile," he said, beaming at me.

That was apparently Hank's cue. He said, "Music time, Pops," and the next thing I knew, father and son were playing together, Pete on guitar and Hank on fiddle. And I was almost overwhelmed by how good I felt, how happy I was to be sitting there, enjoying the last of a great day. "Overwhelmed" is overly dramatic, but I really was close to being both giddy and teary.

Most of the songs they did that night were 1960s and 70s rock and folk hits, with just a few newer ones, and a few old country songs, including a rollicking rendition of the Johnny Cash hit, "Ring of Fire." On that one, while Pete stayed in his chair, playing and singing, Hank got up and danced while he fiddled. He looked like a drunk man in danger of falling into the old ashes in the fire ring, but he never missed a note or beat.

After a few more songs, Pete announced he was ready to "put his bones to bed," and we said our goodnights, which included, much to my surprise, hugs all around, led by Hank. When he hugged me, he thanked me for coming with them and giving him somebody other than his dad to talk with on the road. I laughed, and Pete said, "I second that emotion."

The next morning, we made coffee on a tiny gas stove and had fresh berries, granola, and yogurt for breakfast. Then, after taking down our tents and repacking the car, and a quick trip to the campground's showers, we were back on the road and Hank called for more of a game we'd played the day before, one my family called Car Scrabble. I'd started it with Pete and Hank as an icebreaker on our way out of Saratoga, explaining that each person had to call out a word that fit a particular theme and began with a letter in the word the previous player had called out.

"You can't take time to think," I told them, as I started worrying that it was too early in the morning for games, too soon into the trip, too awkward, too childish.

"If a count of three passes before you say your word, you're out," I said. "If the theme is wacky old-fashioned words, for example, you have to be fast and call out something like 'skedaddle!'"

That was enough for Pete. He jumped in with "K—kerfuffle" and the game was on. And I was saved from my worrying ways. Both guys were good and played hard, but Hank had been the first to falter and called for a rematch as we drove out of Woodstock. He picked the theme, "Foods you can grill that aren't beef, pork, or chicken," and started us off with "S—salmon." That would have been the end for me if I'd had to go next because I blanked and couldn't think of anything, but it was Pete's turn and he called out "A—apples."

I said I wanted to try a slice of grilled apple, which was true, but I was also trying to buy a few seconds. Hank started chanting, "One! Two!" to pressure me, and in the nick of time I shouted, "E—eggplant!"

An hour and a half later, when we got to where we were going next, Bethel, we were playing a new game Pete cooked up, which involved calling out rhyming words, real and made up, that could be split into two other words—hotdog, hedgehog, skunkfog. And we were arguing about what was acceptable, what worked as one word formed from two. "Skunkfog" was one of my contributions, so it worked for me, but Hank, determined to win, tried to disqualify it. He said, "You can't put 'skunk' and 'fog' together. You just can't." So I pushed back on his "foodhole" and insisted that, like "pie hole," it was irrefutably two words.

Bethel, New York, where the Woodstock festival actually happened. Being the educator by trade and nerd by nature that I am, I was excited to visit the museum on the exact site of those three historic days in 1969. We all wanted to see the museum, the Bethel Woods Center, but the guys each had another item on their agenda for the day. Hank wanted to roam around outside and try to imagine for himself what it would have been like to be there in '69 when the Center's grounds were a dairy farm and suddenly swarming with music makers and lovers. And Pete wanted to find a good place to play a tune on his harmonica. He joked that he could then say he'd been at Woodstock and performed after Jimi

Hendrix. He ended up doing his one-song set at a spot overlooking the field that had been a sea of young people during the festival— nearly half a million kids packed together, listening and dancing to the music, huddling in the rain, playing in the mud, smoking weed, tripping on acid, sleeping on the ground.

"So who'd you opt to do for your big gig here?" I asked him when he finished playing and put the harmonica back in his pocket, "Whose song was that?"

"I couldn't cover somebody else at a time like this," he said. "That was a Pete original. Composed in the moment for the momentous occasion."

FIFTEEN

For three nights and two days, we camped at a campground filled with families and Woodstock fans. We spent a bunch of hours at the Bethel Woods Center and a day hiking and swimming in Lake Superior State Park. On the first night at our campsite, we were sitting around after dinner and the guys were noodling around on guitar and fiddle, showing each other things they were working on, songs with complicated chord progressions and melodies they were trying to learn. But then Pete started playing a tune on the guitar, Roger Miller's "Walkin' in the Sunshine," and Hank jumped to his feet and began fiddling along with his dad. Together, they erupted into a rowdy rendition of the song. Hank was dancing as he played and coaxed me to my feet. Pretty soon, all three of us were up dancing and singing. Hank and I joined Pete on the chorus. I didn't know the words, but picked up a few and sang those, and Pete kept me going by acting as if we were sharing a microphone. From the other side of our invisible mic, he locked his eyes on mine so I couldn't quit. From that song, he segued right into another. It didn't have any lyrics, but he kept me on my feet and singing non-words with him, probably ten verses of things like "La" and "Da" and "Dee."

When the guys wrapped up that one with a big guitar and fiddle finish, we all laughed like maniacs. Still laughing, Hank stuck the fiddle bow under his arm so he could give me a high five, after which he grabbed my hand and hoisted it up over our heads like I was a boxer who had just won a championship bout by knockout.

It was a generous gesture, given that my singing isn't anything to applaud.

Pete and his wife raised that boy well. He's a tall, tattooed sweetie. All heart. Always the first to hug, and when he does, it isn't a light, polite gesture. When he hugs you, you can feel that he means it.

Every night, after we were settled in our sleeping bags, in our separate tents, Hank would call out, "Goodnight, John Boy," from the old television program, *The Waltons*, and I'd reply, "Goodnight, Mary Ellen." Then after a second or two, Pete would say, "Goodnight, Irene." The first time he did that, Hank and I yelped, "Wrong show!" It was a corny ritual but made me ridiculously happy.

On our second night in Bethel, the guys once again started playing music after dinner, and almost as soon as they got going, some young people from another campsite appeared with guitars and a banjo and asked if they could join us.

"You bet," Pete said, "let's go." And without much discussion, they all found their way into a tune they seemed to know. An instrumental. A traditional folk song, I think, but I don't remember what they called it. Pretty quickly, Pete decided I should be playing with them, that it wasn't okay that I was the only one not playing. While everybody else kept strumming and picking, he put down his guitar, went to the car, and pulled out what looked like two regular soup spoons with their handles stuck into a piece of wood to form a handgrip. Walking back to the rest of us, directly toward me, he tapped in rhythm with the music, bouncing the spoons between his open palm and flat belly. I knew what he was thinking, and I started shaking my head back and forth. He nodded his up and down.

"Come on, Isla," he said when he reached me. "You're on percussion."

I shook my head again and shoved my hands behind my back.

He dropped down on one knee and said, "If you don't play these spoons, I don't play my guitar, and we both look bad."

"That's blackmail," I told him.

"You could call it that," he replied.

I know it's crazy that I'd be terrified about banging spoons together in front of people I didn't know and would never have to face again, while I was fine going off on a road trip with two guys I'd known for just two weeks, but such were the workings of my mind. Or further evidence of how oddly comfortable I was with Pete and Hank, while still a mess in general.

I said, "Pete, I can't. I do not and cannot do this."

"You can," he said. "You've got great rhythm."

"I don't."

"You do. We're making an awkward scene here, so take these things and have some fun with us."

So I took the spoons and joined in, tapping my knee instead of my belly because my stomach was neither flat nor firm. I stuck to a simple rhythm because I had no choice, given my lack of experience, and I was nervous as hell for a few minutes, but then got a feel for my goofy instrument and I did have fun. It wasn't the same sort of thrilling good time I'd had singing face-to-face with Pete, but it was good. It was really nice to let go and let wary Isla have another night off. She'd reappeared when our campsite neighbors came over but left again when I got into the music.

The next morning, we repacked the car and got back on the road. Pete had his sights set on an open mic in Brooklyn, and the plan was to spend two nights at an Airbnb so we could have a day to wander around the city before heading to Philadelphia for two nights at another Airbnb. I was going to fly home from there, so no more camping for me. I was sad about that and queasy about going back to Brooklyn and Manhattan for the first time since the last time I'd been there with Scott, but I did what I could to prepare myself. The last thing I wanted was to have my mood affect the fun the guys could have in the city.

When we arrived at the apartment Pete had reserved months earlier, a studio with a Murphy bed and a sofa, the guys tried to insist I take the bed, and said they'd flip a coin over the sofa, but I refused, and in the end, we all decided to bring our sleeping bags and pads up from the car and sleep on the floor. Leaving the bed folded up in its cupboard would leave more room for navigating to the bathroom in the middle of the night, which Pete and I appreciated. He didn't make it onto the open mic list, but we went and stayed to watch everybody who had, and after a round of beer, he and I had switched to water and went through enough to float a fleet of ships.

In the morning, we made Hank choose our entertainment for the day, and he wanted to start with a walk through Central Park and a visit to the Museum of Natural History. I'd spent lots of time in both places with Scott, but being with Pete and Hank, who hadn't been to either one, made me see everything through their eyes, and I didn't think of Scott more than once or twice for a fast second.

After the museum, we walked some more—lots more—so the guys could, as Hank put it, "feel the city's vibe." We cut a path that took us past the Chelsea Hotel because so many musicians had lived there, and we made our way to Greenwich Village for the same reason.

When we finally got a Lyft back to Brooklyn and walked up the three flights of stairs to the apartment, we were happy to hit our beds on the floor, and ready for sleep after saying our goodnights.

Hank: *Goodnight, John Boy.*

Isla: *Goodnight, Mary Ellen.*

Pete: *Goodnight, Irene.*

In Philadelphia, the apartment wasn't big, but it had two tiny bedrooms and a sleeper sofa in the living room. The guys tried to get me to take one of the bedrooms, but there was no way that was going to happen. They had many more nights of camping and sleeping on the ground ahead of them, while I was going home to a pillow-top mattress. So I slept on the sofa. In the morning, when Pete heard me up and in the kitchen, he came out and we had coffee while Hank slept in. It was the first time we were alone, but it felt like we'd always done our morning coffee together. Like we had a comfortable routine. I was reading the newspaper on my phone when he came through the kitchen doorway and asked, "Any bombshell headlines?"

"No," I replied. "But my media addiction is a problem. Starting the day with the news is never a good idea anymore."

Pouring himself a cup of coffee, he said, "No, it's not. But I'm a junky too when I'm at home. I'm on a hiatus now, while we're on the road. I'm trying to take a break from worrying about the world my kids are going to inherit."

I started to run with that and bring up the worst of what I'd just been reading, but caught myself and changed the subject. I asked him if he had any pictures of his daughters, and for the next few minutes, we looked at photos on his phone and talked about our families. Of course, the pictures of his girls were mixed in with some of Hank—and Lainie, his wife. I had to resist the urge to linger on those. I did pause and comment on one.

"She was beautiful," I said. And she was a beauty, with the gleaming eyes and smile of a prankster, and a riot of chestnut curls that made me think of Glyn's glorious copper hair. Lainie's was past her shoulders in older photos and very short in more recent pictures, including the one I hesitated to swipe past. In that shot, she was lying on a lawn, leaning back on her arms with her tanned legs and bare feet stretched out in front of her, looking as if there wasn't a thing wrong in her world. If I hadn't just seen several older snapshots, I wouldn't have noticed that the front of her dress was flat across her chest. The breasts she'd had in earlier photos were gone.

"Beautiful," I repeated.

"She was," Pete replied. "A real Rita Ballou."

I didn't get the reference in relation to Lainie, but I remembered "Rita Ballou" was the name of one of the songs in Pete's road trip mix, and I remembered how he'd sung all the words and tapped on the steering wheel when it came on the stereo. When it was over, I asked him the singer's name and texted his answer to myself.

"That would be Guy Clark," he said.

Hank added, "One of the best things ever to come out of Texas, present company included." Then he grinned at me and said, "I mean, *excluded*. Wink, wink."

Remembering that exchange, I smiled and took another look at Lainie on Pete's phone.

"Your turn," he said. "Show me some of your family."

I handed his phone back and scrolled through mine for pictures of my sisters. While I was scrolling, I skimmed over my parents' story, saying only that they'd had a good life and dodged the challenges that often come with aging. I made it sound, I hoped, as if they'd lived to ripe old ages, instead of dying with time left on their meters.

Then I moved on to Glyn and Dale. "You must have met both of them at Evie's party," I told him.

"I did," he replied, "Eve Ellen introduced us. She called them her bonus sisters."

"Here they are at the track on opening day," I said, as I showed him a picture. Then I told him about our family's racehorse names for one another.

"For Dale, the family baby and bruiser, the one who's quick to use words like left hooks, my father mixed together her birth order, horse racing, and brawling to come up with 'BAM!' It's abbreviation for 'By a Mouth!' Which is short for 'Last Out of the Gate and First to the Fight—By a Mouth!' My mother protested that it was too contrived, but it stuck. For my middle sister Glyn, we all agreed on 'Zipper,' as in something that brings two sides together, because she was always the peacemaker between me and Dale. That name still fits her. She grew up to be a career coach specializing in helping people bring together their personal and professional lives, their inner and outer worlds, and she's still the peacemaker between me and Dale, who's still mouthy."

He laughed at that, and asked, "Does your name still fit too? What is it?"

"It's not as good as Zipper or BAM!" I answered. Then I showed him another photo on my phone, and said, "Look, isn't this a great shot of Eve Ellen and Greg?"

He tried to get my pony nickname out of me, but I didn't give in. Withholding it was my version of coy flirtation, I guess. Each time he asked, I showed him more pictures instead, including some Glyn had just recently texted, scans of old snapshots from when we were kids. He paused on one of Evie and me as teenagers, our eyes and mouths open wide with guilty surprise. He wanted to know what we'd been up to, and I told him about the pilfered beer we'd been drinking down on the dock after dark one night when Dale snuck up on us with my mother's camera and snapped the picture. The camera's flash fired just as we turned to look at her, and lucky for us, the photo was such a close shot of our faces, the cans of

Budweiser in our hands were out of the frame, so when my mother had the film developed, she couldn't see them. Even more fortunate, Dale didn't tell on us or force me to buy her silence. She wasn't above tattling or blackmail, but she didn't tattle that time, and when I told her I didn't have any money, she said, "Okay, but remember this picture next time I want a favor from you."

From there, Pete and I went back and forth, swapping stories and hopping from one subject to another. After a while, prompted by something he said, I told him it sometimes felt surreal to look out at the lake from my kitchen windows at the camp and see that the view hadn't changed at all since I looked at it through young eyes. I told him it felt like I'd moved through time and aged, but the world around me hadn't.

He laughed and said, "Your eyes aren't old now, Isla darlin'— you're still far from old. Not that there's anything wrong with being a vintage model."

I said, "You mean like your car, which has had lots of nipping and tucking?"

He snort-laughed at that, then asked, "What do you enjoy most and least about living alone?"

"Most?" I replied, as I was thinking but not saying, "There's something I should enjoy?"

Reading my thoughts, he said, "Yeah. There has to be at least one thing you've found you actually like. Or if that's too strong, something you don't mind."

"Okay, I most enjoy not living in a perfect house anymore. My husband was an architect and every inch of our place was meticulously designed and curated. I only said no to one thing he tried to do. A couple of weeks after we moved in, which we didn't do until he thought he had everything just right, I walked into the living room and found him standing at the built-in bookcases, turning all the books backwards, so their spines were to the wall, out of sight, and the paper ends faced the room. I said, 'Uh, no. No. No. No. No. No. We're not going to do that here.'"

Pete, with a puzzled look on his face, said, "So you couldn't see the titles and tell one book from another?"

"Nope," I replied. "It's an absurd design thing. Hopefully only on home design shows and in magazines, but I'm not sure. Apparently, the look it achieves, unspoiled by covers of varying colors and title text in different styles, is more important than finding the book you're looking for."

Pete, still looking puzzled, nodded and said, "Okay. I don't get why anyone would do that, but okay. We all have our ways. What's the thing you enjoy least?"

"About living alone?" I stalled.

"Yeah," he answered.

"Well," I said, and then stopped to buy another second before starting again. "I guess that would be the alone part. I'm good with living but less good with doing it by myself. Sleeping, eating, doing everything alone. What about you? What do you like most and least?"

"I like being able to turn on the light and read in bed when I have insomnia."

"Did you ever try reading books on your phone or a tablet so you wouldn't need the light?"

"My phone? God no. The tiny little screen would hold two sentences. It would be like trying to get through a whole pot of coffee drinking from a thimble. Besides, I like paper."

"You might be surprised by how much a phone screen can display, and how readable the text is," I told him. "But I'm on your side. I like everything about real books—the paper, print, jacket or cover art."

"Exactly," he agreed.

"So what do you enjoy least?"

"About books?"

"You're stalling."

"As you stalled," he replied, smiling, and reaching across the table to clink his coffee cup against mine. Then he said, "Everything but my reading light. Everything else."

"Name one specific thing you don't like."

"Okay, my wife's sink. Not long before she was diagnosed, we remodeled our bathroom and put in a double vanity. I don't like looking over and seeing her side unused. Mine's always wet, with drops of water everywhere, hers is always dry."

"I think I'd have to rip out the vanity and go back to one sink," I said, "I'd have to."

"Oh, but then there'd be no room for the vase she put on her side. It's still there. Handmade, unpainted white clay, with "HT" on the front, carved like you'd write your initials in wet cement. It was an inside joke between us. She once asked me if I missed Texas and I told her she was my new hometown. Sappy, but she liked it and always signed her notes to me with "HT" after that. So I went to one of those pottery places and made the vase for our second anniversary."

"What would she say about this trip?" I asked, though I was thinking about how hard it must be for him to stand at that sink, first thing every morning and last thing every night, and see what he'd described to me.

"She'd think it was a hoot. Besides the fact she loved a long road trip, she got a kick out of Roger and really loved a lot of country music. The older stuff. I grew up in Texas listening to and trying to play rock and roll, and didn't get into country and folk until Lainie turned me onto them. She was a military brat and grew up all over, but went to high school in Imperial Beach after her dad decided to stay there when he retired. He was a Navy lifer and did his last duty at the Coronado base where Greg and I met. Lainie should have been into California rock or surf music, but she's the one who introduced me to a bunch of Texas songwriters. Go figure."

On that note, Pete got up and refilled our coffee cups, and started another pot, so there'd be something for Hank when he rolled out of bed. And we talked some more about being single at a point in our lives when we hadn't expected to be. How it was like having to "learn a new way to be in your skin" (my words) and "find a new rhythm" (Pete's words). I told him about my foray into the world of online matchmaking, and the swinging chiropractor interested in open marriage. I did my best to make it an entertaining story, playing up my rusty dating skills, my scheming and dashed plans for a rom-com night with Mr. Free Love, though I played down (completely omitted) the part about preparing for fireside sex. I laid the humor on thick when I told him about how I'd swerved around the swinging subject and dodged the chiropractor's attempt to talk about it, how I'd brought up the camp's tree swing and served an apple tart that couldn't have been any more wholesome if it had been an apple pie.

Pete had a good laugh, and before he was through, Hank appeared, stretching and yawning, and said, "Why the giggles, Woody Woodster? Morning, Isla."

Pete said, "Maybe you want to go back to the bedroom, come out again, and give that greeting another try?"

I said, "What *is* it with the Woody thing? I can't see it and I don't get it?"

Hank just smiled, shook his head, and went for the coffee pot.

Pete said, "It's his way of saying I'm a doofus, like the Woody character on *Cheers*."

Neither confirming nor denying his dad's explanation, Hank asked, "So what time do we have to leave for the airport?"

"Too soon," Pete answered. "Then it's just you and me again, so you better get back on my good side."

And with that, the bubble I'd been in popped. It was time to bring my crazy little vacation to an end and get ready to go home.

My sisters spent some time at the house while I was away and made sure the garden got enough water, but they couldn't stay past the weekend. They had to go to work, and I'd soon have to do the same. The start of the new school year was so close, I could almost hear the bell ringing and the kids talking in their squeaky little voices. Not to mention, the farther I went with Pete and Hank, the more expensive it would be to get back. Pete wouldn't let me share the cost of our campsites, the apartments, or the gas, but the prospect of having to return the money I'd received from Craig for Scott's practice made me nervous about my last-minute plane ticket. No early bird discount for me.

I wasn't ready to leave Pete and Hank. I wanted to stay on the road with them, talking, listening to music, playing car games, camping. I fantasized about having just a few more days. They were taking a southern route home and I loved the idea of seeing some of the South together, including Nashville and Memphis, where they were going to visit Graceland and pay homage to Elvis. I imagined taste testing our way across the barbecue belt. Going all the way to Pete's native Texas. I still wish I'd gone that far with them, but I didn't. My last night was the first of the two nights Pete had planned for Philadelphia. From there, I'd decided, I would fly to Albany, where Evie would pick me up.

At the Philly airport, Pete and Hank hugged me. Hank first. He wrapped his arms around me, squeezed tightly, and said, "We have to stay in touch." Pete squeezed more gently, but held on longer, and said, "Isla, you're a rare gem. We'll miss you. I'll miss you."

Then they were gone. And as busy and buzzing with activity as the terminal and the packed plane were, I was back in the silence of my solo life. I had a window seat and spent most of the flight just staring at clouds and sky. I tried to read and made it through less than a page. I tried to write in my journal, and did get down some of the conversation I'd had with Pete that morning, but mostly I just stared out the window.

SIXTEEN

What do you do when find yourself back in your solitary life, post-road trip and post-Pete? First, you swim laps in the lake for so long you become a mindless machine. Then you pickle every vegetable you can get your hands on until your kitchen cupboards look like jewelry boxes, with every compartment loaded with gems in Mason jars—emeralds, rubies, pearls, green and violet amethysts, yellow and orange topaz. When there aren't any more green beans or red beets or carrots or other plant life left to pickle, you go back to work on the book you're supposed to be writing and hardly stop to eat, sleep, or shower. The book is a good distraction for a couple of days, then it's time for your barn sale.

With my professional house stager, photo stylist, flower arranger sister Dale directing the show, we transformed her barn with fresh straw on the dirt floor, big bunches of flowers tied to the wooden posts, and my purged possessions, along with my sisters' own cast-offs, arranged in artful groupings. Dishes and other dining treasures were displayed on tables draped with pristine tablecloths. Nearby, in the center of the barn, we had a home décor and furniture department with some side tables and chairs, a chest of drawers, a few lamps, lots of knickknacks—but only things that Dale said didn't scream or even whisper "garage sale junk," which ruled out the dust-crusted model of a wooden sailing ship with a busted mast that Glyn wanted to evict from her house but couldn't bring herself to throw in the trash because it had belonged to one of our grandfathers. Her hope was that if somebody was willing to pay a few bucks for it, they'd be willing to clean it up and repair the damage. She'd accepted that she wasn't ever going to find the time or will to mend or dust it herself.

Dale deemed my brass table clock worthy and it sold immediately. It had been a gift from Scott on our first anniversary, but I'd never tried to figure out how to read its complicated face, which displayed the time in each time zone around the world. I was willing and able to keep up with my own zone, so I could be where I was supposed to be when I was supposed to be there, but I just couldn't see any reason to know the time in Mozambique or Mongolia. I'd glued the card Scott gave me with the clock into the journal I was keeping that year. I don't purge journals, so there's no getting rid of the card, or the note my husband wrote inside.

I'm so glad we're just getting started, Isla, and still have fifty years to be together. Or even sixty, if I'm lucky. That's a half-million hours that I get to be married to you, and I'm looking forward to every one of them.

Along one wall of the barn, we had clothes and handbags hanging on racks. Along the opposite wall, we displayed books on long tables and arranged a couple of comfortable chairs so shoppers could sit and flip through the pages of any volume they wanted to consider for purchase—travel and art books, cookbooks, gardening books, novels.

Dale said we'd sell more if we created "an experience" and treated our stuff like it was valuable, rather than castoffs we wanted to unload. I was a tad afraid the *experience* would come off as pretentious, but I knew it would make the day more fun, so rather than resist, I added my own touch—background music. I brought the small sound dock and speakers I sometimes used in my classroom and a playlist of songs I'd been collecting since I came home from the trip with the guys. I'd become music-obsessed or possessed since meeting Pete. I'd always enjoyed having the radio on or stereo going, but I didn't subscribe to any streaming services and hadn't bought any new music in ages. After the trip, I started loading up my phone with Pete-inspired songs, and whenever I added another one, I also put it on an iPod one of my sisters had abandoned at the camp and I had adopted so I could keep it in my car, plugged into the stereo à la Pete's set up. His music became my soundtrack at home, around the house, in the car, driving to and from school. It made me think of him, though I sometimes also thought about how he'd obviously been thinking of his wife when he made the mix, when he selected the songs. There were some rock tunes, some rhythm and blues, but many more country songs, and a lot of them were about love and longing, so I couldn't help but know he'd had his wife in mind.

Dale wasn't sure about having background music until I told her my playlist was heavy on country. "Bring it on," she said. "It'll be really ironic on multiple levels." Oh, cynical little sister.

I can't know how much we would have sold if we'd just put everything out willy-nilly, like a standard garage or yard sale, but I was surprised by how well we did with Dale's set up. And with her promotion of the big day via the massive social network she'd built to promote her freelance stager-stylist-florist services. She'd been teasing the sale and doing a daily countdown for two weeks, posting photos of some of the things we'd be selling and a series of artsy shots of the barn, with its big doors closed and emblazoned with "Opening Soon." When it was all over and I was lying in bed that night, I thought about how I already felt less weighed down and like I'd taken a step forward. I didn't know what I'd stepped toward, but I was traveling lighter, making progress, and I'd eventually get somewhere good.

In the meantime, I had just a few days left until school started again and I hoped that would be enough to finish the first draft of my book. I thought it might be because I wasn't writing a hefty epic full of blab about why you should practice what I was preaching. I was doing a fat-free guidebook to take readers through the process of renovating their food lives, with each chapter providing succinct steps for one stage of the process. I'd already written more than half the chapters I'd mapped in my outline, and thought I could get through the rest quickly, once I focused—but finishing in less than a week, while also getting my classroom ready for the first day of school, had been a pipe dream.

Or as Dale said, "The peeps in hell hope for frozen yogurt with rainbow sprinkles but it's not going to happen for them. They need to get real. I'm just saying, Isla. Don't set yourself up for disappointment. Or, you being you, for a guilt trip."

I didn't finish before school started, and I was disappointed, but just a little. And I didn't feel guilty.

Once I was back in class five days a week, I started a daily practice of taking a half-hour break when I got home, to wind down before making dinner. I'd sit and drink mint tea, think about what I wanted my future to be, and write in my journal. It was the time of day that Scott and I would have our post-work, pre-dinner drink and catch up. Living alone at the camp, I turned it into a time for sitting on the porch, or at the kitchen table, filling pages with the contents of my mind.

After dinner, I'd sometimes rouse myself to go for a walk along the lake and then try to work on my book, but more often than not I'd watch an episode of my latest favorite food program. Or, truth be told, get lost online watching music videos, feeding my new obsession. Then I'd go to bed.

I'd discovered that a room full of five- and six-year-olds can drain you dry when you're in a funk or depressed. Yes, the kids were a daily dose of joy, but there were also days I'd come home so spent, when I climbed the porch steps, I could almost hear a sucking sound as the last of my energy drained away and left my body like used bathwater leaving a tub. The tea break would revive me enough to make dinner and eat, which would revive me a little more, but I still wouldn't have enough oomph left to do anything but stare at a screen.

Thankfully, because I'd been teaching for years, I didn't have to spend enormous amounts of time preparing lesson plans and activity materials. I did have to do some of that, to supplement or refresh the plans and materials I'd created and collected over the years, but I had it down to an efficient routine I could cover in a few hours on occasional weekends. Or, if necessary, a weekday evening. Unlike teachers in higher grades, I also didn't bring home piles of homework assignments and tests to correct. Altogether, I had less work than I might have to do between the end of class in the afternoon and returning to my classroom the following morning, so I fell into a pattern that repeated, Monday through Friday—school, journal, dinner, down the music rabbit hole on YouTube, bed.

I didn't try to reach Pete.

I didn't text or call Tom. I knew it was just a matter of time before Eve Ellen brought him up, but in the meantime, I didn't get in touch with him. In part, that was because of the snark I feared I had heard in his reply when I let him know I had to cancel our dinner date in order to go rambling with Pete and Hank, and because I felt flaky for the way I'd handled that situation. But the real decider: It felt like pursuing him would be cheating on Pete. Logically, I knew that was nuts. Literally crazy. Nothing had happened between me and Pete. There was nothing to cheat on. Still, I had a sense that I'd be betraying something true and genuine—what I was feeling for him—and I'd be going for something that wasn't true or genuine, simply because it was available.

More sanely, I thought I should pause the partner quest and finally figure out what I wanted in a new relationship and in life. Finally focus, think it through, form conclusions, and define goals. Feelings are great, I told myself, or they can be. And overthinking isn't good, particularly obsessing about relatively trivial things while overlooking others that might be more significant, or refusing to look at anything that might be uncomfortable. But some rational thinking was in order. Unexamined feelings and assumptions got me my failed relationship with Scott. I didn't want to repeat any mistakes I may have made with him. I suppose it's considered outdated or unsophisticated to see the end of a marriage as a failure, but there's no getting around the fact that Scott and I failed to fulfill the wedding vows we wrote together and exchanged before our families and friends.

I vow to be your partner in *and* for *life, to walk through this world with you, to live and learn and grow with you, to be by your side through whatever comes our way.*

Scott—I didn't get in touch with him either. I figured he'd let me know when he knew something about Craig. Until then, there was nothing I could do but wait. And try not to worry.

I did exchange texts with Hank. He sent one to me on my first night back at the lake. *"Miss you already,"* he wrote, beneath a photo of Pete on stage at the Philly open mic. Then nearly every day after that, he sent long road reports to me, Eve Ellen, and Greg, and we'd reply with shorter texts. He included his dad too, but Pete chimed in just once.

Hank: *With our music man at the wheel I'm free to sit here and take in the amazing views. Virginia and the Blue Ridge are rolling by to the tune of Pop's trip mix. Courtesy of its alpha order we just heard... My Darlin' Hometown by John Prine... My Favorite Memory by Merle Haggard... My Favorite Picture of You by Guy Clark. If you can listen to those three songs back to back and not have your heart fucking feel something I'm sorry to break the bad news but you don't have a heart. Apologies to my genteel Pop for the language and to any of the rest of you if you're offended but there's no other way to say it.*

Pete: *To He Who Lacks Vocabulary... there actually are other ways to say what you said about the Prine, Haggard, and Clark songs yesterday, but I'm glad you at least don't lack taste in music.*

Occasionally, Hank texted just me, apart from the group. Sweetheart that he is, on my first day back at school, he sent a sweet message and photo of the empty spot in the car's backseat, where I'd sat, except when he or Pete insisted on swapping so I could enjoy the view from the front seat.

We're still missing you. I hope your kindergartners are good and your new school year gets off to a great start.

Whether Hank texted me alone or all of us, I was glad to stay connected. I reread every word he sent and looked at every photo again and again. I tried to recapture the feeling of being with him and Pete. I summoned the sound of their voices, remembered how Pete always smelled like eucalyptus leaves because of a balm he used to keep his hands in shape for playing guitar and fiddle, but he sometimes also smelled a little like one of my favorite spice mixtures—cumin, coriander, cinnamon, and mint. Heavy on the cumin, which some people say smells like man sweat, in a less than good way, but makes me imagine a guy who's worked up a clean steam hiking in the woods on a winter day, or splitting firewood, and then come inside trailing a whiff of outside. The fragrance of pines and spruce and cedar trees, snow, fresh-split wood, smoke from the chimney.

I've always been an ardent fan of cumin, but oh how smitten I was with Pete—how yearning. If I'd still had the refrigerator poetry magnets Scott couldn't abide in our kitchen, and if I'd used them to describe Pete's scent, I would have said something so over-the-top, I'd make my own eyes roll.

Confession: In my journal, I did write the eye roller I would have put on my refrigerator if I'd had the magnets.

Summer scent of fresh eucalyptus and blue sky with distant memories of winter woods and wood smoke

Oh, pining poet Isla. In each text from Hank, I looked for what I could learn about Pete and loved when Hank reported on the music they were listening to in the car as they drove. One day, not long after I left them, he sent a beautiful photo of an old wooden building and water wheel beside a pond, followed by three long text messages that came so fast his fingers must have flown over the keyboard on his phone.

See what we just saw! Mabry Mill and pond... one of the most photographed places in the US. It looks like a painting of a scene too pretty to exist.

Pop played Roanoke last night. Today he's taking a break and we're headed to the Blue Ridge Music Center in Galax. Tomorrow we go to Maces Springs. It's the home of folk and country's original royal family... the Carters. Old Pete is so thrilled to be traveling the holy land of American roots music he can hardly speak but every few miles he groans about someplace we to have to skip.

We just heard two versions of Sugar Moon... K.D. Lang's beautiful cover and Willie Nelson's toe-tapper as Pop would say about it. Good old Willie is another stellar gift from Texas to the world. Whether he's doing his own songs or somebody else's he's flat out masterful.

Another reason to love Hank: He uses full words when he texts, rather than writing an alphabet soup full of cute abbreviations. And when he writes about music, he includes complete titles and the names of the singers or bands that recorded the songs. For that, I'm especially grateful because I bought every song he mentioned in his road reports, along with all the ones I could remember from when I was with him and his dad. Knowing Lainie inspired a lot of Pete's mix didn't stop me. Two or three tunes at a time, my playlist grew as the guys made their way through the South and Southwest, doing open mics and visiting places associated with music. At ninety-nine cents a song, or just pennies over a dollar—prices too easy to dismiss as nothing—I kept buying as the guys' pilgrimage kept moving, cutting through Tennessee to Nashville and Memphis, zig-zagging down through Mississippi to New Orleans, crossing Texas and then Arizona, where Tucson was their last stop.

I was particularly thrilled to get a report that arrived with a great profile photo of Pete, driving with his arm out the window and his hand open to catch the passing breeze.

Hello New York friends. Goodbye Louisiana. We're headed to Houston then Austin and Kerrville and appropriately listening to Waltz Across Texas Tonight sung by the insanely great trio Emmylou Harris, Dolly Parton, Linda Ronstadt. Before that it was Wake Up Time courtesy of Pop's historic fixation with Tom Petty. Then we had some walkin' songs... Patsy Cline went Walkin' After Midnight... and Pop's current fixation Roger did his Walkin' in the Sunshine. Isla we'll always have Bethel!

I loved that Hank remembered when he and Pete played "Walkin' in the Sunshine" at our campsite in Bethel and got me to sing and dance with them. If I had to pinpoint the moment I knew I had a thing for Pete, it was then, as we sang into our invisible mic.

My text back to Hank:

I seem to recall hearing Wildflowers by Petty when we were driving into Philadelphia. If you're back to songs that begin with W, you must be listening to music more than making it. I miss hearing you two play together.

Hank's next text:

Pop says he misses singing with you!

Patting my chest, I said, "Be still, my beating heart, Pete was just being a nice guy." But my imagination could and did fantasize that there was more to his reply.

SEVENTEEN

Three-and-a-half weeks after I said goodbye to the guys in Philadelphia, my journal entry was a diagram that looked like a child's line drawing of a sun radiating nine rays. In the middle of the circle, I wrote, *"Isla's New Life,"* and along each of the rays, in tiny print, I described something I wanted in my future. For good measure, I repeated those things in a list on the opposite page.

House in Saratoga
Light, bright, white rooms
Lots of windows
Music indoors and outside
Sunny garden
Music through windows into garden while I work
Big table outside for dinners with family and friends
Two chairs out by veggie beds for morning coffee
Pete in one of the chairs

Earlier that day, before I made the diagram and list, I received a text from Hank with a video of Pete doing his last open mic the previous night, in Tucson. Then a second text with just four words.

And so it ends.

For his final set, Pete changed it up. He did "Kansas City Star," modified to "Tucson City Star," and then "It Takes All Kinds to

Make a World," before finishing with the fiddle tune he'd played in Saratoga. The crowd responded with nice applause, but with less enthusiasm than Pete had received at Caffe Lena. I hoped he didn't feel it was an anticlimactic end to his trip. He looked happy as he took a quick bow, but I knew a smiling face doesn't always indicate genuine happiness.

When he left the stage and disappeared from my phone screen, I was slammed with the thought that I should have asked Hank for videos from the beginning, all along the trip, and I cursed both myself and him.

"Damn me! Damn you, Hank, for not thinking of it! Oh, sweet Hank, what *were* we thinking?"

I would have again rolled my eyes at how high school silly I was being, but I was too busy watching the video a second and third time.

I'm not one to drink alone, but that day I traded my usual cup of tea for a glass of wine. I swiped a bottle from the supply Dale kept at the camp and hoped it wasn't one she was saving for a special occasion. I picked a Zinfandel because it was the only red wine from California in Dale's stash. I usually go for Cabernet Sauvignon, and there were two Cabs in the cupboard, but Pete was in California, so I went with the Zin.

EIGHTEEN

Five weeks after I last saw Pete, I heard from him. I got a card, an actual paper card with a photo of an ocean sunset on the front and a handwritten note inside. Standing in the post office, at my open mailbox, I read the note twice. Then I read it again out in my car in the parking lot.

Hi, Isla Frances!

Let me know your racehorse name and I'll call you that if you'd prefer.

I'm finally back into a rhythm here at home, adjusted to living in a house, rather than the car and tent and rented apartments, and I want to thank you, way too belatedly, for making our trip extra wonderful. Thank you for your hospitality at the lake and letting us descend on you without much warning.

Thank you for the Saratoga history tour. It couldn't have been better tailored for me, but Hank really enjoyed it too. If you're ever out our way, we'll do some West Coast history. Imperial Beach isn't Saratoga Springs, but this corner of the country, San Diego County, has had its interesting moments.

Thank you for making the too few days you spent with us on the road immeasurably more fun and memorable. I enjoyed every minute and hope you had a good time too.

Wishing you well always,

Pete

Old school Pete. I loved seeing his handwriting. It wasn't ornate but looked wonderfully elegant in a world where cursive is a dying art and kids learn keyboarding skills in grade school, at around the same age they once learned to produce flowing script.

I loved that he'd written the note, but I wished he'd texted so I could reply immediately and then hold my breath while I waited and hoped for more from him. I fantasized that we could be at the beginning of a conversation that would soon move from texts to phone calls and continue nightly, and on weekend mornings. I wondered how I could still make that happen.

Should I take the initiative and call him? I had his phone number, thanks to Hank's group texts. But I didn't have the guts.

Should I reply to his note with a thank you of my own, via text, and hope it would get a conversation going? Some back-and-forth talk that would lead to *what?*

I mulled my options for a week and changed my mind multiple times, then I sent him a Saratoga Race Course postcard featuring a lone horse in full stride on the track, running hard, the competition nowhere in sight. On the back, I carefully copied a note I'd composed and revised, and revised some more, on a separate piece of paper.

BACK OF THE PACK? OUT IN FRONT?
One of the above might be my racehorse name. And might not. Thank you for the card. It was a treat to get real mail.

Sincerely,
She Who Knows But Isn't Telling

Every day after work, I stopped at the post office on my way home, checked my mailbox, and hoped for another note. Or a long letter. I started monitoring my mail before it was even reasonable to think Pete had received my postcard, so, of course, nothing came. Nothing but the usual bills and junk. Eventually, I went back to checking only occasionally. I accepted that Pete's note had been a polite "thank you," rather than a flirtation in disguise, and I tried to believe there was a very good chance he didn't realize my postcard was a cringe-worthy attempt to flirt with him.

NINETEEN

After Pete and Hank got home, I heard from Hank less often, but he occasionally texted "surf reports." Which rarely mentioned actual water and frequently mentioned Pete.

Surf report... He's riding a new wave. Pop's doing Petty. Acoustic Tom Petty. Roger has left the house.

Surf report... Choppy water today but burgers are on the grill. Wish you guys were here.

Surf report... Pop lost his razor or decided to go for a beard. This shot shows three days growth.

Surf report... As you can see, Pop found his razor or decided against the beard.

Naturally, I added more Tom Petty to my playlist, but I calmed down about Pete and didn't make a habit of mooning over the two new photographs of him. He didn't leave my head entirely—I still played his road music every day and it would sometimes trigger thoughts of him—but I had so much going on, I couldn't devote swaths of time to fantasizing. The school year was taking longer than usual to shift from herky-jerky first gear into a smooth cruising speed. I had some challenging kids. And I was working like mad to finish the first draft of my book, putting in six hours every Saturday and another six on Sunday. Once I had all the chapters roughly written, I went right into edits and polishing and tried to get every word right. I was determined to send a flawless manuscript to my agent by Thanksgiving. She'd told me she'd try to start reading it as soon as her family's focus turned to football and they were glued to the television. She said she couldn't promise she'd finish before the holiday weekend was over, when other commitments would claim her time and slow her progress, but she'd try. That was pure kindness on her part because I wasn't a big earner for her or one of her prestigious authors, so I wanted to send a book she wouldn't regret reading when she could have been doing something else.

I'd also heard from Scott. Long story short: Craig had pleaded guilty to embezzlement after weeks of huddling with his lawyer and considering the terms of a plea bargain, weighing whether he might come out better if he went to trial. He hadn't been sentenced yet, but he wouldn't be returning to the practice, even if he avoided jail time. I wouldn't have to give back any money, but I wasn't going to get the rest of what Craig was supposed to pay me. And I was once again financially entangled with my ex-husband. Scott and I went back to negotiating through attorneys, working out a payment plan we would abide by until he finished paying for my half of the business, or he found a way to take care of the remaining balance in one lump sum. The only good news, besides not having to give back what I'd already received, was that I wouldn't end up in the middle of anything Scott might cook up with another architect. My new attorney said, "Under no circumstances will that happen on my watch." She was appalled by the terms of the deal with Craig that I'd been encouraged to accept by my old attorney. A part of me wanted to just move on and let Scott have the practice, but I listened to my legal eagle and took her advice. She said she'd push me to go for full payment if I were her daughter, given that my income was much less than Scott's and I'd made it possible for him get started when he went out on his own. I'd supported us with my teaching income through his first lean years in Saratoga and I hadn't asked for spousal support in our divorce settlement. She told me I'd been more than fair, splitting everything equally with Scott—assets and debts—and she cautioned me to think about my future security. She was chic and very high-fashion and didn't look like anybody's mom, but I knew both my parents would tell me all the same things. They'd urge me to be as fair to myself as I was to Scott. I could almost hear my mother saying, "He made choices that are costing you dearly, and more than monetarily, Isla. Don't cover any of his costs too." So I went along with the wise counsel of my elders. The attorneys wrestled, mine kept coming back to me with questions, and I fielded what felt like constant emails from her.

All of the above left little time to obsess about Pete. It was enough, but there was more—I got an email from Mr. Free Love, the Albany chiropractor.

Hi Isla,

I've been thinking about you and wondering whether you've had any second thoughts about me. I really enjoyed the time we spent together and would love to see you again. What do you think?

Lyle

He caught me at the wrong time, at the end of an intense week. My students were out of their little minds with full-moon fever or God knows what. Unrelated to their madness, I'd had conferences with their parents, and a few, who were more exhausting than their kids, came in with loads of demands disguised as suggestions.

And my ex-husband had turned angry. Frustrated that my attorney was being such a stickler, treating every detail as if my life depended on it, he texted me directly and I could hear his caustic voice in my head as I read his words.

Scott: *Really, Isla? We're back here?*

Me: *Looks like we are.*

Scott: *We're not trying to launch a NASA mission to Mars and make sure the astronauts come back alive. Your lawyer lady can ease up on questioning every nut and bolt.*

When I didn't respond to that text, he sent another one:

Scott: *I'm trying to run a business and keep clients happy while I deal with this shit. I'm supporting four people with one income, so who has Craig screwed worse? Who's been hit hardest?*

I let that one go, too, and instead vented my anger in an email to Mr. Free Love. I told him what I thought. He asked. I answered. Without a polite opening greeting or closing sign off.

Hmmm. What do I think? Well, as I recall, the last time I saw you, you said you wanted to be honest with me and didn't want to waste my time. I think that was either a calculated load of crap or a delusion you bought into before trying to pass it on to me. You waited to bring up what you were looking for because it served some selfish purpose for you to wait. You took my time and used it to suit your agenda. You took hours I'll never get back. Bravo to you for figuring out what you want, but you should have been honest with me about it before we met for that first coffee. I wouldn't have gone out with you if I'd known. Don't contact me again.

I knew I shouldn't send such an ugly reply and I'd be sorry if I pressed the "Send" button, but I pressed. And, as expected, I was sorry. I regretted letting Scott bother me and wished I hadn't reacted to his texts with an overreaction to the chiropractor's email, which I should have just ignored.

My lack of control was beyond juvenile, but in the grand scheme of things, I decided it wasn't worth losing sleep over. I had other concerns.

TWENTY

On November 2, I drew another diagram in my journal. I made it the shape of a target, and in the center, in the bull's eye, I wrote, *"New Partner."* In the rings that circled the center, I described my ideal guy, starting with attributes that were absolutely essential in the first ring, closest to the bull's eye, and working out from there, ring by ring, to things that would be nice but might not be necessary, depending on the guy's other gifts and charms. Then I repeated the attributes in a list on the next page.

ESSENTIAL:
Interesting & fun
Thoughtful & kind
Honorable
Sane

VERY IMPORTANT:
Good conversationalist
Good sense of humor
Reader/curious
Happy outdoors
Adventurous

ICING ON THE CAKE:
Food lover/not finicky
Not finicky in general

Tidy but not obsessively so
Physically magnetic
Warm hands
Smiling eyes
Doesn't snore
Does snuggle & spoon

Limiting myself to what I was able to squeeze into the rings forced me to focus and hone my wish list, but it also meant lots of erasing and reworking, until the paper practically had holes in it. If it had been less worn, able to take more erasing, and had I not gotten hungry for dinner, I might have made more changes because reading the list again later, I decided I'd wasted space on things that overlapped or covered the same ground. For example, if you're "adventurous," you're not likely to be "finicky."

Where I really wanted more room was in the first ring, the essentials. To make the diagram, I had traced around the lids of bottles and jars—a small ketchup lid for the bull's eye, mustard for the middle ring, and mayonnaise for the largest circle. The result was very little space for the things that were most important to me.

I agonized over leaving out "Available," after I erased it to make room for "Honorable." I knew I wanted nothing less than availability on every level—heart, mind, body, and soul. I'd started thinking about that because of how Pete lived thousands of miles away and was physically absent, and from there my mind wandered back to Scott and how he had been physically present, but gone from me in every other sense in the last months of our marriage, even as we ambled around our old stomping grounds in the city and ate ice cream two days before he told me he was leaving me. That afternoon in Brooklyn and Manhattan, I thought we were still a couple, but his body just hadn't yet left to rejoin the rest of him, which was with his running friend. So I'd thought about restoring "Available" and losing "Sane," my sarcastic shorthand for the multitude of ways a person might be damaged and might deal with their damage—including shutting down, closing off, lashing out, stepping out and sleeping around. But the paper's fragility and my desire for happiness I could trust won the contest. I convinced myself that availability went without saying.

Plus, I didn't have enough room left for more than four letters and couldn't think of any other essential attributes that were that short.

Looking at the diagram and list again as I ate dinner, all I could see was Pete. It seemed glaringly obvious that he'd loomed large in my subconscious as I filled in the diagram's rings and then listed what I wanted. Maybe I was wishfully projecting, but it seemed he was a match for nearly everything I put on those pages. There were a few things I couldn't know for sure, but more that I could. I knew he didn't snore because our tents had been only a few feet apart when we were camping and we'd slept in the same room, inches apart, in Brooklyn, but I couldn't know whether he was inclined to spoon in bed. He might be. I knew from hugging him that our bodies fit together nicely. I knew he hugged well. He didn't give the power squeezes that Hank gave, but he didn't do the light, polite pat on the back thing either. There wasn't any Yankee reticence in his hugs. Maybe he'd spoon well too.

And maybe I'd left "Available" out of the diagram and off the list because I didn't want to truly accept that he was out of the question. Life had moved on and I'd gotten busy, but not so much so that I completely forgot how good and comfortable it felt being with him, and how much I missed him.

TWENTY-ONE

On November 30, I saw Tom again. Eve Ellen had been pestering me to get in touch with him for weeks. I always told her I was too tired after work on school nights and too busy with my book on weekends. But I sent a finished manuscript to my agent just before Thanksgiving, as I'd hoped to, and Evie was done with my excuses. She took me out to celebrate with my sisters and conveniently picked a pub where she knew Tom and a group of his Skidmore buddies met up on the last Friday of every month.

Seeing him for the first time since I flaked on our dinner date back in August was awkward, and having him and his group join us for a toast to my book was embarrassing. I would have strangled Eve Ellen, but other than those few uncomfortable minutes, it was a fun night. I was so happy to be through with weekends working at my desk, shackled there, I felt free and light enough to float.

A few days later, I was at home decorating my Christmas tree, and he called. He asked me to dinner and I accepted because it was the most comfortable thing I could think to do, and seemed like the polite response, in light of how I'd canceled our first date with a text as I took off with Pete and Hank.

When I said yes, I wasn't thinking about anything more than one evening at a restaurant, where I would do my best to be a good dinner companion for a couple of hours. I thought that would be as far as it would go. I didn't factor into my plan the effect Tom's gifts and charms would have on me. He arrived at my door at six o'clock on the dot on Saturday, December 8, with a wheel of cheese he'd made. It was a gift, he said, to celebrate my manuscript milestone. As he handed it to me, I thought, "Hmmm. Beekeeper, canner of vegetables, cheesemaker."

But I said, "Maybe I need to have some of this now."

He replied. "Don't do that to me. You might not like it. Put it in your fridge and let's stick to our pizza plan."

So the cheese went into the refrigerator and we went out to Tom's car, where we were talking before we had the doors shut. I asked about his cheesemaking and made him tell me about that before I let him ask me any questions. He wanted to know about my book. I tried to make short work of that topic and told him I was waiting to hear from my agent, so I didn't have any news to share. He wouldn't let me stop there. He asked a bunch of questions about the book's content and my writing process. So we talked about that for a while and it led to talking about our divorces after I told him how I'd tossed the chapters I'd written before my split and started over with a new idea.

I told him I hoped to be married again one day, but not until I'd tended to other things on my to-do list, and I let him know I wasn't open to anything more than platonic friendship. I hadn't meant to do that and didn't have anything specific in mind, in regard to those "other things" on my to-do list, but I believed what I said as I was saying it and managed to say it in a way that didn't ruin the nice time we'd been having.

Then we were back at my place, standing on the dock, and Tom was telling me the end of a story he'd started on the drive home, one about how he and some of his high school friends had celebrated their graduation at his family's camp. Other than being the longest he'd talked about himself before steering the subject back to me, it wasn't anything that should have had an effect on me beyond making me laugh, but standing there beside him, I started to feel the same surge of heat I'd felt at Eve Ellen's party. I would have peeled off my jacket if I could have done it without him seeing me. It was a cold night, but I'd become that hot. We'd gone down to the lake so he could point to where his family's place sat right at the water's edge up the shore a few miles. All I could make out was a small cluster of lights against an inky black backdrop, but the moon was bright enough that I could see his face, with the grin and the squint lines, which were growing more attractive by the second. I was probably doomed by then but hadn't yet let myself acknowledge it.

He finished his tale with a finale involving a wooden raft rigged with dozens of fireworks that were meant to go off in a series of beautiful bursts in the sky over the lake, but instead exploded all at once in a blazing bonfire on the water's surface, incinerating the raft, he said, "like a floating funeral pyre." I was blazing like a human bonfire and desperately wanted to fan my face and take off both my jacket and shirt.

Then he said, "Brrr, it's cold," and turned toward the house. I followed a couple of steps behind him and frantically fanned myself until he reached back and offered me one of his hands. The path had swung to the right, toward the side of the house, and passed through a patch of trees, where it got so dark it was hard to see where we were stepping, so he took my hand. He hadn't turned around, so he didn't catch me flapping air at my hot face, but I'd been going at it so frantically, the movement surely rippled through my whole body and he would have felt it if I'd kept flapping. I had no choice but to quit.

When we got to the edge of the light from the front porch, he said "Brrr" again, let go of my hand, shoved both his hands deep into his pants pockets, and stepped aside so I could get ahead of him. From there, I took the lead and he followed me across the lawn and up the porch steps. After I had the door unlocked and open, he leaned over, kissed my cheek, and said, "Goodnight."

As he was pulling away, his hands still in his pockets, I put my free hand on his arm. He stopped, his face just inches from mine, and looked at me, as if checking for my consent, then kissed me on the mouth.

So much for platonic friendship—I'd left that idea down by the water. He didn't stay the night but did stay a while, and we made use of the sofa. And then the rug by the fireplace, once he got a fire going. When we were done, we stayed there on the floor, beneath a blanket, and talked about the consistency of perfect pizza crust, whether a good Caesar salad dressing could be achieved without anchovies, whether wheat beer is worthy or earns the scorn some beer snobs pour on it. We agreed on thin and chewy crust, the necessity of anchovies, and the worthiness of a good wheat beer.

Around eleven o'clock, he kissed me one last time, got dressed, and left.

Remarkably, I didn't start worrying right away. I didn't fret about where that night might lead, what it meant, where I wanted it to go, what I should or shouldn't do next. I climbed into my bed and for the few minutes it took me to fall asleep, I just enjoyed remembering how good it felt to hold and be held by a guy again. How good it felt to have someone's warm skin on mine. How wonderful it was to be kissed. Even though Scott and I had less frequent sex after the miscarriage, we never quit altogether, but I couldn't remember the last time our lips touched for longer than a quick greeting or farewell peck, and those pecks never involved eye contact. Tom was an eye-contact marvel, master, wizard with magical powers. He seduced with his eyes. I'd shared an intense kiss with the Albany chiropractor, but it had been more like a blind feeding frenzy than a seduction.

When Wizard Tom texted me the next morning, just before I left for school, I hesitated for only a fraction of a second before I replied.

Tom: *I don't know what to say, except I'd like to do what we did again.*

Me: *It's not out of the question.*

Tom: *Name the date and time, I'll be there. Have a good day today, Isla.*

And so it began, my complicated next chapter.

TWENTY-TWO

It had become such a habit to listen to Pete's road music at home and in the car, I turned it on automatically. It got me ready for class in the morning and brought me back home from school at the end of the day. It accompanied my tea breaks after work, kept me company while I cooked dinner, and played in the background while I wrote. It had almost become my music, rather than Pete's, and didn't automatically make me think about him anymore.

But there was no way Pete and Tom weren't going to collide in my mind when I turned on the stereo in the car the Monday morning after that Saturday night. I was backing out of the driveway, thinking about the texts I'd just received from Tom, and I hit the stereo's power button. Out of the speakers came a song that always stood out as exotically distinct among the others in Pete's mix and in my playlist—an instrumental rock number, rich with Latin rhythms and sounds, and oozing sensuality. Santana's "Samba Pa Ti."

Startled, I grabbed the key in the ignition and killed the engine. That song never failed to affect me. It had been the soundtrack for my most sensuous Pete reveries. Once when it came on while I was at the stove stirring a pot of polenta, I stopped stirring, closed my eyes, and started swaying, with the wooden spoon still in my hand but up in the air over the pot and dreamily waving like a wand. I just swayed, listened to the music, and imagined Pete standing behind me, kissing my neck while I tried to cook. It's not a short song, nearly five minutes long, and by the time it finished,

I'd let the polenta burn on the bottom and get stiff as half-set cement. I never smelled it scorching.

After the rough start, my drive to school that day was silent. Or the car was quiet while my mind was a racket of competing thoughts. They darted and hummed in my head like hummingbirds fighting for territory and jabbing at me with their sharp little beaks. I ordered myself to cut it out and get ready to give my students the undistracted teacher they deserved and required. I tried running through my lesson plan for the day and planning what I'd make for dinner when I got home. I practiced the Zen breathing exercises I'd learned from a CD my un-Zen sister Dale had given to me.

The thing that finally worked was seeing the kids. Once I was in their all-consuming and happy presence, all else retreated. Put another way, I retreated into my class and used it to put off thinking about Pete versus Tom.

When the school day was done, my reprieve was over. I got back into my car, unplugged the iPod loaded with Pete's music, stuffed it into my school tote bag, and turned on the radio. I distracted myself with the latest bad news and planned my evening. I would spend an hour drinking tea, thinking, and talking to my journal about what I was doing with Tom, and then I'd cook some comfort food. A browned butter fettuccini Alfredo with an extra big pile of freshly grated Parmigiano-Reggiano on top. I wouldn't skimp on the cheese—budget be damned. After dinner, I would bundle up and go for a long moonlight walk, then go to bed and read until I fell asleep.

That agenda held up for only so long. I did make the tea and sit down at the table, and I opened my journal, but I couldn't pick up my pencil and write right away. The silence was too loud. It felt like I could hear the absence of the music I'd grown so used to having on in the house. I tried to get started by asking myself, "What are you doing with Tom?" But then I wrote, "Why the hell do you have to think so much?"

I drank the tea, stared out the window, then decided to make a new music playlist for myself. It would be some of the music I used to listen to before I met Pete, and some from his mix, but only women singers. I thought a whole playlist of just women might help me stay focused and steer myself to where I wanted to go. It might help me avoid getting carried away by fantasies that would never be reality, daydreams that kept me from thinking rationally about the reality I could create for myself if I pulled my head out of the clouds.

While it was the instrumental "Samba Pa Ti" that prompted my dreamiest Pete reveries, certain male voices were also triggers. Most especially, until a certain point in time, Kris Kristofferson's. I've heard Pete sing one of his songs only once, and since then, it's somebody else my mind goes to when I hear Kristofferson sing or say anything, and even when I hear his name mentioned or see a photo of him. It's Evie and Greg I think about. But that's now. It used to be automatic that every time I heard Kris Kristofferson's voice, I would be back in my Pete fantasyland. I had to stop that—stop thinking about Pete if I wanted to see more of Tom.

So I changed the plan I'd made on the way home and decided I'd work on my new playlist after dinner, instead of taking a walk. While I made the fettuccine, I went back to my pre-Pete cooking music and listened to Ella Fitzgerald, but as much as I love her, and loved that she evoked my parents, she was only a short-term solution. So I ate and did the dishes, then fired up my computer and started picking songs for my women-only mix. When I was done, it was past my bedtime and the process of scrolling through my music library, selecting songs and moving them to the new list, one by one—scroll, point, click, drag, drop, repeat—had calmed my mind so much, I fell asleep within minutes. In my dreams that night, my mom and dad danced to music I'd never heard before, in a kitchen I'd never seen, while I stood at the stove stirring a big pot of something. The only thing I recognized, other than my parents, was my yellow stand mixer. It was on the counter. Pete and Tom were nowhere in sight.

On the Tuesday morning after the Saturday night with Tom, I plugged my updated iPod back into my car's stereo and pressed the power button. The first song that came on was the last one I'd added to my new playlist—Barbara Lynn singing "You'll Lose A Good Thing." It was from Pete's music, and it was another song with a very sensuous vibe, but it also had lyrics about a woman with a healthy sense of self-worth telling her partner she'll leave and he'll lose her if he doesn't do right. Singing as the woman warning her lover, Barbara had an immediate effect on me. In my mind, I wrapped my hands around my life's steering wheel and sat up straighter in the driver's seat. In my actual car, I said, "Oh yeah, that's what I'm talking about," and started backing down the driveway.

It had been only twenty-four hours since I'd texted Tom that I was open to more of what we'd done on my sofa and the rug in front of my fireplace, but the mental shift that had happened in my head was huge, and I wanted it to last, so on the drive to school, I decided I wouldn't see him again until I could answer the question, "What do I want with this relationship?" I decided I would think about that after work and I wouldn't reply to any texts or calls from him until I had an answer.

That night, I was out walking after dinner and he texted. I was ready to respond. My journaling before dinner had started with the idea that I didn't know him beyond a collection of basic facts and funny stories, and from there I'd spent several minutes thinking about my original question, by way of a few more.

Question: *If I don't really know him, isn't it premature or plain stupid to decide what I want from a "relationship" with him?*

Answer: *Premature and stupid.*

Question: *Do I want to get to know him, and in the meantime, do I want to keep having sex with him, or would it get in the way of getting to know him?*

My next answer was longer and less direct and took a while to come together because my thinking took a turn I hadn't expected. I figured out that what I wanted more immediately than anything else was to move back to Saratoga and quit the isolated life I was living at the lake. No more daydreaming about moving, I wanted to do it. I wanted to get a house in town, and instead of waiting for my single life to be over, try to take it on. Live it.

"Divorced, middle-aged, childless woman" wasn't an identity or a status I'd ever anticipated for myself, and when I ended up there involuntarily, I'd hid at the lake. Though I didn't move to the camp to hide, hiding had become part of what I was doing there. I was saving money and saving myself from having to face people. But then Eve Ellen's party invitation came along, and the instant excitement I felt when I discovered it in my mailbox, and the great time I'd had at the party and with Pete and Hank afterwards, and then the business with Tom, convinced me I was ready to risk leaving my hideout. I might not be totally fear-free about going back to Saratoga, where I'd been half of a couple for so long, many people never knew me as anything else, but I was ready to rejoin humanity. With my new book done—or the first draft, anyway—I wanted to work toward making the move during my school break that summer when I would have time to settle into a new place.

As for Tom, I decided I wanted to be friends with benefits, and I wanted to have fun with him while I got to know him well enough to know what more I wanted and what we could have together. So when I got his text, I stopped walking, stuck my flashlight in my coat pocket, and texted him back.

Tom: *Hey there.*

Me: *Hey. I'm out walking. What are you up to?*

Tom: *Wishing you were here.*

Me: *Aww. Come for breakfast on Saturday?*

Tom: *Yes! Or drive directly to your place after my evening class on Friday and make breakfast together? In the morning.*

Me: *I like that idea. Come Friday.*

Tom: *See you around nine!*

I resisted the urge to answer that last text with something embarrassing, something about how I'd be holding my breath or pawing the ground until I saw him again. But I was so giddy, I turned back to the house and forgot to take the flashlight out of my pocket until I'd fumbled along by moonlight for several yards.

TWENTY-THREE

Waiting for the overnight with Tom was a wild ride. My anticipation doubled every day and would have pushed everything else out of my mind if I'd let it. I like to think I was professional and didn't make my students suffer, but there's no denying that I didn't try too hard to hold back on getting worked up. It was too fun feeling that way. When Tom finally came through the door on Friday, I was so excited to see him, I could have done the movie scene thing where two characters rush at one another, tear off their clothes, and go for it.

But that's not how *it* went with us that night. Tom put his hands on my hips, his forehead to mine, and just smiled. When our clothes did start coming off, piece by piece, it went slowly. With each piece he removed from me, and then from himself, he kissed me twice. First somewhere on my face—a cheek, my mouth, an eyelid—then on whatever part of my body he'd just exposed. We were down to our socks before we had the movie moment, when he picked me up and carried me into my bedroom, where I'd turned on the bedside lamps while I was waiting for him, and draped silk scarves over their shades to make the light rosy and romantic.

We did have dinner, eventually, after a midnight bath—O*h, who knew what two could do in a bathtub built for one*? But we didn't do breakfast in the morning. We overslept, and when we finally woke up, Tom had to scramble to get on the road in time to make it to his eldest son's hockey game. It wasn't the finish I'd fantasized about, but not unexpected. He'd let me know via text, the previous afternoon, that he wished he could spend the whole weekend with me but would have to leave right after breakfast. He said his son had just joined a new hockey team and would be playing in his first game. He hadn't known about it when we made our plans or he would have told me then.

After he was gone, I poured another cup of coffee and took it back to my bed to do some thinking and get a grip on the melancholy I could feel creeping up on me, even as I was still buzzing with excitement and already looking forward to my next round with Tom. I needed a plan that would keep me too busy to think about being alone for another silent weekend.

The plan I devised: Get my butt up and out into the world. Do my Christmas shopping. Hit all my favorite vintage and thrift shops between home and Brooklyn, and find unique treasures for my sisters and their tribes, for Eve Ellen and Greg and Annie. Then spend the next day, a Sunday, baking and making candy. I was behind on holiday prep, I reminded myself, so I should be relieved Tom couldn't stay.

Half an hour later, I was in my car, heading for the closest vintage treasure chest, and an unfortunate song came up on the stereo. Again. When I made my all-women playlist, I couldn't bring myself to lose "Wildflowers," so I replaced Tom Petty's version with a cover by three women who harmonized like angels but called themselves The Wailin' Jennys. It wasn't a wise cheat on my part because, even with female voices, that song made me think of Pete. Perhaps, I confess, because I had sometimes used it to conjure him. To entertain myself with reveries in which we sang its beautiful lyrics to one another while gazing into each other's eyes over another imaginary microphone or across a glowing campfire on a romantic camping trip.

Yep, fantasies can be so very helpful. So easily fashioned to suit your needs and cravings. But my "Wildflowers" fantasy wasn't one I needed that day. Hearing the song rattled me and added a third conflicting emotion to the mix of melancholy and Tom-titillation I was already feeling.

I switched the stereo from the iPod to the radio and listened to somebody talk about a topic I never really registered. I tried to keep my mind on what was coming out of the speakers but still hadn't gotten into the story when I reached my first destination, where, with much desperation, I threw myself into shopping like it was a lifeboat bobbing in the water alongside a sinking ship.

TWENTY-FOUR

Between mildly dreading my first date with Tom and then eagerly looking forward to our first sleepover, I'd done a good job of not thinking about my literary agent and agonizing over what she was thinking about my manuscript, or when she would get back to me about it. I'd put my book project on her plate and was glad to have it off mine for a while. So I wasn't expecting to hear from Agent Bean when my phone rang while I was out rowing away in my shopping lifeboat. I knew she often worked from home on Saturdays and caught up on client calls from the comfort of her bed, but I was so busy checking out a pair of candlesticks and considering whether they'd make a good gift for my sister Glyn, I was caught off guard.

Agent Bean's news: She thought I'd done something fresh and original with a topic that wasn't fresh. However, there was an issue I'd have to address before she would shop my book around to publishers. She told me to check my email when I got home, look through her notes, and let her know when I could get a new draft finished. I looked at the notes on my phone as soon as she hung up, right where I was standing in the middle of the Ribbons for Birds vintage shop, right where I almost sat down on the floor because I was so daunted by the nature of the problem Lillian said I needed to solve, but resisted sitting, composed myself, and resolved to carry on with the weekend I'd planned. I decided I would wait and work on the book when school was out for winter break. Until then, I would mull possible solutions and get ready to hit the ground running.

The next day, I'd just pulled a sheet of shortbread cookies out of the oven and put another one in when I heard a car come up the driveway. I knew it was Tom. Nobody else ever showed up at my door without warning. I wasn't dressed much better than I had been the time he caught me with wet spots over my breasts, but I was glad for that unexpected appearance.

Did we fall immediately into bed? We did not. He helped me with my baking and candy making, and he made sandwiches for our lunch, so I could keep cranking out the sweets. While we worked, we talked about gardening and what we hoped to do when planting season returned. We talked about summers at the lake when we were kids and discovered we'd both worked as counselors at the same sleepaway camp between our junior and senior years in high school. It was light chitchat, and he made sure I did most of the talking, but it was nice.

Later, when we finished with the cookies and candy, we made dinner together, did the dishes, and continued the chitchatting. Then it was time to call it a day because we both had school in the morning.

But first, before he left, he kissed me and we did a lip-locked shuffle to the sofa for a brief interlude—brief but highly enjoyable, right up until it ended with a thud after I mentioned my father.

Tom and I were entwined on the sofa, and he noticed a plaid Pendleton shirt hanging from a wall peg by the front door. He asked about it and I told him it was my dad's. I told him my sisters and I left it hanging where our father had always kept it so we could feel like he was still around.

Tom said, "My ex-wife gave that same shirt to my father on our first Christmas together, before she knew he didn't wear plaid or any prints, or colors that weren't beige or gray. When he pulled it out of the box, my mother's eyes went 'eek!' because she expected him to say something impolite. But he said, "Now, that's handsome. Let's see how it fits." And he put it on while we all watched. His gratitude to my wife for marrying me and potentially giving him grandsons was so immense, he would have worn anything she gave him. It could have been covered in purple and gold sequins and he would have been fine. He was so grateful to her, he overlooked the fact she wasn't Catholic. That would have been unthinkable before I went off to the Benedictines. Maybe not as unthinkable as plaid, but not okay with either of my parents."

We both laughed. Then he said, "So it's like our fathers are here with us now. That's awkward."

"On that note, you better get going," I told him.

He had another idea. Another round of sofa polka. He looked over at the Pendleton and said, "Watch this Dad," and stuck his tongue in my ear.

I yelped, "Leave my father out of this!"

"I was talking to *my* dad," he said, as he slipped a hand between us and took hold of a boob.

"You're creepy," I replied and pushed away from him so hard I fell off the sofa and thudded on the floor like a sack of flour, bringing our day to a graceful end.

TWENTY-FIVE

Journal entry, Saturday, December 22:

Thursday was the last day of school. Yesterday I did some more Christmas prep. Tomorrow I might start working on the book edits. Today I saw Tom. I spent the morning at his house in Saratoga. It was the first time I went to him instead of him coming to me. Going to his place made sense because he had an afternoon flight out of Albany, but I was nervous about being seen. I still haven't told EE, G, and D about whatever it is he and I have started. Naturally, he lives west of central Saratoga and there was no way to get to him without going through town. Not without a winding and miles-long detour that even I could recognize as neurotic. Luckily, as far as I know, I made it there and back undetected.

But heavy sigh of resignation. He's spending the holidays in Florida with his boys, parents, and ex-wife (hmmm). And I'm doing another Christmas alone. G and D and company will come up and spend a night, but I'll still be a solo camper among their tribal units.

Stay busy, Isla. That's the key. Stay busy.

Teacher Tom took his end-of-semester work with him, the exams he has to correct and grades he has to calculate, and he'll be done with all that when he gets back, so we can spend the last of my school break together. When I got to his house this morning, he greeted me at the door with a mimosa and a kiss, then made brunch—eggs scrambled with smoked salmon, spinach, and goat cheese. While he cooked, I perused the piles of books he has on nearly every flat surface. Mostly nonfiction. Predominately science and philosophy. But a few spy thrillers too. When we finished eating, he showed me his dormant garden beds and greenhouse and had me put my ear to the side of one of his beehives so I could hear the bees humming inside. He explained that they survived winter by clustering around their queen and flexing their flight muscles nonstop to create a collective vibration that generates heat and keeps the hive warm—hard work they fuel, he said, by eating the honey he leaves in the hive when he harvests the rest for himself. If he doesn't leave enough for them, he'll lose the colony to the cold. The bees will die.

After the bee lesson, we went back inside. To his bedroom.

When it was time for Tom to go pick up his boys and ex-wife for their flight to Florida, and we were saying goodbye in his driveway, he leaned down to my open car window, and said, "Don't disappear while I'm gone."

I told him, "I'm not going anywhere. I'm a Yankee freshwater fish. Adirondack spawn. Don't you decide to stay down there and go ocean on me." I was thinking of how, on the night we met, he told me not to disappear when he went in search of a bathroom, then I didn't see him again until Eve Ellen pulled me across her yard for a whirl with her on the dance floor. He was listening to a guy at the beer and wine bar just off the deck, which had been cleared for dancing. With Evie dragging me by the hand, I let myself look for too long and he caught me. Meeting my eyes, he held up a fresh beer and pushed his eyebrows to the middle of his forehead. I figured there were at least two ways to interpret his expression—he wanted to signal that he'd been waylaid by the talker, or he'd been snagged by the lure of a drink he was powerless to resist. I left it at those options and avoided thinking about it anymore. Except to note that I was glad he wasn't talking with another woman, and I was embarrassed about being glad, and even more embarrassed he'd caught me looking at him.

During the two weeks before our holiday separation, or three weeks, if you count back to our first official date, we saw one another as often as we could. Always at my place because his parents had been loaning their lake house to their church for spiritual retreats every December and January since he was a boy. He didn't seem to mind the drive up to my funkier camp after his last class, or the trip back a couple of hours later—I wasn't ready for sleepovers on school nights. Facing a classroom full of five- and six-year-old brains demanded a teacher whose mind was undivided, and I didn't think I could pull myself together and deliver if I woke up with Tom. On Fridays and Saturdays, he did stay over, but on workdays, on cold and dark winter mornings, getting myself out the door was challenging enough without having him in my bed and bathroom making it harder.

One of those weeks before he left would have been his turn to have his boys, per the joint custody he shared with their mother, but she'd kept them because her parents had come from Michigan to celebrate Chanukah. That left him to me, and other than working around our school schedules, the only commitment that kept us apart was the few hours I was at Glyn's Christmas party. He made plans to join friends for drinks that night because there was no way I was going to take him to Glyn's as my date—because there would be no way to stop my sisters from gawking and talking. They wouldn't care that he was just across the room as they hounded me for every juicy detail, and they wouldn't wait to share what they learned with Evie. They'd burn up their phones texting her in Paris, where she and Greg were doing the holidays with Annie. Or they'd FaceTime her and hound her for what she could tell them. He said he hoped my "glow" told them everything they wanted to know the second I walked into the party, and he started doing things I know he meant for me to remember when I was mingling, making party chat, and trying to look like there was nothing new going on in my life. I got through the evening, but it wasn't easy. Trust me when I say fingertips tracing the lightest of lines on bare skin can leave marks that are hard to hide. And lips touched to the soft places between your hips or where your hips and thighs meet or even the backs of your knees can leave visible prints on your face. They can make your voice change.

When he came up on weeknights, we fell into a routine of eating dinner and then heading to the bedroom. A couple of times, we talked about watching the cooking show I'd told him was my usual after-dinner fare, but it never happened. We started to watch an episode once and he lost interest before the opening titles were finished. I didn't need much persuading to go along with what he wanted to do instead. I was fine with him finding me irresistible and everything else less enticing.

On weekends, we stayed out of bed long enough to make popsicle stick frames for the photos I'd taken of each of my students—snapshots of the kids doing their favorite classroom activities or goofing off with their best buddies. When we were done with the crafting, we filled treat bags with the framed photos, the notes I'd written for each child, and the cookies we'd made and I'd stowed in my freezers earlier in the month. He seemed happy to help, but joked that he was pitching in so the work would get done more quickly and we could go back to doing "grownup things."

"You really meant it when you said you left the monastery because you didn't want to give up sex," I said.

He responded with a wicked grin.

Our day at his house, before he left for Miami, was just three weeks after our first date, so it could be argued, I thought, we were still in the initial hot and heavy phase that new romances go through, and that would explain the first three texts I received from him while he was away. Rapid-fire, like horny missiles launched from Florida, they came just after midnight on December 23, less than half a day since we'd said goodbye.

Do you want to sext?

If you send a nudie selfie to me, I'll send one to you.

Just joking. No nudies. If we got hacked, it wouldn't be good. Especially for a kindergarten teacher.

My reply back to him:

But what a juicy story. Kindergarten teacher, former monk, and compromising photos. It would go viral on the internet and inspire memes galore.

He didn't reply to my reply and I resisted texting him again. I doggedly kept my attention on my book until it was time to get ready for my sisters—it was my year to host the Christmas Eve dinner that had been our family's tradition when our parents were alive, so Glyn and Dale were coming to the camp with their kids and husbands, and they were all going to stay the night, and most of the next day too, to open presents and go sledding.

Only after I was rolling with the meal prep, did I let my mind go back to Tom. As I cooked, set the table, and obsessively tweaked the table decorations, lest Dale find my arrangement of pinecones and boughs and winterberries substandard, I thought about him and whether we might move to another level soon, whether the time apart might magically propel us to something deeper than the physical fun we were enjoying. There's nothing like the holidays to make you forget you were going to embrace being single.

Thanks to my highly associative mind, those thoughts made me remember the conversation Mr. Free Love tried to have with me about the sort of relationship he wanted, and it wasn't a pleasant association, so I reminded myself to quit thinking so much.

Then I jumped to another thought and did some more thinking, which induced another association. I remembered how Tom had told me he was helping with the holiday treats for my students so we could get back to "grownup things." At the time, those two little words had niggled at me and made me wonder whether they carried condescending judgment about my teaching career. They'd catapulted my mind back to when I was a new teacher in Manhattan, newly married and living in Brooklyn, and Scott's colleagues at the architecture firm would look at me with blank, uninterested eyes and chirp things like, "A kindergarten teacher! How great is that? Your days must be so full of everything cute and adorable." And then, at the next cocktail party, they'd say almost exactly the same thing. They wouldn't bother to come up with new blather, and I wouldn't resist responding in a sarcastically cheery chirp of my own, with lines like, "Well, puppies are pretty unbeatable when it comes to cute, but we don't have any in my classroom."

Fussing with the pinecones, boughs, and berries on the table, just before my family blew through the door in a pack, shouting "Ho! Ho! Ho!" and shoving Tom out of my head, I thought about the education conversation he and I had after his "grownup things" comment. Testing him, I asked what he thought kids got from kindergarten, and he replied, "It's the most important school year for all of us. It lays the groundwork for everything that comes later. It introduces kids to classroom learning, and shapes how they feel about school and education."

"What about pre-school?" I continued the test.

"I forgot about that. Scratch what I said about kindergarten. Pre-school is the key. The foundation upon which all else rests. Kindergarten is about snacks and naps."

I pinched him and said, "Are you ever serious about anything?"

"Everything always but never too serious about any one thing. Moderation across the board."

"I wouldn't say you're moderate when it comes to sex, but come on, are you being serious now? Snacks and naps?"

"I'm just trying to do my part and talk, trying not to retreat back into the hermitage in my head. My mental monastery, as my wife called it."

I said, "Points for the alliteration, but it's hard for you to stay out here and engage with other people?" I purposely didn't say, "engage with *me*." Broad and impersonal felt safer for both of us.

He replied, "Sometimes. Do I get points for being aware of that and working on it?"

"I guess," I said, "but I'm not sure you mean what you're saying even now. Maybe it's just more banter."

My inner warning whistle was blowing at top volume. I was thinking about how Tom was supposed to be the available guy, the accessible option, as opposed to Pete, who lived thousands of miles away. I was wondering whether I'd ever get real conversation from him, something more than quippy chat.

"I'm not always serious, but I'm always honest," he said. Then, rolling over and hovering above me, he asked, "Points for honesty?"

We were back in bed, but we'd been taking a breather from the grownup things we'd been doing since we finished filling the bags for my students. We were lying there, doing our usual bantering, until I went past his comfort zone. When I did that, he started some more adult business to avoid conversation. Later, though, he circled back to what we'd been talking about and sounded more earnest than I'd ever heard him sound. He said, "I believe any nation that chooses to have an economic system based on competition, as capitalism is, and wants to claim it's a moral system, has to ensure everyone has access to a good education because they'll need it to compete. They'll need it to have any chance at a job that'll provide a decent living. A good education begins with pre-school and kindergarten. They're the foundation."

It was a mouthful, but I believe I remembered and put close to his words in my journal. When he said them, we were on our backs with our faces turned to one another. I can still see the look in his eyes and hear his voice, as it sounded for those few minutes. He was obviously trying to show he could and would come out of his head for me, as well as trying to assure me he respected my job, but I could tell there was a tall monastery wall between his mind and the outside world, and behind the wall, a serious Tom that the playful Tom would rather leave behind when we were together.

His effort at unguarded engagement didn't last long before he escaped to the bathroom to pee, and then to the kitchen for food, but it was enough that I decided he didn't deem my career "cute," and, as Evie had told me, he was interesting. There was a lot going on with him. It was hard to get to or to bring out of him, but it was there. That's the exact thing I was thinking when my door flew open and the house filled with bodies and noise. "Ho! Ho! Ho!"

Tom's fourth and final text from Miami, a panicked warning, came the following day, on Christmas morning, as the gang at my place opened gifts.

Isla, sorry. I just realized it might be awkward for you if your sisters are there when you find the present I put under your tree. Really sorry. Talk soon.

I'd heard my phone buzz but didn't read the text until after my family was gone, so the warning reached me too late. Not that I could have done anything about the wrapped cookbook—or rather, sourdough baking book—Tom had hidden beneath some gifts from me to my nieces and nephews.

"It's Aunt Isla's turn," one of my nieces called out, as she dove at the tree to get a gift for me to open.

"To lovely Isla from adoring Tom," she read aloud from the name tag on the gift. Then she asked, "Who's Tom?"

Glyn and Dale said, "Adoring Tom?"

Cat out of the bag. No getting it back. It was off and running.

TWENTY-SIX

As I knew they would, my sisters grilled me without mercy and wasted no time filling in Eve Ellen, who then cross-examined me via a flurry of texts, followed by a FaceTime call when she grew impatient with my cagey replies.

I tried to calm everyone down and temper their hopes. I said my priorities had changed and a relationship wasn't something I wanted right away. I told them I'd decided to enjoy life as a singleton for a while. Not just abide it but get into it, enjoy myself, and get used to feeling and living like I was a complete person on my own.

"Imagine that," I said. "I don't need anyone to make me whole. A real revelation and growth spurt on my part, right?"

I wasn't entirely honest with them. I couldn't really believe being alone was something I'd ever "get into" and relish. And, at the same time, I'd never felt like an incomplete fraction of a person. My mother wouldn't have let that happen or let me leave home until I was cured if I'd picked up even a mild case during my formative years.

I wasn't entirely dishonest either. I knew who I was as my parents' daughter, my sisters' sister, and Evie's friend, but I'd lost touch with who I was for myself. I'd give anything for another day with my mom and dad, another day being their daughter, but maybe it was time to be Isla's Isla. And maybe I'd be a better partner to my next love if I had that experience.

Nobody's hope was tempered, but Glyn and Evie backed off when I insisted I needed peace while I tried to tackle the book revision Agent Bean encouraged and required. Dale tried to respect my wishes but popped up at random times with text queries.

So how is it to bed a monk?

Missing holy communion with Tom?

Wrong kind of doc to play doctor with you but how about hands on anatomy lessons?

Somehow, I did get focused and finish a new draft for Lillian. I shut out all distractions and spent eighty hours over the course of four days totally immersed, eating nothing but cold leftovers, drinking gallons of reheated coffee, taking just one shower, and never leaving the house except to bring in armloads of firewood. I hardly slept between writing sessions that ran from three or four in the morning to eleven or twelve at night. Once I got into a groove, it was easy to stay there because of Lillian's vision. I wasn't sure I was comfortable with the changes she wanted, but I knew she was pushing me to do something richer than I'd attempted. She saw unfulfilled potential in my manuscript and was pushing me to fulfill it. That was heartening and spurred me on because when I proposed my original idea to her, back in my former life, she wasn't interested and offered no suggestions for tweaks that might make her reconsider. I'd worked really hard crafting a proposal to sell her on that idea, which could be summed up as "here's how to grow a garden, pickle what you produce, and stock a winter pantry," but after she read it, she told me she couldn't do anything with the book I had in mind. My concept and content outline didn't add up to "a standout," she said. She knew I'd been struggling since the miscarriage, and I was hoping a project would be my medicine, so she kindly said she would look at my manuscript if I went ahead and produced one, but she gently warned me it might not make her feel any different.

The manuscript I handed over to her just before Thanksgiving wasn't the book I'd proposed roughly three years earlier, as I explained in a cover letter that briefly summarized my new idea, my food life makeover manual. The summary didn't mention the personal anecdotes I'd included at the start of each chapter. I didn't say anything about those because I hadn't considered them fundamental elements. As far as I was concerned, I was doing a practical guidebook, and the personal bits were extras.

The bit about growing my first tomatoes in a tiny backyard in Brooklyn because my new husband worked long hours at his new job and I thought pursuing the perfect tomato would be a good way to fill my free time. The bit about planting my first full garden behind our first house in Saratoga and learning to preserve what I grew to save money when Scott was trying to get his practice going and my teaching job provided our only income. The one about taking over the yard at the house we built and making it my domain because the house's interior was Scott's, even the kitchen, though I was our cook.

My hand was lightest with references to the roles gardening and cooking played for me during the years I struggled with trying to have a baby, lost my parents and grandmothers, lost the hopeless pregnancy, lost my marriage. I hadn't avoided those times altogether, but I'd skimmed over the losses and focused on delicious victories and humorous debacles I'd had in my garden and kitchen. Such as my successful mission to grow superb blueberries and turn them into plate-licking great syrup the first summer my parents were gone because pancakes topped with blueberry syrup had been my father's favorite meal. And the frazzled scarecrow I created when I was weary from another round of embryo transfer and failure, only to have birds claim its head for a perch—a roost from which they could survey my garden and choose what they wanted to eat next.

I'd treated all the anecdotes like garnishes you would add to a dish for a more appealing presentation. In Lillian's view, that was a serious mistake and a missed opportunity. She said they were some of the best things I'd ever written, but invariably left her feeling dissatisfied, as if I'd given her "a nibble of something good" and refused to let her have "a full bite."

She told me, "I'm not talking about turning this book into a memoir or adding a great deal of length. Just give me a complete forkful in each chapter intro, one that makes functional sense in relation to the chapter's topic, but also within the arc of the book as a whole and the arc of your life. Don't tease me, feed me. And don't shy away from being candid about whatever your emotions were at each juncture. Commit to being open and honest. Do that and you'll have a standout."

It was scary, but I did commit, and I found I enjoyed reworking the stories from my life, trying to make each one feel complete and satisfying, trying to figure out the puzzle of making each "forkful" make "functional sense."

I worked without coming up for air until the wee morning hours of December 30, when I emailed a new draft to Agent Bean, put my parka on over my pajamas, stepped into my boots, and went outside into the freezing dark to look at the stars and moon and remind myself there was a world beyond my computer. I stood out in the yard, looked up at the sky and down at the lake, closed my eyes and breathed in the cold, then hustled back inside where it was warm and my bed was waiting. I hoped to fall asleep immediately and stay there for a solid eight hours. Then I'd give the house a good scrub before welcoming 2019, and start practicing the patience I was going to need to get through what could be many weeks of waiting to hear from Lillian and learn whether she liked what I'd done.

TWENTY-SEVEN

By early evening, December 31, I'd finished cleaning the house and started getting ready for my New Year's Eve celebration. It had been my choice to usher out the old and welcome the new by myself. It was a decision I'd made weeks earlier, before Tom entered the picture, and I was sticking to it. With Evie and Greg in Paris, and my sisters doing their thing with their husbands and kids—their traditional potato soup supper and board games—I'd decided to decline their invitation to join them, and start some new traditions of my own to replace the ones I'd had with Scott. I'd stay at the camp, stoke the fire, light some candles, put a stack of my parents' vinyl records on the record player, take a long bath, then open a bottle of wine and make myself a wonderful dinner of elaborate dishes I'd never attempted. I'd just lit the candles when I received a text from Hank.

Tardy happy holiday greetings to you Isla. I hope your Christmas was great and the year ahead will be everything you want it to be and better. I finally got around to organizing my photos and videos from the trip and came across this one. Enjoy! And stay tuned for another surprise… it'll be coming your way soon!

The video was of me and Pete singing into our invisible microphone at the campsite in Bethel. I'd been so into what we were doing, so focused on Pete, I hadn't noticed that Hank had paused his fiddling and recorded us.

I replayed the video several times, pausing it at key moments so I could study Pete's face as he looked at mine from the other side of our mic. What had he been thinking? Feeling? Had he watched the video? Replayed it? Had he thought of me at all since sending his thank you note?

I thought hard about how I wanted to reply to Hank, and I settled on safe—no mention of Pete by name.

Happy New Year! And thank you! I love how the video brings back the trip and a few moments of summer. It's freezing here. I hope you guys are having a great holiday in sunny southern California. Even though I think you're cruel to announce a surprise is on the way and not tell me what it is!

He responded with two emojis—a devil's face and a heart. I watched the video again, then went to the kitchen for a bag of potato chips, took them to the sofa, flopped down, and ate while I tried to figure out what Hank's surprise might be. A digital album full of photos and videos from the trip? Some of Pete doing his new Tom Petty homage? A new music mix?

When I'd had enough of the salty chips and needed something to drink, I got up, guzzled a glass of water, and tried to get my celebration back on course. I ran a bath, but instead of my parents' old jazz, I turned on my Pete playlist. Then, because my luck or my fate or my idiocy is what it is, as I lowered myself into the steaming tub, a Kris Kristofferson song started up, with that voice that still made me think of Music Man Pete.

The song: "Help Me Make It Through the Night." I had to laugh because it was so perfect, given my situation, and because I knew I was about to hear it six times. Six versions, one right after the other. I bought the first one because Pete had it in his trip mix and because it was one of Kris's later takes—he'd gone back and done a new recording after his voice started sounding more gravelly. Like Pete's. Then I bought five covers recorded by Sammi Smith, Elvis Presley, Tammy Wynette, Willie Nelson, and a band with the awful name Lady Antebellum. Because, apparently, I have a thing for the song. I guess I should have been glad I stopped at a half dozen because half the singers who have ever sung a note of anything have done "Help Me Make it Through the Night."

So I laughed, but my laugh was bittersweet, and, after soaking and listening to my Pete music until the tub water got cold, I made the dinner I'd planned and drank so much wine while I cooked, I woke up late the next morning with a throbbing head and a kitchen full of dirty dishes. *Happy New Year to me. Happy 2019, Isla.*

In penance and desperation, I threw myself into dishwashing, but it didn't help me avoid thinking about Pete or wondering how my attraction to him could reappear so strong and unchanged after the three weeks with Tom. Scrubbing pots didn't stop me from wondering how I was going to feel when I saw Tom again. We were supposed to spend his first weekend back from Florida together. How was it going to feel being with him?

TWENTY-EIGHT

Of course, at the start of 2019, I didn't know 2020 was going to turn the whole world upside down. I still didn't know twelve months later, when I wrote the last lines in my 2019 journal.

This has been a year of changes I'd hoped for and one I didn't want, didn't see coming, wish I could cancel. How do I reconcile being glad I got something I so craved this year, something that feels so right and immeasurably better than I could have imagined, something for which I'm grateful beyond words—how do I reconcile that with desperately wishing I could turn back time?

If I could, how far back would I go? How far would be enough? Five years? Then I'd still be with Scott and wouldn't have what I have now. There are no right answers and there can be no reconciliation.

And so it ends, this year of years.

On January 4, 2019, Tom returned from Florida, but we didn't see one another right away because he'd brought back a souvenir case of the flu, which he'd started to feel mid-flight. I asked if I could deliver soup to his bedside or doorstep, but he told me to freeze and save it for when he felt better and could come to the lake. He said having it handy would save time in the kitchen and give us more time for "cooking in other rooms. We can work on our bathtub recipes." I laughed and told him he was incorrigible, but I felt a jumble of anxious anticipation and relief that I'd have some more time to put my feelings for Pete back in the lockbox they'd apparently been hiding in all along.

Just days earlier, I'd been unhappy that Tom's next break from school wouldn't correspond to either of my next recesses. I'd have time off in February and April, and his spring vacation would be in March. Until summer, I'd see him only for the occasional weeknight or weekend visit, and only every other week, when his boys were with their mother. I'd been fretting about having so little time with him, then Hank sent the video of me and Pete, and my fretting and dreading shifted.

Among other things, I dreaded Evie coming home from France. I knew she'd beat a fast path to my door to pump me about Tom, and I worried she'd detect there was more going on in my head. I'd been telling her almost everything since we were kids, but I didn't feel I could tell her how I felt about Pete. It was one of my rare holdbacks. If he hadn't been one of Greg's oldest and closest friends, and recently widowed from a woman Greg had also counted as a good friend, I wouldn't have kept quiet, but those pieces of the picture made me clam up.

A jet-lagged Eve Ellen did indeed come to the lake, with a bottle of French champagne, and questions. Starting with, "Adoring Tom?"

Then she shoved the champagne at me and demanded, "No more secrets, sister. Tell all. Now."

Her interrogation could have been disastrous for my hope to hold back the Pete information. She knew me so well, she could usually tell when I was off-kilter in any way, for any reason. But I got lucky. I think she read my caginess as reluctance to talk about Tom and didn't suspect anything about Pete. She grilled me for full disclosure about what "TomTom" and I had been doing, got what she wanted about that, and was satisfied. Though she did ask, "Is there any other news you haven't shared?"

So I told her about my book. I hadn't been purposely mum about it, just skittish about jinxing Lillian Bean's efforts to get me a publishing deal. Plus, it had only been two days since I received the news. Lillian called me precisely one week after I sent the new draft to her, told me she loved what I'd done with the personal stories, and was sure I had "a winner" on my hands. She said, "I hadn't meant to do more than peek at one of the revised chapter introductions until I'd crossed some other things off my to-do list, but once I peeked, I was so impressed, I couldn't stop."

Still too happy to be modest, I repeated Lillian's praise to Evie.

Evie said, "Hot damn! I should have brought two bottles of bubbly. Here's to you and a fabulous 2019, Isla Frances!"

One bottle was more than enough—I had class in the morning.

With the new session at school underway, I resumed most of my old workweek routines but swapped my evening YouTube time for cruising real estate listings and posting "for sale" ads online to sell everything I hadn't already sold—my wedding and engagement rings, the diamond earrings Scott gave me on our tenth anniversary, the jewelry I'd inherited from my grandmothers but never wore. I was determined to sell it all, drain my savings, and scrape together a down payment for a house.

I met with a woman at my bank to learn whether I could get a mortgage loan, and if so, how much I'd be approved to borrow.

I texted my sisters and Evie and told them I was looking for a place. Dale protested and Glyn stepped in between us, per usual.

Dale: *We just moved you to the camp and now we move you back to SS???*

Glyn: *It's been nearly three years, Dale, darling. Isla, just say when and where and I'll be there.*

Dale: *Thanks for the backup goody goody Glyn the good sister and patron saint of us*

Glyn: *You're welcome. I'm too tired to be the zipper between you two today, but I'll be fine tomorrow, Isla, and ready to help whenever you move.*

Me: *Thank you, but I'm good, Glynnie. I don't want either of you to lift a finger this time. It'll be easy peasy doing it myself because my stuff is whittled down and ready to go. You'll have all that space in your barn back, Dale.*

Dale: *Hooray for me*

The rest of January flew by, and though Tom and I talked on the phone, and texted, we didn't see one another because his flu turned into pneumonia. By the time he was well, his classes were starting and he had to catch up on prep work.

The first week in February, I got the astounding news that Agent Lillian Bean had two offers for my book—one from the editor who had bought my first gardening tome, and one from an editor with another publisher who was ready to sign me to a deal for two books and pay a bigger advance. I'd get only half of the money for the book I'd just finished, and the rest would come later, after I wrote another one, so my old editor's offer would put more cash in my hands to start, but both scenarios were dreams come true. I was floored. The publishing world just didn't work that way or move that fast for writers like me.

The next day, Tom drove up after class and we had the soup I'd put in the freezer when he was sick. As we ate, we talked about whether I should stay with the editor I knew and trusted, and take the larger of the two advances on the table for the book I'd just finished, or work with an unfamiliar editor and get more money over time, if I wrote book number three. Lillian was in favor of the two-book deal because she thought it showed the publisher believed in me. And because, as she said, "your next project will have a home waiting for it, if they like what you do with that one, and a fresh start would be good." By which she meant good for both my emotional life and my writing career—or my hope to have a career that included people buying and reading what I wrote. But she told me to think it over and let her know what I wanted to do.

Tom asked thoughtful questions and never gave even the vaguest hint he was ready to quit talking and move to the bedroom. I told him how selling my book would seal the deal on my plan to move back to Saratoga, and about a couple of the houses I'd found online. Neither was realistic, given the loan I qualified for, but both had helped me refine my thinking about what I wanted to look for and to avoid, what I had to have, no matter how long it took me to find and afford it.

He asked, "What's at the top of your list, what do you have to have, no matter what?"

"A patch of ground for gardening," I said. "No condos with only a paved patio, no upper-floor apartments with only a balcony big enough for a few potted herbs. A kitchen plumbed for a gas stove. I will not cook on an electric stovetop."

The conversation felt like a relationship milestone for us. It was the first time we relaxed into an extended normal discussion, with no underlying sexual sizzle and tension, no flirtation, and no sense that Tom was forcing himself to engage or prove he could. He was clearly happy for me and put anything he may have hoped to do that night on hold.

"You've got this, Isla," he said, smiling with what looked like pure delight. "Whatever you decide, you're making your new life happen and I'm really excited to see how it unfolds."

Since we had work in the morning, he was supposed to go home to his own bed, but we fell asleep in mine after we did eventually make our way to it for what was supposed to be just a few minutes—for one episode of his favorite "cooking show," as he'd started calling sex. When I felt his lips on my forehead kissing me goodbye, I thought I was still asleep and dreaming, but then I heard his car start outside. I looked at my phone and saw it was nearly six o'clock. My alarm was going to ring at six-fifteen, so I turned on the light and went to the kitchen for coffee.

And I made my decision—I'd stick with my old editor and publisher. I didn't want the pressure of a two-book deal. I knew I'd push myself to do a third book and I didn't want that. When and if I was ready to write, I would write. Until then, I wanted to be free to tend to other things. I wanted to spend time with Tom, keep looking for a house, and put out feelers for a teaching job in Saratoga. I'd taught there for years, before taking time off after the miscarriage, and I still had plenty of district contacts and friends I could ask about positions that would be open for the next academic year, beginning in September. My plans to buy a place and move didn't depend on a local job—I was willing to commute—but it would be really nice to avoid driving the extra hours every week.

TWENTY-NINE

Friday night, February 8, Hank's surprise arrived. He called and told me he was in Saratoga.

Completely unbeknownst to me or anyone in our group when we went to Caffe Lena to hear Pete play, Hank had met a young woman when he went to the bathroom, and they'd stayed in touch and fallen for one another. After months of texting and talking on the phone, he'd come back to New York to be with her.

He hadn't met just any young woman—it was the singer who had performed just before Pete and had blown us away with her amazing voice. Hank saw her outside the bathroom, told her how much he'd enjoyed her set, and they'd talked music for a few minutes before he came back to our table with her name and number. Fast-forward six months and one of her roommates moved out of the big old farmhouse she shared with friends, and Hank decided to move in. He took the vacated bedroom, so he and Zoe could take the next step toward finding out whether they worked as a couple in person.

I asked him if they could come for brunch the next day. "Yes, for me," he said, "but Zoe has to work. Are Greg and Eve Ellen going to be there?"

I told him they had plans with Evie's father, who was visiting from North Carolina. Then once again, I let something in my head leak out of my mouth—an unnecessary, unkind, and bitter explanation. I said, "He's lived there since his midlife crisis when he walked away from his marriage to Eve Ellen's mom and abandoned their family. He's a New Yorker, born and bred, who went south to Chapel Hill for college and came home with his degree and a teenage bride. Eve Ellen's mother was a Chapel Hill girl by birth, but after their divorce, he went back down there and she spent the rest of her life up here. Evie hasn't seen him in years, so they have some catching up to do, or I'd invite all of them."

Hank replied, "Got it. I remember her mentioning him when we FaceTimed last week before I left California. But, hey, the big reveal on that call was when Pop asked how you were doing and Eve Ellen said you and Tom, the guy who with us at Caffe Lena, are together now. Congratulations!"

Both ashamed of my bitter leakage and annoyed with Evie for her loose lips, I fumbled for something to say and came up with, "Thank you, but Eve Ellen's more hopeful than factual. I'm so busy teaching my tots and planning my move to Saratoga, I hardly have time to get together with my shadow, much less anyone else."

"You're moving to Saratoga?" Hank asked.

I rattled, "Hoping to. Trying to. Working on it. Looking at house listings."

"That's so cool, Isla. You'll be closer to Eve Ellen and Greg, and to me and Zoe. I really want you to meet her soon, but what time do you want me to come tomorrow?"

"How about ten? Too early?"

"I'll be there."

As soon as the call was over, I wanted to text Evie and give her hell for telling Pete about Tom, but I couldn't because she didn't know about my infatuation with Pete and I didn't want her to know. So I texted her, but I didn't mention him, or even that I knew she'd FaceTimed with him and Hank before Hank came back to New York.

Me to Evie: *Hank and the girl with the voice, who knew? Let me know how it goes with your dad.*

Evie back to me: *Sly boy, our Hank. Let's try to get together Friday. Dinner here. It'll be great to see him and check out Zoe. My father leaves on Wednesday.*

Talk about a development I hadn't seen coming—Hank back in New York. He came over the next morning and lifted me off the ground when he hugged me at the door. Then he ran back to his truck, doing all but the first couple of porch steps in one sailing leap, and returned with a gift from Pete, a wicker basket full of musical instruments crafted, in part, from beautiful wood. Spoons similar to the ones I'd tried to play at our campsite in Bethel, but with a prettier wooden handgrip. A tambourine shaped like a crescent moon. A pair of shakers shaped like goose eggs. And a pair of claves, or "rhythm sticks," as we called them in my classroom.

On a slip of paper tucked in between the instruments, there was a short note in Pete's handwriting.

You got rhythm, Isla. Here's hoping you'll make more music with friends, soon and often.

I knew I needed to say something appropriate to Hank, but my mind was scrambling, trying to remember whether I'd told Pete that Ella Fitzgerald's "I Got Rhythm" was one of my mother's favorites. I didn't think I would have told him it was the one Ella song I couldn't listen to anymore—that I couldn't handle her chipping singing about being happy because she had her man and everything she could ask for—but I may have told him my mom loved it.

Hank said, "Pop says they'll look pretty in your house even if you can't be persuaded to play them, but he told me to get you playing and singing and dancing again. I promised to try."

"Good luck with that," I said. "Let me get you eating."

Over a brunch that lasted two or three hours, Hank and I talked and talked. I asked him about Zoe, of course, but also how Pete was doing and what he was up to, whether he'd been doing any more of the things he'd put off when he became a father.

Hank laughed and said Pete had just come home from another road trip. He'd gone to see his daughters—Hank's older sisters. First, the younger of the two, who lived in Oakland, where she played in a punk band and worked at a tech company. And then his eldest daughter, who was married to a naval officer, but had been home alone in Bremerton, Washington, and getting ready for her first baby to arrive, while her husband was "on a cruise, courtesy of Uncle Sam."

"Did your dad stay long enough to see his grandbaby enter the world?" I asked.

"He did. Good thing he was there because my sister went into labor early. Everybody's fine, but it would have been a bummer if she had to be by herself. And Pop got to hear his grandson's debut performance. He has some powerful lungs, my sister says."

"You're going to be a fun uncle, Hank."

"Thanks, but I'm not sure when I'll even see the little dude. Little Weston, who's not so little, I guess. For a premature baby, I guess he's pretty hefty."

"I like 'Weston.' It's nice a nice name and not one that every other boy at his school will have. So you didn't do the trip with your dad?"

"I was working a construction job and saving up for my own big move. When do you transplant to Saratoga?"

"As soon as I find a house I can afford. I'm looking."

"What are you going to do with this place?"

"It'll go back to being our family retreat. It belongs to my sisters too. So, back in California, your Pop's going to be alone?"

"Yeah. I feel a little bad about that, but he really encouraged me to go. He said now's the time I should try things like this."

"Well, maybe we can get him here for a visit, if nothing else."

"He's talking about going back to work."

"His old job?"

"I don't know. He says he's exploring his options. I think he should just chill. He was offered early retirement and he'd put in enough years to draw his full benefits, so why not enjoy them?"

"He enjoyed his job working on planes. Maybe he's bored."

"He's constantly busy doing other things that I know he loves, including volunteering at a shelter, teaching kids to make music with improvised instruments. He could consider that his job. It's a great one. I went with him a few times when I was out of work, and the first time, on the way to the shelter, I said something about 'homemade' instruments. He told me, 'Don't call them *homemade*. It doesn't make the instruments or the music sound exciting, and these kids don't have homes. But treat them like you would any kid. Laugh with them and have a good time.'"

My Pete-seeking questions and shallow digging for news about him slammed to a stop. I said, "Wow. It does sound like that's a good job for him. And valuable work." I suddenly felt frivolous and self-centered. Which isn't to say I was done with Pete.

After Hank left that day, I worked on a note to his dad, to thank him for the basket of instruments, and I wondered whether I was being dishonest with Tom—whether I was guilty of making myself physically available to him while my mind, or part of it, and possibly my heart, were elsewhere. His boys were going to go back to their mother the following night, and he was planning to come to my place again after work the next day, on Monday. Would it be dishonest to spend another evening with him? I was still stewing about that when I went to bed, but I'd finished my thank you note.

Dear Music Man,

What a gift! Thank you so much. I have the basket sitting in the center of the coffee table for all to see. And to remind me to use the beautiful instruments whether friends are here making music with me or not. Who's to say I can't try to play along to tunes from the stereo or one of my playlists? (I have one from the Pete Does Roger Road Trip.) I surely need to practice if I'm going to be a passable percussionist by the time you come for another visit, which I hope will be sooner rather than later.

Come see your boy and his girl, your old pal Greg, and my old pal Eve Ellen. Time with friends is good medicine and making music with them makes the medicine even more potent. I learned that from you. Come see us and give me percussion lessons. I need them. I ain't got rhythm. Not yet.

Yours truly,

She Who Loves Her Spoons, Tambourine, Shakers, and Sticks (I Mean, Claves)… and the Horse (I Mean, Basket) They Rode in On

To ensure I didn't spend a week rewriting and agonizing, or trying to add something about how Evie had overstated my relationship status, which I knew I shouldn't do because it would be awkward and deceptive and unfair to Tom, I planned to drop the note in the mailbox outside the post office on my way to school in the morning, where it would be safely beyond my reach and ability to revise, and I'd have no choice but to begin the excruciating wait for a reply.

THIRTY

Partial journal entry from Sunday, February 10:

"That's the end of that tale, but don't forget, once upon a time there was a dad who loved to tell his girls bedtime tales and would have a new one for them every night because he hoped his stories would help them sleep soundly and have sweet dreams so they would stay in their own beds until morning."

That line, and then "Sleep soundly, my loves," always followed my father's bedtime stories when I was a kid. He started every story differently, but always ended with that line. Referring to himself as "a dad," he'd sweetly hint that he hoped G, D, and I would refrain from crawling into bed with him and Mom, who slept super lightly and could never get back to sleep once she was awake.

After finishing my note to Pete last night, and giving myself fully to fretting about Tom and my moral obligations where he's concerned, the last thing I remember thinking before I fell asleep went something like, "Once upon a time there was a dad who was my father and an honorable man. Truly, wholly honorable. What would he think if he knew I was pining for Pete but planning to spend the night with Tom? What would you say, Dad, if you knew I was thinking of lying to buy a little time, telling Tom I wasn't feeling well and had to give him a rain check? What would you think of my secretly divided mind and my dishonesty?"

Monday morning, there was no getting back the note to Pete after I let it fall from my hand into the mailbox. But I still had time to get out of seeing Tom that night. I hated the idea of once again texting him to cancel because of Pete, but I wasn't sure which would be the worse violation—texting him or seeing him. I also wasn't sure I wanted to cancel. I really did care for him, and there were still those three thousand miles between New York and California. Pete's availability status hadn't changed.

Ultimately, I figured women and men have surely entertained private thoughts about people other than their bed partners since our species did its bedding in caves, and their thoughts haven't always constituted betrayal or dishonesty. They aren't always and necessarily dishonorable. So I decided I would see Tom, and while I was with him, I would be wholly present for him.

When he arrived and I met him at the door, my smile was absolutely honest. Over dinner, we bantered and laughed about nothing memorable and I was right there with him. Though, when we finished eating, I did try to keep him out of the bedroom and talking at the table a little longer. I tried to get him to open up by asking him to tell me more about why he decided to leave the monastery. I said, "What changed?"

He started to reply with another deflection, grinning as he said, "You mean, besides realizing I didn't want to live without women who aren't the Virgin Mary?"

But then he flinched ever so slightly at his own words and tried to counter them with something serious. The gist of what he said was that he was working in the monastery garden one day, found himself saying the Lord's Prayer, and realized he'd rewritten it without noticing what he was doing. When he did notice what he'd done, it led him to think about his beliefs, and the Catholic church's teachings, and where he and the church were no longer on the same page.

He said something to the effect, "Realizing I'd revised a prayer created by Jesus Christ for his disciples when they asked him how they should pray stopped me in my tracks. It made me step off the path I'd been on and into an existential crisis. I'd thought I knew what I knew and what I believed, and I'd figured out what my life was supposed to be, then suddenly I wasn't sure about any of it anymore."

I replied, "That must have felt like a profound unmooring. How old were you?"

"Twenty-six. Not a kid, but young. I don't think my new and improved Lord's Prayer would have offended the guy who supposedly came up with the original, but the fact that'd I'd subconsciously felt the need to change his work, to improve on what he is said to have told his disciples, put me on a road to a dark place. In hindsight, I'm glad I traveled that road, but it was wasn't fun."

Then he went back to grinning his charming grin and said, "I eventually knew what I had to do. It's been all good ever since."

He was done discussing his life, so he stood up, took our plates to the sink, and that was the end of that. For the moment.

I started washing the dishes. He looked through my parents' record collection, put on a Billie Holiday album, and asked me, "Did any of your kids say anything priceless today? Anything that proves kids do say the darnedest things?"

I said, "No zingers that I remember. But I've got a good haircut story," and I told him about the two Harpers in my class, how they'd come to school with their bangs mangled and so short they hardly constituted bangs. They'd had a playdate and put scissors to one another's hair.

It was a short story, even though I tried to draw it out and make it funny. When I finished, rather than wait for his next question, his next attempt to keep the conversation focused away from his life, I told him I was thinking I would rent in Saratoga if I didn't find a place I could buy before July 30. "That would leave me some time to get settled before school starts up again," I said.

He replied, "You know what else it would mean?"

"No, what else?" As sincerely as I'd meant to stay present, I'd lost interest in our talk and let my mind drift to what I had going on with my class the next day.

He nodded his head toward the bedroom, and said, "We'd have more time for—"

I snapped him with the dishtowel and asked, "Are you really a sixteen-year-old boy disguised as a middle-aged man?" Then I said, "Wait, I get it—you're taking Viagra, aren't you?"

"No need for that," he said. "I'm making up for lost time."

I snapped the towel again to keep him from coming for me, and I said, "You didn't lose all that much if you left the monastery at twenty-six."

"I didn't just bolt. It was another year after I opened that existential can of worms for myself. Which means I lost a solid decade if we say boys typically lose their virginity at around seventeen. I'd decided by fifteen I wanted to be a monk or a man of science. In case I chose to go with religion, I remained chaste. So I was a virgin until I was twenty-seven."

I had the towel in position, threatening him, and I said, "This is interesting to me, Tom. I want to hear how you decided at fifteen to be a monk or a scientist."

He took a step forward.

"Stop!" I ordered.

He stopped, and said, "My grandfather gave me three books for my birthday—*Walden* by Henry David Thoreau, a collection of essays by Einstein, and Thomas Merton's autobiography."

"Thomas Merton?" I knew the name, but couldn't remember anything more than that.

"He was a Trappist monk in the 1950s and 60s, and his life at a monastery in Kentucky sounded to me like a Catholic version of Thoreau's life at Walden Pond in Massachusetts. They both lived surrounded by nature and had lots of time to read and ponder weighty things. I decided I was meant to live that way too."

As determined as I was to keep Tom's mind off sex for a little longer, he was determined to thwart me. He said, "I was a good Catholic boy, so I chose to follow in Merton's footstep, but reading about him, I missed the parts where he fathered a child out of wedlock before he entered the monastery, and he fell in love with a nurse after he'd been living his Benedictine vows for years. They met when he was in the hospital for surgery, and who knows how far their relationship went, or where it would have ended up if he hadn't died at fifty-three, but at twenty-seven, I knew the celibate life wasn't for me. Speaking of which, come here."

Before I could whip the towel, he grabbed me by my hips and pulled me close. With our noses touching, tip to tip, he said, "Can we make up for my lost decade now?"

And I consented.

When my alarm went off in the morning, Tom was still there. I hit the snooze button. He got up, pulled on his clothes, kissed my forehead, and said, "Have a good day, but miss me."

I'd consented willingly, and happily enough, but clearly didn't yet feel completely okay about seeing Tom while harboring feelings for Pete.

THIRTY-ONE

Proof of a Higher Power looking out for me, or how lucky coincidences can be: The next Friday, which was supposed to be one of Tom's free days, without his boys, he was going to have them for the night so his wife could accept an invitation from a friend who had an extra ticket to a play in the city. That meant he had to decline Evie's invitation to dinner at her place. Hank and Zoe were going to be there, and Evie hoped Tom and I would come together too.

She told me, "Since you're out of the closet now, you can bring him and make your debut as a couple."

I told her, "You need to relax. It's still very early days and I'm not sure where we're going. If you don't want to jinx us, you'll back off."

"Backing off," she said. "See me moving back? Step, step, step. Back I go."

Before the dinner with Hank and Zoe was done, they had talked Evie, Greg, and me into coming to their place the next afternoon for a potluck and music by their "house band and guest performers." Zoe told us a bunch of her friends got together at the farm almost every weekend, and everybody brought food to share and an instrument to play, or their voice primed for singing.

Hank said, "Isla, you and Eve Ellen will be on percussion, so bring your basket. Greg can play his harp."

"I'm not sure anybody is ready to hear my banging," I replied.

"You'll be great. Don't make me break my promise to Pop."

Evie said, "I wish he was here. Get him to come back, Hank. With you and the girls gone, he's free to pick up and move, right?"

"Well, it's not like he has no life in California. He stays busy. He has friends. My sisters are on the West Coast, and now his first grandkid is there."

"How often would he really make that trip by car, all the way to Washington? If he flew there from here when he needs a grandbaby fix, he'd be in the air just a little longer than he would be flying from San Diego, and the airport hassle would be the same either way."

"Take it up with him," Hank said. "I'd love the idea."

"I just might," Eve Ellen replied. "As for tomorrow, count me in. It'll be fun."

Early the next morning, I woke up smiling and happy about seeing Hank and Zoe again. I literally whistled while I made a butternut squash gratin for the potluck and filled a box with jars of pickled vegetables to take as a gift. And I whistled some more while I showered, dressed, and pulled on a pair of cowboy boots, in case we did any dancing. I'd impulsively purchased them for a party Evie threw, a western-themed affair several shindigs prior to our anniversary bash, and I discovered they were great on the dance floor. I knew they probably weren't the best footwear for snow and icy ground, but I wanted to wear them, so I did.

When I pulled up to the farm at around noon, I gave an appreciative whistle in the car. I was smitten with the place at first glance. The house was a white Victorian, with peeling paint, but still pretty. There was a twig wreath shaped like a peace symbol on the front door, a row of mismatched rockers on the porch, and several rows of raised garden beds in the side yard. The beds were empty and blanketed with snow, but clearly hadn't been abandoned because some were patched with wood planks that looked new. Beyond the garden, there was a chicken coop and a congregation of fruit trees that were bare for winter but expertly pruned.

I parked beside Evie and Greg's car, glad to see they'd arrived ahead of me, and made my first trip to the house with the gratin. The box of veggies and basket of musical instruments would have to come in a second trip. I wasn't going to try to do it all in one load in my slick-bottomed boots.

I was still on the porch steps when the front door swung open and Hank said, "You made it!"

"I did. A little bleary-eyed after last night's festivities at Evie's, but I made it. How about you take this pan, so I can go back for the rest of what I brought."

"No, you're going to go inside to get warm. I'll take you to the kitchen and then run to your car. You brought Pop's basket?"

"Yep. Bring the box in the backseat too," I said, as we made our way down a long hallway to the back of the house, passing door after door, and squeezing past young people Hank introduced without stopping.

"Isla, meet Tyler. Joshua meet Isla. Proper introductions coming soon."

At the end of the hall, we emerged into an enormous kitchen that extended the full width of the house and opened to what looked like a newer addition, though it also looked like a parlor from another century, with an old velvet sofa, overstuffed chairs, and an upright piano. Hank put my pan on the table and handed me over to Zoe and Evie, who were shaping dough into dinner rolls, then he started out of the kitchen but quickly turned back and gave me a tight hug before he left.

Zoe held up her doughy hands and said, "I'd hug you, but *this*." For punctuation, she wiggled her fingers and made a funny face, and I thought, "You and Hank are one adorable pair of lovebirds."

That day at the farm was beyond fun. Everyone crowded together at the long kitchen table to eat. When we were done, a crew of two guys and two girls said they were on cleanup. While they got started clearing the table, another couple of guys started playing music in the parlor—one on the piano and the other on a banjo. In short order, the table and chairs were moved to the side of the kitchen, space was opened up for dancing, and more instruments got going. Hank was one of two people on fiddle, there was a guy on standup bass, a girl on banjo, Zoe sang and played guitar, and Greg played his harmonica—it was the first time I ever heard him play. Together, they seamlessly segued from one song into another, from bluegrass to blues and rock. They gave classic rock songs a bluegrass spin and country songs a reggae beat.

Evie got me to dance and we kept going through three songs. After we exhausted ourselves and sat back down, Hank came over and put the spoons in my hands and the tambourine in Evie's.

He said, "Time to play."

And we did. Depending on how you define "play." We made some noise, and I'd call it joyful, but not music.

Later, I discovered Hank had once again put down his fiddle, picked up his phone, and recorded a video—this one was of me and Evie working the spoons and tambourine. He texted the video to us, Greg, and Pete. I saw the short thread just before I started for home that day.

Hank: *You should have been here Pop!*

Pete: *I wish I had been. Keep it up, Isla. You too, Eve Ellen.*

THIRTY-TWO

I was supposed to have an overnight with Tom after spending the day at Hank and Zoe's, but I called him and canceled for an honest reason. Evie had asked me if she could come to my place for breakfast. We were walking to our cars, with Hank and Greg trailing behind us and talking music, when she put her arm through mine and said, "That was fun but I could use a quiet day at the lake now. Can I come up tomorrow? I'll bring scrumptious pastries for breakfast."

Something in her voice worried me. It wasn't unusual for her to come up to the camp when she wanted a break from the world—I have lots of memory images of her sitting by herself at the end of the dock, sometimes reading a book, more often just sitting—but I could tell there was something going on with her, and it worried me enough that I knew I needed to cancel with Tom. So I kept my voice cheery and told her she could come.

"Of course, my lake is your lake. I'll take an almond croissant," I said. "Make that an almond croissant and a bear claw, just in case."

"Just in case what?"

"In case I decide I need to store the calories for next winter."

Then, as soon as I was in my car and driving away, I called Tom and asked him not to come. I told him I had "a family situation," and I'd explain later. I said I couldn't talk while I was trying to find my way home from the farm or I'd get lost.

Pastry box in hand, Evie arrived just after nine. I was still in my pajamas, but the fireplace was going, there was a fresh pot of coffee and two fruit smoothies on the table, and I had a skillet of scrambled eggs just about ready to serve.

I'm convinced we were in telepathic agreement to say nothing until we'd settled on the sofa, put up our feet, and spread a blanket across our laps and legs, for both warmth and a tablecloth. We each had a plate of food, though I'm not sure we ever touched them. I know we didn't finish them. I remember scraping the eggs into the trash can and feeling like I wanted to throw the plates in too. Or break them. I'm religious about not wasting food, but tossing the eggs and pastries was all I could manage. By then, Evie was asleep on the sofa.

She had come to tell me she had cancer and the prognosis wasn't good. She wanted me to have my mid-winter school recess, which started the following day, to absorb the news. I remember only pieces of our conversation. I have more visual memories, but they're also patchy. I didn't write anything about that day in my journal, and I'd be glad to forget all of it.

At some point, we quit talking and just sat. Evie laid her head on the back of the sofa, with her cheek pressed to the corduroy slipcover, and I remember thinking she was going to have lines on her face when she sat up. A weird thing to think about at a time like that, and a weird thing to remember.

She'd brought her legs up underneath her, and she was turned toward me, sitting on her feet. I was still facing the fire, but I'd pulled my legs to my chest. After she dozed off, I spread my half of the blanket over her and took our plates from the coffee table to the kitchen counter, then went to the bathroom to cry, muffling the sound with a towel as well as I could. The next thing I remember is scraping the plates.

Before she left, Evie asked me to go back to Saratoga and spend a few days with her and Greg, but I told her I'd come the next day. That was selfish, but I needed to get my bearings. I asked her who else knew, and she said just Greg and her father. She'd thought about telling Annie, when they were together for the holidays, but had decided against it.

"Merry Christmas, Annie honey! I've got the big C, the cancer," Evie said to me. Her eyes welled up and she swiped at the tears before they could fall. I hugged her and held on until she pulled away. I asked if I should tell Glyn and Dale, and she nodded. I texted them after I was in bed, then we did a three-way phone call and talked for a while. It could have been an hour, two hours, or ten minutes. I have no idea. But one thing is for sure, I never went to sleep that night.

The next morning, my sisters showed up looking like they hadn't slept either. They could hardly remember when Evie wasn't part of their lives. We drank coffee at the kitchen table, and they brought up memory after memory of things the four of us had done together or to each other. I laughed at the funny ones but wished they'd leave so I could be alone. After they did go, sometime around noon, I went back to bed and pulled the covers over my head to shut out the light, hoping the dark would help me fall asleep. I didn't have any luck with that, so I was just lying there when Tom texted to check in on me.

Tom: *How are you doing? Feeling better, I hope.*

Me: *Sisters just left. We're dealing with some hard news. I'll talk to you in a few days. Until then, I'll be missing you and hoping you're having a nice time with your boys.*

Tom: *I'll be missing you and hoping for the best for you and your sisters. Call me when you can.*

Giving up on sleep, I showered, dressed, put a few things in an overnight bag, and texted Evie.

Me: *Do you still want me to come down?*

Evie: *If you feel like it.*

Me: *Do you want me to come for you or for myself?*

Evie: *For both of us.*

Me: *I can leave now. Okay?*

Evie: *Yes! I should have my makeup on and hair done by the time you get here. I'll be ready to receive you in style.*

Evie doesn't wear makeup and doing her hair means pushing it behind her ears or putting it in a ponytail.

THIRTY-THREE

Greg was outside shoveling snow when I got to the house. Letting the shovel drop, he came to my door and opened it. When I got out, we hugged but didn't say anything. I took my bag from the back seat and went inside. He picked up the shovel and went back to work.

For the next three days, we binged on Netflix and ate takeout. Evie and I would tell Greg what we wanted, and he'd go get it. Tacos, Thai food, roast chicken and mashed potatoes with gravy. When he was doing the Thai run, I asked Evie whether she might reconsider treatment. She said she wouldn't, that two different doctors told her chemotherapy might slow the cancer and buy her a month or two, but not likely any more than that. She wanted to feel as good as she could for as long as she could, and chemo would make her feel lousy.

In other words, she had too little time left to give up any of it to being sick with the side effects of a treatment that wasn't going to cure her. Chemotherapy wouldn't buy her any good days, any *quality* time, and there was zero chance it was going to save her, so she wasn't going to do it.

"What about your classes?" I asked.

"They think I have the flu," she said.

Then she turned back to me with an accusatory smile and said, "Giving you the big news threw me off my game. I hadn't missed a day until this week. But I'll go back on Monday and let them know, then finish the semester. Hell, I may try to do another one. I'm not going to stop before I have to."

The next day, I went home. I thought it would be a good idea to go back and have a few days to get used to being alone with Evie's news before I had to return to work. I tried to resume some semblance of normal life. I worked on activity materials for my class, cooked and froze food until my freezers were practically bulging, and tried to watch food and gardening programs but zoned out during those. In the middle of the night, when I couldn't sleep, I looked at online real estate listings and rental ads.

I called Tom. I'd asked Evie what she wanted me to tell him, and she said, "The truth. But tell him to keep it quiet until I've let my Department Chair know. I'm going to talk to her first thing on Monday morning."

So I told him what was going on. He was silent for several seconds, then said, "I can take the boys back to their mother and be up there in two hours. Do you want me to come?"

I thanked him and said, "Let's wait. They go back to their mom on Sunday, right? You can come up then. Or Monday after work."

He replied, "Let's make it Sunday."

I texted Evie and asked about Hank and Pete.

Evie: *I left it to Greg to tell them. I don't think he has yet.*

Me: *I'll probably hear from Hank. He's an avid texter. I wrote a letter to Pete to thank him for the music basket and I can see him replying to thank me for thanking him. He's so… well-mannered. I don't really expect to hear from him, but I might. I won't say anything to either of them if you'd rather I didn't, but I'll tell them if that would make it easier for Greg.*

Evie: *Play it by ear and do what feels right. I'll nudge Greg and let him know so he can decide if he wants to talk to them before you do.*

The next few days passed and I didn't hear from Hank or Pete. I was grateful that Hank was busy looking for a job and surely spending every free moment with Zoe. And I was glad Pete wasn't a texter. I knew he'd want to know about Evie, but I didn't really want to be the one to tell him. I also didn't want to hear from him or Hank and have to pretend nothing was wrong.

Then on Sunday morning, the last day of my school break, Pete called. Greg had given him the news the night before. I was in the shower and missed him, so he left voicemail.

Hi Isla, this is Pete. I just wanted to tell you I'm sorry. I know how important Eve Ellen is to you. I'm thinking about you and everyone back there. If you want to talk, call anytime. Don't worry about the time difference, I'm up at all hours. Bye for now.

Then Hank texted and asked if he and Zoe could come over. They brought a pot of stew and we had lunch together. We went for a snowy walk and I showed them Evie's old house. After the walk, they left and Tom arrived. I heated up some of the stew for him. I told him everything I knew about Evie's diagnosis and prognosis, and what she wanted to do. Then I asked him if it would be okay if we made it a short visit. I said something like, "I know it's a long drive, so I hate to ask you to turn around and go back so soon, but would it be okay if I did? I think I might actually sleep tonight, and I'll need it tomorrow when I'm back in class."

"It's completely alright," he said.

After he left, I put the rest of Zoe's stew in the fridge, pot and all, and was in bed by eight.

My kindergarteners were so thrilled to see one another after being apart through the school break, one of the Harper's peed her pants, which made the other Harper, her best friend, cry a flood of tears, such was her empathy and shared agony. Lucas, usually an empathetic boy, laughed and pointed at the two girls, and said, "Run, everybody! The Harpers are going to get us all wet!" That made Ollie, who was in love with the blonde Harper, fighting mad, so he shoved Lucas, who went down and took tiny Abigail with him. It was a bona fide melee, with more shoving and shouting all around, and more tears.

In my head, I was hollering, "That's enough! Shut your damn pie holes! Do not move another muscle!"

Outside my head, in the presence of my sensitive young students, I did not holler. I told the kids we were going to begin the day again, and I used the melee as teaching material.

That evening, I texted Evie and asked how it went when she talked to the head of her department. She texted back, "Nice and easy. I'm naked and about to get in the shower. Talk soon."

Life returned to something close to standard operating procedure. We went to work, talked occasionally, but mostly texted during the week. We sent photos of food. No miserable news articles from online newspapers or funny animal videos on YouTube, but enough food shots that I wondered how much Evie really was eating. I kept cooking but consumed little of what I made. I reorganized my freezers to free up space and stuffed every inch with soups, stews, enchiladas, and ravioli in single-serving containers.

Evie's doctor had said she had eight months to a year if she didn't try chemo. She'd received that news in early December, which left roughly five to nine months. I texted her again and asked her to change her plans.

Don't do another semester. My kids graduate June 25 and your spring classes will be done by then, right? Let's spend the summer drinking on the dock.

If she made it for only the short end of the time she was told she could expect, there probably wouldn't be any summer drinking at the lake or elsewhere, but I was banking on her getting a full year. At least.

THIRTY-FOUR

The last days of winter and first weeks of spring passed like a steady trudge through deep snow, one foot in front of the other, day after day. At the same time, I felt suspended in a state of waiting. Things were happening, but not the thing I was watching for and dreading—the first sign that Evie was starting to decline.

During her spring break, she and Greg took a short trip. They flew to Berkeley, where they'd met. Greg had gotten into the university after he left the Navy, and he and Evie ended up living in the same co-op, where they became good friends, though not a couple until later when they were in graduate school.

When I was driving them to the airport, she said, "Like my dad, I return to the scene of my collegiate glory days. But I take my spouse with me."

They hadn't been back to the Bay Area since they finished school, and had fun sampling some of what was new to them in Berkeley and San Francisco, as well as visiting places they remembered. Then they rented a car and drove north to spend a few more days at a beach house in Mendocino, near where they used to camp when they were students. Back then, in a letter Evie wrote to me after their first camping trip, she told me about Greg.

He's older than our fellow co-op dwellers and he was in the military, so he knows what it's like to live with lots of people sharing close quarters, but this house, the co-op, is something else. It doesn't exactly offer the military hygiene he's used to, with everything ship-shape, spic and span. He's not really a camper but says he'll take a patch of dirt and some trees over filthy wall-to-wall carpeting and bathrooms every day of the week. If only we could be in Mendocino every day. The redwood trees made me cry. They're so beautiful, Isla. You'd love them. You'd love Greg too.

When I picked them up at the airport, Evie looked happy and didn't seem to have lost anything to the stress that always comes with air travel, but I kept watching for signs and spending as much time with her as I could, without intruding on Greg's time. I always said yes when she asked me to come down to their place, and I invited them up to the lake as often as I could without feeling greedy. So on weekends, we were often together. During the week, we kept going to work, which sometimes felt surreal. I knew there were people everywhere getting up and going to their jobs while they were dealing with cancer, their own or a loved one's. While they were caring for aging parents, trying to raise kids, struggling with depression or something else. When they were nearly overwhelmed by all they had to juggle to get through each day and keep paying their bills. But it felt surreal to do "business as usual."

One afternoon we were at my place watching something on Netflix from our usual positions on the sofa—I was at one end, with Greg next to me, and Evie was stretched out from the other end, with her feet in Greg's lap so he could rub them. When the closing credits started to roll, Evie said she wanted to go for a walk and have a look at her family's old house. It would be empty until summer, or whenever the owners got around to coming up again, and she wanted to see if she could peek in the windows.

We couldn't see inside, as it turned out, because the curtains were pulled tight, so Evie tried the doggy door and discovered it had already been pried open by somebody else and didn't latch anymore. She then got the brilliant idea that I should squeeze through, unlock the back door, and let her into the house. She started needling me and wouldn't stop.

I told her, "It isn't going to happen. No way, no how. I'm not going to do it, so save your breath."

"Please, please, please. I won't fit."

"If you won't fit, I won't. I'll get stuck. Even if I made it inside, there could be a security camera. A motion-sensor alarm."

"If we get caught, we have a great excuse."

"Which is what? You forgot you don't live here anymore? You lost the last marble in your head and forgot your own address?"

"No, much better than that. I've got *the cancer* and I'm doomed."

Greg, who'd been quiet until then, said, "That's too much. Too much, Eve Ellen. I'm gone."

He started back to my house and Evie started pleading with him to stay.

"Greg, sweetheart, cupcake, pumpkin, please don't go."

He kept going. Evie looked at me, I looked away and wouldn't meet her eyes. She started after him. Neither of them was moving very fast, but by the time she was close enough to reach out and grab the back of his jacket, she was breathing hard. She yanked him to a stop and got him to turn around. At first, he just stood there with his shoulders slumped and his arms hanging at his sides. She pulled his face close to hers and I could see she was talking to him, but I couldn't hear what she was saying. Eventually, Greg put his arms around her and they held each other for a long time.

Then he called out, "Come on, Isla, I'm hungry."

Back at the house, he made sandwiches for all of us, but Evie was asleep before he had them ready.

When Evie and Greg weren't at my place, or I wasn't at theirs, and I wasn't at school, I worked on another round of book edits with my editor after I signed the one-book contract offered by my old publisher. When I was done with that, I often spent evenings sitting on the porch, wrapped in a blanket and rocking in one of the chairs out there, staring at the lake, or in the direction of the lake if it was too dark to make out the water. Sometimes, while I rocked, I'd quietly hum, which isn't something I'd ever done before.

I stopped my manic cooking after I'd filled Evie's freezer too. Sometimes I'd heat up frozen food for dinner after work, but I often ate only one meal a day—lunch, which I ate only because I didn't want my colleagues to know I was struggling, or to ask me if I was dieting, which would then require me to tell the truth or have a fake conversation about which diet I was doing.

After every visit or phone call with Evie, I replayed her words in my head and wrote them down. I reconstructed my best approximation of everything she said, but it wasn't just her words that I wanted to record and remember—I wanted to lock the sound of her voice in my memory. I hated that I couldn't conjure my parents' voices anymore. No matter how hard I tried, I couldn't hear them. I could retrieve only the empty capsules of silent space their voices once filled. Like when a painting is removed from a wall and you can see the patch of wallpaper that was hidden behind it, blocked from the light so it hasn't faded, and in that patch, you can see the painting's outline, its shape and size, but you can't see the painting itself—that's how it was with my parents' voices. I could hear the empty spaces where they'd once been, but I couldn't hear them. I didn't want to lose Evie's voice too.

When I was staying in Saratoga, she went with me to look at houses. She insisted on driving, and I wondered whether that was because she knew her driving days were numbered, or because it gave her a sense of control when she couldn't control where her life was going.

We were out in the car, after looking at a house, when she started pumping me about Tom.

She asked, "Any progress I should know about? What's happening with you two?"

I said, "Nothing's happening. I needed a break."

I didn't tell her that I could no longer bear for him to touch me, that I felt as if the skin had been ripped from my body and left my nerve endings exposed. That sounds melodramatic, but it's how I felt. She didn't need to hear about it. Didn't need to hear how I was hurting. She was the one with cancer. I was a healthy bystander.

But she wouldn't let the Tom subject go. She kept pushing until I gave her a dose of her own dark humor. I said, "Look, I know it sounds crazy, but worrying about your best friend biting the dust isn't an aphrodisiac. It's a libido killer."

She was usually the one to say things like that, to joke about situations that were anything but funny, to use humor like a pressure release valve. My attempt to take up her tactic didn't go well. Her face twitched and she looked sad for a second before she pushed on and kept asking questions, pumping me.

"So you guys aren't humping, but you're talking? Right? You're keeping the love spark alive?"

"Evie, you're killing me. Wait, forget I said that. Do not run with it."

"Okay, you get one free pass. Now, forget about where things are with you and Tom today—what do you see in your future? What do you want to see?"

"I don't necessarily see us together. I've had a lot of fun with him and I care about him, but I don't see us ever living under the same roof. So I don't think he's Husband Number Two."

"Well, it's early days, you said so yourself. It can still happen."

"Maybe. I don't know. I don't think so."

"Is there something you're not saying? Some reason you know you'll never live with him? A disqualifying factor?"

I snapped, "Evie, I can't give you a forensic analysis! I just don't feel it. I get that you want to get me hitched again. You want to check that off your list. But I don't think it's going to happen with Tom. You need to let it go."

"Now I know there's something you're not telling me. You always snap when your head is festering with something you've got bottled up. You don't bottle without suffering. You never have. What are you not saying?"

"Look, Tom isn't my future. He's not who I'm feeling. You really need to quit. Please."

"He's not *who* you're *feeling*? Who is? Tell me."

"I really wish I could make it happen with Tom. I really do. He's here, he's fun, he shares a lot of my interests. Or some of them. He's most of what I thought I wanted. He doesn't spoon in bed and he snores. Lightly and only sometimes, but there's definitely some snoring. And talking with him isn't—"

She interrupted me and said, "That's too bad, but let's back up. *Who* is it that you're feeling? You have to let it out, for your own good and for mine. I'm your best friend and I have the big C and it's the big T, so I need you to tell me who you're feeling."

"The big T?"

"Jesus, Isla, you're the queen of word games and puzzles, figure it out. T, something you don't want C to be. Rhymes with G—germinal."

"I'm not in the mood for games."

"T—terminal. Airport terminal for flights to the great beyond."

"Goddamn it, Evie! That really is too much."

"Give me the goods, then. The timer is ticking and my C is past the germinal stage. I don't have forever. *Who, who, who* are you interested in?"

"You don't play fair. You really don't. I'll tell you who it is, but you can't tell anybody else, not even Greg. Especially not Greg. You know I never ask you to keep anything from him, it's against my policy to ask partners to keep secrets from one another, but this time you will not say a word to him."

Evie swerved to the curb, jammed the car's gearshift into park, and said, "We're staying here until you tell me everything. I don't care if we have to call Greg to bring us food and adult diapers, we're not going anywhere."

She wore me down and I finally spilled the big secret. I told her, "I think I have a thing for Pete."

"*Pete?* You *think?*"

"Yes, *Pete*. Yes, I *think*. I mean, I know I should go for Tom and would if I had half of my kindergartners' intelligence. Tom is available, Pete isn't. He lives three thousand miles away. He lost his wife and he's dealing with that."

Evie stared at me with her mouth hanging open. She was still processing the Pete news and probably wondering why she hadn't seen clues that I was falling for him.

I asked her, "Do you think it really could still happen with me and Tom? He's who I should want, right?"

Before she replied, Evie literally shook her head to shake off her surprise. Then she said, "It might be possible that you'll still fall for Tom, but he deserves more than somebody who's settling for him because you don't think your first choice is an option. You deserve more than that, and you wouldn't be happy if you tried to settle. Have you been in touch with Pete?"

"Just a thank you note from him last summer, and then my thank you to him for the music basket. Maybe I'm just attracted to what I can't have."

Evie raised her eyebrows as if to say, skeptically, *"Really?"* Then she asked, "Are you and Tom still in touch?"

"We talk on the phone once in a while. The break has been good for that. He's opening up a little, talking about things he'd avoided. His default mode is to shift the focus away from anything about his life or what's going on in his head, anything serious, but I'm getting to know him better than I probably would if we were seeing each other. And he's been good about the time apart. Really understanding."

"But you're thinking about Pete."

"Evie, rewind. Pete isn't the reason I'm not seeing Tom, or not the primary reason. You are."

And that's when I started crying. I said, "What am I going to do without you? What's Greg going to do? And Annie. She should be here. Why won't you have her come home?"

"I want her to finish her term. This is going to be difficult enough for her without screwing her up at school too. If she can stay on track with that, it's going to help her down the line. What do you want to do about Tom and Pete?"

"You are so goddamn relentless. I don't want to do anything about them. For once, I'm telling the truth when I say a relationship isn't my top priority. How's Greg doing?"

"Having a hard time."

"Why don't you just quit working and be with him? Take another trip. Go see someplace you've always wanted to see but never got around to."

"Maybe if it was going to be two or three years, I'd want to go to the Galapagos and look at turtles, or go suck up some ramen at the source, wherever ramen comes from. I can never remember which country it is. But all I want now is just to be here enjoying our normal life. It's what I love best."

"For a couple who went from being platonic friends for a long time to falling in love and eloping overnight, you guys have been really solid."

Evie started to reply, but then stopped to switch gears. I saw something so clearly shift in her, it made me quit crying and listen intently for whatever was coming.

She said, "You know, it wasn't what you think. I wasn't ever going to fall into anything or be swept off my feet by anybody. There wasn't any big epiphany that Greg and I were in love. In some ways, it was more like an arranged marriage with us, only it wasn't our parents who did the arranging. My engineer husband and I decided to engineer a good partnership and a good life, and we eloped because it was the easiest way to deal with our friends and families."

I couldn't have been more confused if Evie had spoken in a foreign language and I hadn't understood a word. I said, "An arranged marriage? What are you talking about? Does Greg see it that way?"

"Not exactly. He's more like you, at least when it comes to romance. He would have been thrilled to sweep me up into a fairytale love story. But he knew who I was, what I was about, and he wanted to be with me anyway. I wanted the life we could create as partners."

"How did I not know about this? "

"I wasn't going to have anyone doubt or question what we have. Or see it as something sad. It's not and never was. I love Greg fiercely and he knows that. I just don't believe in fairytales."

I asked, "You don't believe in them or you don't trust them?"

"Slice and dice it any way you want. I don't do them."

"You never wanted or wished for romance? I mean, we were never the girls who played Barbies and talked about marrying Ken, but haven't you ever had secret fantasies? Romantic hopes and dreams?"

"I dreamed of having a steady Freddy guy I really liked as a person and enjoyed as a friend. A guy committed to commitment, who thought I walked on water, and would happily rub my sacred feet every night. That's what I wanted and what I got with Greg."

"You really did. He still thinks you walk on water."

"And I still think he's the man of my dreams."

Evie looked sad but smiled as she said, "I want you to have something as wonderful as I've had. You're not going to get it by rationalizing your way into a relationship. You can't just decide you're going to be with Tom and then be happy with him."

"It sounds like that's exactly what you did with Greg."

"That's *not* what I did. It wasn't that simple."

"I'm just going by what you said yourself. You just told me that's how it was with you."

"Look, it doesn't matter what I did because you're a different person. You've said you believe love is something we choose to do, while attraction is something that happens to us, and attractions can end but love never does because that would be contrary to its nature. You've told me you believe love is always unconditional, never about getting anything in return, and once you truly love somebody, you can never again not love them. If what you felt goes away, it was something else. Not love. I'm way out of my depth here, but I can tell you I didn't choose to love Annie. When she was born, love came over me like a force. Like a tidal wave, it rolled in from the ocean, caught me, and carried me away. With my dad, it *was* a choice. I chose to love him a second time, after losing what I'd felt for him as a kid and then feeling nothing for a lot of years. Not even anger about the way he abandoned us. I decided to cultivate new love for him and I'm actively working on that. With Greg, it wasn't an external force or an internal decision. It wasn't work or something I had to cultivate. I chose to be with him, but my love for him grew from our friendship like a tree grows from the forest floor—it just happened. And it became so deep-rooted and rich, I've never felt like I missed out on anything. I'm sure you're going to love whoever you end up with because you're a lover. You love by both conscious choice and innate bent. It's your factory default setting. But you're also someone who has to have romance. You have to feel your relationship is something involuntary and—"

Evie stopped talking, but held up one of her hands to tell me, "Wait, I'm not done." When she was ready to continue, she put both hands to her face, rubbed her eyes, and said, "Lord, I really am out of my depth." Then she looked at me, and added, "Here it is in your own language: I believe you're someone who needs to feel a magical, mystical connection the way bread has to have yeast to rise. Without it, any relationship you have will feel flat and you'll always feel something's missing. You won't be happy."

I replied, "Tidal waves, trees, and bread aside, are you trying to tell me I should let Pete know how I feel about him?"

"I'm saying you should listen to the wee small voice inside and do what it says. Not the neurotic voice in your mind—the other one, the one in your guts and in your bones."

Then somebody tapped on the car window, right behind my head. An old man had come out of the house to tell us we needed to shut off the car. I hadn't realized it was still running. He said he could smell exhaust in his living room, even with his windows and doors closed. That was highly unlikely, given that his house was shut up and Evie didn't drive a clunker that spewed fumes, but we apologized and told him we were leaving.

Driving away, Evie said, "The only thing I'm going to add about Pete is don't rule out anything. Don't think he's not ready or too far away."

"So I should get in touch with him?"

"Watch my lips! Don't rule out anything based on reasons that may exist only in your head."

"Maybe I'm only drawn to him because I'm pining for something like he had with Lainie. He said his road trip was about paying homage to Roger Miller, but I think it was all about her. He adored her. Maybe I just envy that. Or maybe it's some other pitiful sick thing like I see him as my fellow heart-broke sad sack, cast adrift and lonely, and figure we can join forces."

"He isn't a sad sack, but do you honestly think that's what your attraction to him is, the only thing you're feeling?"

"I don't know. Tom made me feel good about myself again, but from the moment I met Pete, I felt good in a bigger or more complete sense. I felt a connection I don't feel with Tom. Don't laugh, but on the trip with Pete and Hank, it was like I was with my people. How ridiculous is that?"

"Not at all. Zero percent ridiculous."

"I wish I wanted Tom, but I do know he deserves more than somebody who's settling and I wouldn't just use him. You know that, right?"

"Yes, I do. That's not who you are. Before all is said and done, you always try to do the right thing."

"I'm a good Girl Scout and Lainie was cool."

"You do have a lot of badges on your sash, what with your love of the domestic arts and outdoor activities, but that's its own kind of cool."

"Yeah, right. You know Lainie was way cooler than I've ever been or ever will be."

"I don't know that."

"I've never punched a shark."

"Never? Really?"

"Screw you."

"Isla, since when do you care about being cool? Since when has thinking about something like that been anything you'd waste half a thought on? Those are rhetorical questions, don't start obsessing over them. You may not be able to see yourself the way the rest of the world does, but I know you know what Scott said to me the first time I met him. Say it with me: *'I love that she's so open to life and isn't held back by fear of how she'll look to anybody. She doesn't give a shit about being anyone other than who she is.'* That was true, Isla. Scott was right. You just went merrily along your wonderful way being you."

I started to interrupt, but Evie snapped, "Quiet! I have more to say that you need to hear. Just as my relationship with Greg wasn't what you or anybody else may have assumed, Pete and Lainie's relationship wasn't either. That's Pete's story to tell, if you two ever get that far, but whatever Lainie was or wasn't doesn't have anything to do with what you might be able to have with him. Yes, she was cool. She was great. But you are too. You're smart, self-aware, empathetic, funny, fun, strong. And you're not defective because you can't make babies—I repeat, *you are not defective.* Let's face it, not only are you not a lemon, you're beautiful and your body is of the variety guys can't help wanting to undress, no matter how enlightened they are. Gandhi may have preferred the anorexic type, but most boys between the ages of fifteen and a hundred want what you have. It's one of the crosses you've had to bear and you've carried that sucker with grace. Your confidence hasn't recovered yet, and you can do neurotic in a big way, but that's not who you are when it really counts. I've seen you come through fire after fire without flinching, without whining about your burns. You've always been game for an escapade, and escapades are still more fun when you're involved. That's never changed, no matter how badly you've been torched by life. You still look out for people, and you take care of them, the way you always have. But you'd slap a shark silly if it needed to be slapped. *Then*, Isla, when you talked about it later, you wouldn't make yourself out to be any better than the fish, you wouldn't say a bad word about the foolish creature. You'd be funny and you'd be kind because *that's* who you are."

"Are sharks fish or mammals?" I asked, to mess with Evie and change the subject.

"It's whales that are mammals," she answered, playing it straight, as she made a last-second turn so fast and sharp her side of the car must have come close to leaving the ground. Rounding the corner, she said, "Let's go to a swanky restaurant, order four desserts, and call it lunch."

"Maybe not," I replied. "I think you just called me fat, a veritable whale, when you said Gandhi preferred anorexics."

"No, I said you have a bodacious body. You're an irresistible sweet roll rather than a saltine cracker."

"You need to stop before you dig yourself deeper."

Whatever or whoever else I am, I can be a worrier, and I was worried about hogging Evie and thought we should get back to Greg, so I said, "Let's make it five desserts and take them to go so we can share with your husband." And that's what we did.

THIRTY-FIVE

On April Fool's Day, Dale texted to tell me she'd just met with new clients who wanted her help getting a house ready to put on the market. Then she blasted a barrage of texts listing the reasons she thought the place was right for me.

It's old and not updated for like a hundred years but that's a good thing

No carpet to peel off the hardwood and no shitty laminate cupboards and counters in the kitchen

It needs some serious cleaning but has huge potential

They inherited from an aunt and want to offload fast

No realtor

So no fees

When she paused, I slipped in two texts with questions:

But is it falling apart? Does it need expensive repairs?

How big is it? Where is it?

She replied with another blast:

I think nothing major to fix right away

Every room is a different color

Easter egg pink yellow lavender

But a bucket of white paint and it would be totally livable

Tiny but three beds one bath

You could convert third bed to a master bath when you have the money

Not a huge yard but big enough for a garden

Great sun outside and all rooms

Downtown walking distance to everywhere

I asked if she could get me in for a look. She replied that she was on it and would get back to me as soon as she had an answer. And I suddenly had to think about whether I really wanted to spend time moving and commuting when I could be with Evie. I would live closer to her once the move was made—she and Greg lived in downtown Saratoga—but I'd burn hours driving to and from school all week. The math was more than I could handle right then. I couldn't immediately figure out which scenario would leave me with more free time. Live close to Evie and commute to work? Stay at the lake, closer to school, and drive down on weekends?

Two days later, I went to see the house and desperately wanted it. The owners were desperate to be done with the place, so our deal came together quickly. They liked that they wouldn't have to pay Dale to clean, paint, and stage, and they wouldn't have to show it to a parade of prospective buyers. I loved that it came with a gas, griddle top, double oven Wedgewood stove, circa 1952. I loved that it was a small but tall vintage cottage, circa 1890, with minuscule bedrooms but enough room in the kitchen for a little breakfast table, plus a separate dining room large enough to seat eight people without excessive elbow jabbing. I was thrilled that the down payment was do-able, without wiping out every cent of my savings, thanks to the advance money from my book.

Superstitiously, for jinx protection, while I waited for escrow to go through, I spent my spring recess looking at other houses with Evie, widening my search to towns that were just minutes from Saratoga, but less expensive. I knew I could get more for my money elsewhere—more house and more yard—and knew I should consider that, but I loved Saratoga's historic district and wanted the cottage so much I couldn't see other properties with clear vision and an open mind. I looked at them only for whatever magical protection they might provide.

When escrow finally closed, the move wasn't easy peasy because no move ever is, but it wasn't as hard or time-consuming as it might have been, given that most of my belongings were already packed and sitting in Dale's barn, ready to go, and I had lots of help moving them. Evie was thrilled I was coming back to Saratoga, and she and Greg insisted on joining me and my sisters in washing all the walls and painting them white the weekend before I moved in. Dale had already refinished the wood floors, as a housewarming gift, and made them beautiful. And Glyn had helped me clean the kitchen and bathroom. We scrubbed away years of grime and made every inch of those rooms spotless, including the grout around the old porcelain penny tiles on the bathroom floor.

On moving day, Hank came with his truck and helped my brothers-in-law and Greg haul my stuff, and Zoe came over with homemade pizzas for lunch, then stayed to help me, my sisters, and Evie unpack enough to make the place semi-functional, and help us drink the wine Dale brought to "sustain us through our labor."

On my first night in the house, after everyone left, after I crawled into bed in my new bedroom, I might have had a blubber if I hadn't been so tired. I felt incredibly lucky to have gotten the place and so much help with the move. I was emotional about that, exhausted, and, most of all, I was wrecked about Evie. She seemed to have fun working with our crew but moved more slowly than her usual brisk pace. I found myself stealing looks at her, checking to see how she was doing. Twice I caught her standing with her eyes closed, taking open-mouthed breaths. I didn't say anything because I knew she wouldn't want me to, not with everyone there.

As she hugged me goodbye, she said, "I'm so glad you're here. For me, but for you too. This nest feels like you."

I asked her, "Am I going to see you and Greg tomorrow? How about I make Sunday brunch on my fabulous stove?"

She asked me, "Don't you want to spend the day chipping away at the rest of these boxes and putting something on these very white walls?"

"I want to test my new griddle. Let me make you guys pancakes and eggs, then you can tell me when I'm hanging pictures too high or low. Or crooked. You can just sit back, with your feet up, and lend me your eyeballs."

"Let's talk in the morning," she said.

She and Greg did come back the next day, but I still didn't ask how she was feeling. It didn't feel like the time was right. When we finished eating, she and I stayed at the kitchen table, and Greg went to work on the bathroom door, determined to unstick its stuck lock, which had caught his attention the day before.

Eve Ellen said, "He has his priorities and non-negotiables. A locking bathroom door is right up there with American league baseball. He'll have no intrusions when he's in the loo and no pinch hitters. I almost didn't marry him because I knew he could never be a Mets fan."

She'd raised her voice so Greg could hear her, and he said, "You should know me well enough by now to know I don't do my business at other people's houses. I'm fixing this door out of the goodness of my heart. For Isla."

After they left, I listened to Ella Fitzgerald, Louis Armstrong, and more of my parents' favorite music while I worked on the unpacking. That night, Tom called and we talked for a few minutes. I had school in the morning and would have to get up even earlier than usual to do the commute, so we kept the call short. He said he wanted to see the cottage when I was ready. I told him it was going to take me a little time to get it presentable, but I'd give him a tour as soon as I had it in semi-order.

THIRTY-SIX

By mid-May, Evie was open about needing to conserve her energy for finishing the semester at school—she still had papers to grade and grades to submit for all her classes—and she'd decided it was time for Annie to come home.

Annie's first week back from France, I didn't call or text. It was the longest Evie and I had ever gone without contact of any kind. When we were kids, during the school year she lived in Albany and I was in Saratoga, but until we turned sixteen and I got my first car, an antique but dependable Ford Pinto, we pestered our parents to drive us back and forth for weekend sleepovers, and on school nights we stayed on the phone for so long her mother set a thirty-minute limit. During college in different states, we called one another almost every day, and when we went on our honeymoons, we sent postcards. Whenever either of us was going through a rough time, we'd talk or text first thing every morning and again at night, at the very least—really tough times called for more. She came to stay with my family during the final ugly convulsions of her parents' marriage and divorce, and when my parents were killed, she dropped everything, sent an email to her students to cancel her classes for the rest of the afternoon, and got to me before anybody else, including Scott and my sisters.

While I gave her and Greg the space I thought they'd need and want with their daughter, I tried not to think about Annie being alone when she got the news her mother was sick, and alone for the long flight home. I tried to stay busy and distracted.

During the drive to and from school, I kept my mind occupied thinking about what I was going to do in my classroom or at home, whichever place I was headed. If I wasn't at school or in the car commuting, I worked on the house, unpacking the last boxes, rearranging things in cupboards and drawers to make the kitchen more efficient, rearranging the furniture in the living room to make it work better in the small space. When Evie texted on a Saturday afternoon, I was pushing my sofa to a new spot and putting all my weight into worrying about scratching the wood floor so I wouldn't think about other things.

Evie: *Your goddaughter wants to know why she hasn't heard from you since she got here. She wants to see your house. Can we come over?*

Me: *Yes! Come!*

Though it had only been a week since I'd seen Evie, she looked less well. Her face was pale, close to colorless. She'd lost weight. I could sometimes see her working to get a good breath while trying to look as if that weren't the case.

Annie looked like a stunned fawn, scared, but trying to appear otherwise. Seeing her, I think I fast-forwarded to grief's anger stage. I was suddenly furious at Evie. Angry that she'd waited so long to tell Annie and to bring her home.

The three of us sat at my kitchen table with a pot of tea and plate of oatmeal cookies we didn't touch. Evie pressed Annie to tell me about what she'd been up to in Paris since the last time she'd been home. As Annie talked, she fidgeted with the mug of tea she wasn't drinking, turning it around and around on the table. I listened to her and tried to ask appropriate questions and make the right facial expressions, but I wanted to scream at Evie, "What were you thinking? What are you doing now?"

After Annie left the room to go to the bathroom, when I heard the door click shut, I exploded. I kept my voice low, but I hissed, "You should have brought her back weeks ago! You were wrong to let it go until now! Wrong! What were you thinking waiting until you look so sick and scary? I don't care if you are her mother, you're not so goddamn much smarter than her and the rest of us that it's your job to engineer our lives. We're not yours to protect from ourselves and from life. It's not for you to dole out information to us as you think we need it or can handle it. You have this wonderful daughter and she could have been here with you. She *should* have been here."

I stopped and stared at Evie, challenging her to respond, but she just stared back, startled. Her eyes looked as scared as Annie's had been.

"You're trying to engineer my future too," I accused her. "Pete called me about staying at the lake, and he told me he'd wanted to be here for you guys, but hadn't wanted to intrude, then you asked him to come. He has no idea what you're up to, but I do. Leave my life alone and leave Annie alone. She doesn't want to tell Paris stories. That's not going to help her."

"I asked Pete to be here for Greg, and for me," Eve Ellen said. There was nothing defensive in her voice, only sadness, but I kept going, kept up my attack.

"Really? That's all? Or is that just what you're telling yourself? I know you want to check me off your to-do list, get me fixed up and taken care of while you still can."

I was shaking, I was so mad. Evie was still staring at me, but then she closed her eyes, her face quivered, we heard the bathroom door click open, and we put on happy faces before Annie came back into the kitchen.

There were no words that could undo how awful I'd been, but I texted Evie later and apologized.

I'm so sorry. I'm the one who was wrong. I love you so much, Evie, and I love Annie so much. It was hard seeing her look scared. But that's no excuse. There isn't any excuse. I was horribly, cruelly wrong. You're the most thoughtful, kind person I've ever met and didn't deserve a word of what I said. I'm so sorry. So very, very sorry.

She replied with a heart emoji.

Ugly truth: It was love and grief that made me lose it that day, that made me attack Evie so viciously, but it was also envy and jealousy. I'd run into Scott and his daughters at the grocery store that morning, in the produce section, surrounded by mounds and bins of fruit and vegetables. I knew it could happen anytime, anywhere in town. I knew that it was sure to happen eventually after I moved back to Saratoga. But I thought I was ready to handle it without a major upset. I wasn't ready.

Scott's twin toddlers were standing up in a parked shopping cart, holding its rim with their chubby little hands, and I saw them before I saw him, before I knew they were his girls. I'd stopped in the aisle to assess whether I could get my cart around theirs, and one of the twins lifted a hand and waved at me. I waved back and she laughed. Scott was facing the other direction, with his head bent over a bin of mushrooms he was picking through, and I didn't realize it was him until he turned toward his daughter's laughter.

"What's so funny, honey?" he asked. Then he noticed me and said, "Isla. Hi." There was an awkward pause between his words.

I said something like, "Scott, hello. I didn't realize it was you. But hey, these two are beautiful bundles of babychild."

"They're bundles of something," he said. "How are you?"

"I'm good. Just bought a place here in town."

"Congratulations, that's great."

Then one of the girls fell in the cart. Her butt landed on a loaf of bread, so she wasn't hurt, but she started crying nonetheless.

Scott said, "Good to see you, Isla," and reached for his daughter.

"Good to see you too," I said, and headed for the nearest cashier with only half of what I had on my shopping list. I couldn't get out of there fast enough, and I was still reeling when Evie and Annie came to my house a couple of hours later. I didn't say anything to them about seeing Scott, but I wasn't over the shock.

Tom called that night and we talked for a while. I didn't tell him about seeing Scott and his twins either, but I told him how scared Annie had looked, and how I'd torn into Evie with rabid, ruthless fury.

I said, "As if I know the first thing about raising a daughter. Even if I did know, even if I was Old Mother Hubbard and I'd raised a giant damn shoe full of happy, healthy, perfectly adjusted kids, Eve Ellen didn't deserve what I did to her today. Didn't deserve it and didn't need it."

Tom listened and made understanding noises on the other end of the line as I talked. When I finished, he said, "Isla, the Eve Ellen I know is really wise. She would understand that it was your grief talking. She would understand, and that would make your anger and your words less painful to her. She would feel the love underlying them."

"Thank you for saying that. Evie really is wise. She had to be hurt today, but I hope knowing how much I love her did help."

"I don't see how it wouldn't. You're wise too, Isla, and you've been around the grief block before. You know there's no getting through something like this without wishing you'd done some of it differently. Your heart is taking a horrible beating, horrible. Be gentle with yourself."

He was so caring, I felt guilty, like I was using him to vent and to comfort me. I said, "Tom, I'm sorry I've been so unavailable and can't tell you when I'll be ready for anything again. I'm not sure I ever will be ready. Everything's going to be different, and I don't want to string you along and make you think our situation will go back to where we were. I'll never be back to where I was before this."

He said only, "I know. But I'm here for you as a friend, when and if you want to talk."

"Thank you. Thank you for everything. Goodbye for tonight, but not for always, okay? No disappearing."

"Not for always. Goodnight, Isla."

THIRTY-SEVEN

The other big development the week I saw Scott and blew up at Evie: I heard from Pete. He texted me and asked if he could rent the lake house. I was in the bathroom, standing at the sink. I'd turned on the water to wash my face, then forgot what I was doing. The phone's buzz brought me back, but I was confused and replied to Pete with a question.

Me: *Rent the house?*

Pete: *I thought it might be available because I hear you've moved. I want to be close, in case I can help Eve Ellen and Greg, but I don't want to be underfoot. No problem if you or your sisters don't want to rent it. Really. I can get an Airbnb.*

Me: *Can I call you? Now? Texting is such a hassle.*

Pete: *It is a hassle and it'll be good to hear your voice.*

It was good to hear *his* voice. I told him my sisters would be happy to have him stay at the camp, and he didn't need to rent it. I filled him in on what I knew about Evie, from seeing and watching her. He told me what he knew from talking with her and Greg. He asked how I was doing. I tried to be stiff-upper-lipped, but my voice wobbled.

I said, "Oh, you know, it's hard. But you just keep putting one foot in front of the other."

"You do. That's the deal," he said.

"How are you?" I asked.

"I'm still trying to wrap my head around the fact that this is happening to them, that they have to go through it too. I'm hurting for them, and glad Evie asked me to come."

"Evie asked?"

"Yeah, though she circled around it, saying that if I had plans to come see Hank anytime soon, it would be good for Greg to see me too."

Eight days later, Pete was back in New York. He'd arranged for somebody to stay at his house and keep the newspapers from piling up on the driveway, and he'd driven practically straight through from California, stopping as seldom as possible for gas, food, and bathroom breaks. And just twice for a few hours of sleep and a shower. We'd made a plan that had him going directly to the lake, where I'd meet him after school, hand over the keys, and show him everything he'd need to know about the place.

Evie had another idea and sent a group text to get everybody on board with it.

Reunion! How about everyone comes over here and we bust out some of the frozen enchiladas Isla stuffed in my freezer? Greg will make margaritas. Annie and I will make guacamole and salad. Isla can bring the camp keys and some of her pickled things. Hank can bring Zoe and introduce her to Poppa Pete. We can play Hearts. Or get the gifted among us to make a little music. It'll be great. What do you say?

We all said yes. And we all stayed so late, it made sense to go along with Part Two of Evie's plan—Pete spent the night with her and Greg, then we all caravanned to the lake the next day to install him in the house and make sure he knew its quirks and workings. When we got there, another party ensued. Hank and I made lunch from the food I'd left in the cupboards and freezer, while Pete and Greg played guitar and harmonica, Zoe sang, and Evie curled up on the sofa with a cup of tea.

Pete couldn't get over how many songs Zoe knew, and he called out to Hank in the kitchen, "Holy moly, Hankster, where did we find her?"

Hank called back, "I'll give you the 'we' on this one, Pops."

Before we all left and went back to Saratoga, all but Pete, I went outside with him to show him where the circuit breaker box was hiding behind a dogwood that grew too close to the back of the house.

When I finished explaining that the breaker switch that was missing its label was for the attic, I told Pete, "That's it, all you need to know."

He said, "Thanks so much, Isla. It's going to be nice being here instead of a strange Airbnb."

"I'm glad you came," I told him, and then without warning, I started to cry. He hugged me close while I sobbed. When I pulled away, he took a blue bandana from his pocket and handed it to me. It was folded into a neat little square, and for some reason that struck me as significant. Like it was a totem with meaning. I was probably caught in the grip of a temporary insanity.

I looked at the little square lying on my open palm, and I said, "A tidy package in our untidy world. I don't want to mess it up."

Pete laughed, took the bandana, and dabbed at my wet face. Then he put it back in my hand, closed my fingers around it, and told me, "There, it's been besmirched. You can use it now."

I said, "Besmirched. Great word."

THIRTY-EIGHT

Like a brakeless car rolling downhill, Evie's decline picked up speed. She left the house less, and then not at all. She spent more time lying on the sofa or staying in bed. Greg had taken a leave of absence from work to be with her and Annie, and a hospice nurse had started coming in a couple of times a week to make sure her medications were working, keeping her as comfortable as possible.

Pete and I were there a lot, at Evie's request. We all played cards, watched baseball, listened to the guys play music. Pete and I tried to keep everyone fed, but nobody had much appetite. We did the laundry. Answered the door when neighbors brought food and flowers and asked how Evie was doing. I picked up her brothers at the airport when they came to see her. Pete picked up her prescriptions. We did whatever we could think to do. Folding clothes late one night, I told him, "I feel like we're bees in a hive, clustered around our queen, trying to keep her safe through winter, but there's no way it's going to work. We can't keep her safe."

The friends Annie had grown up with were away at school or too hard for her to face, but Hank and Zoe got her out of the house for hikes with them.

One day, Zoe had a gig singing at a club in town, and Evie insisted the rest of us "go hear and cheer her." The guys took Annie, but I stayed with Evie.

As soon as everyone was out the door, she said, "I want to take a bubble bath and go to bed. Let's go, little sister. Talk to me while I soak."

"I'm older than you are," I corrected her.

"One month older and two inches shorter," she corrected me.

I drew a bath while she undressed. Taking off the few clothes she was wearing—sweat pants, pullover hoodie, panties—took so much of her energy, once she was naked, she had to sit on the edge of the bed to recuperate before coming into the bathroom.

I helped her step into the tub and held onto her as she eased herself down into the water. I was shaken by how thin and frail she'd gotten.

Once she was settled and had the bubbles arranged where she wanted them, hiding her breasts and boney body, she asked, "So what's your current thinking about Pete and Tom?"

"No current thinking. I did sort of tell Tom we weren't going to go back to whatever it was we had. That it's over. God, that sounds dramatic. I didn't say it that way to him."

"So you're sure you're ready to close that door? You're positive he's not the guy and never can be?"

"You know I'm rarely sure about anything. I'm the world's worst equivocator. And when I am, I'm not always right. Surprise, surprise. I was certain Scott and I were an indivisible unit, bonded for eternity. Oops."

"You *can* waffle," Evie replied, "though sometimes you leap first and leave your waffling and worrying for the way down." She let the mention of Scott go by without comment.

Suddenly struggling to keep my voice steady and my tone matter of fact, I said, "But I'm unequivocally certain I don't know how to do life without you and I don't want to learn how."

She smiled, shook her head, seemed unable to speak, but then said, "I love you, sister."

Afraid I'd cry if I tried to say anything, I left it at the best smile I could manage. It probably looked more like a grimace.

Evie laid her head back on the edge of the tub and worked to get some good breaths, then scooped up some bubbles and blew them at me from her cupped hands. They made it as far as the floor beside my feet. She leaned over to look at them, said "Damn," put her head down again, and closed her eyes. Dropping her voice, she whispered, "This is a real pickle I'm in, right? The pickle of pickles, oh Pickle Princess Frances, lover of alliteration and words and fermented vegetables. I don't know how to do what comes next. My next big adventure. The great beyond. I don't know the first thing about it. What am I going to do without you when I get to wherever the hell it is I'm going?"

"That's possibly your worst pun ever," I told her. "And one of your reeking-bad worst attempts at humor."

"The hell part or the pickle?"

"Both."

"So shoot me."

I didn't have a comeback for her, so I didn't say anything, and after a while, she changed the subject and said, "You would have been a great mom, Isla. Better and more natural at it than I was. I wish it had happened for you."

"I would have been too neurotic to give my kids the exact right balance of guidance and freedom you've given Annie. You've always known when to let her wander on her own and when to force-march in a particular direction. You've been a perfect mom to her."

"There's no such thing as perfect. No perfect parents or anything else, but I've tried to be good with my girl."

"You *have* been good."

"I'm not ready to be done. I want to be here to celebrate her graduation, her first job, her wedding, her babies. If she gets married and has babies. I'm angry that you couldn't have kids. I'm angry about a lot. I really do believe it would be greedy and ungrateful to feel anything but fortunate for the life I've had. It would be like you were invited to a fabulous party and got pissy because you wanted to stay for three hours but had to leave after two. I know I should just be grateful that I got to be here at all, but I'm mad about having to leave. I am. I can't help it."

I was crying by then, she was crying.

She asked me, "Are you still angry I didn't tell you Scott was going to be a father as soon as I found out?"

I shook my head in reply and felt a new wave of shame about exploding on her the day I saw Scott and his girls.

She said, "I wish you'd heard it from me instead of Dale. It was just going to be so sad to see what it would do to you, I kept putting it off, waiting for the right time and rehearsing different ways to tell you. Then Dale did a Dale move."

"Evie, please never think about that again. I know why you waited and I'm sorry you were ever in that position. It must have felt awful."

She smiled in lieu of "thank you," and announced, "I need more hot water. Or up and out of here."

I reached for the faucet, but she stopped my hand.

"I'm done. Help me up. Pretty please."

I helped her out of the tub and handed her a towel.

"Thanks, love. Now can you get me one of Greg's t-shirts from our dresser, second drawer on the right, and some undies from the top drawer on the left?"

I went for the shirt and underwear as she dried off. When I brought them back, she was leaning over the sink, brushing her teeth, but looked up at me in the mirror. With toothpaste foam covering her lips, she asked, "Is my lipstick on straight?"

Once she was settled in bed, she said, "Isla, I want to ask you to do something for me."

"Okay," I replied.

"I want a party at the lake, at your place. No traditional funeral. A big party, and then my ashes spread on the water."

I started bawling again and couldn't look at her, but I nodded.

"Between now and then, I don't want to go back to the hospital, no matter what. If Greg or Annie panic and want me to go back, speak up for me if I can't speak for myself. Don't go ballistic on them, but help them stick to what I want."

I nodded again.

We didn't talk anymore. She fell asleep. Then I fell asleep beside her, lying on top of the covers. She was under them but hardly made a bump.

When everybody came home, Greg put a blanket over me and left me where I was, and he and Pete took the two sofas in the family room because they couldn't agree on who should take the guest bedroom. Hank and Zoe had gone back to the farm, and Annie went to her own bedroom, but then came back sometime in the middle of the night and crawled into bed with Evie and me.

In the morning, when Annie and I woke up, we looked at each other across Evie, who must have felt our eyes meeting above her. She opened hers and growled, "Who's been sleeping in my bed, Mama Bear said."

It was a Sunday, so I had that day with her, and then had to go back to work. It was the day she started saying no to food and stopped getting out of bed to go to the family room, to her spot on the sofa. She slept off and on until around four that afternoon, then asked me to help her take another bath. I thought she might want to talk again and might have something else she wanted to ask me to do for her because it was almost always Greg who helped her in the bathroom. But she told him, "Isla can take the bubble bath shift. Go make some music with Pete. Make it loud enough that I can hear you."

Once she was in the tub, the only thing she said was "Perfect," when I asked if the water was warm enough, and "All done," when she was ready to get out. She didn't talk, so I didn't talk.

After she was back in bed, I sat on the edge beside her and tidied the things on her nightstand to keep busy. I took a tissue from the box and unnecessarily polished the spotless glass in a framed photo of Annie. As I rubbed and checked to make sure I'd eliminated spots and dust that weren't there, I heard a voice in my head say, "Put the damn picture down and be real. Be honest, Isla."

So I put the photo down and asked, "Is there anything else you want me to do, Evie, anything you want besides the party?"

She said, "Keep Greg and Annie close. Keep them in your life. Love them."

I nodded and she smiled faintly. After a minute or two, I asked, "Are you scared about what comes next?"

The smile left her face and she said, "Just sad about leaving."

Her eyes were still open, but they were starting to droop.

I asked, "Ready for a nap?"

"I think so."

"Could you drink a smoothie first? You haven't had anything to eat today."

She shook her head and said she felt worse when she ate. I don't doubt that was true, but in hindsight, I believe she had also decided she didn't want her exit to drag on. She didn't want everyone waiting and fearing every breath might be her last, so she stopped eating and drank only small amounts of water after her decline reached a certain level.

Every day after school, I drove directly to her house and stayed until I needed to go to bed and try to get some sleep so I'd be ready for the reverse commute the next morning. I didn't qualify for family leave but called in sick for a couple of days until Evie told me that was "bad form" and if I was going to do it again, I needed to stay home, at my house, and at least pretend to be sick.

She said, "If you're too ill to teach, you're too ill to be around me. I have a vulnerable immune system, you know."

The night before my last day of school, she told me and Pete she needed some time with Annie. She said, "I need a few days with my lovely Ann Elizabeth, so I want you two to go have an adventure together and then come back and regale me with stories about it."

I turned so Pete couldn't see my face and gave her a look that said, "Are you kidding me?" Then I tried to sound cheerful as I choked out, "Right-tee-oh, Engineer Evie."

She moved her head back and forth on the pillow as if to say, "I'm not engineering anything. This isn't that."

I didn't doubt that she was being honest about needing time with Annie, and I was glad she was going to have it, but I also knew it would be just like her to take another shot at getting me hitched while she still could.

"Make it a real caper," she said. "Promise?"

I shook my head, "No," but Pete told her, "We'll have stories."

I asked, "You'll call when we can come back?"

She nodded, "Yes."

The next day, after the kindergarten graduation ceremony, I went to the lake and sat with Pete on the porch. We talked for hours. I told him about the party Evie wanted, and how worried I was about Annie. I asked how his kids were doing. He said they were much better than they had been for the first year or so after they lost Lainie. The new baby had been good for his daughter in Washington, and his younger girl, his punk rocker, had gotten engaged to her boyfriend, a wonderful guy, and she was up to her eyebrows in planning her punk rock nuptials.

Pete said, "I think it was hardest for Hank. You know you never get completely past it, but he's good now. What you see is what there is with the Hankster, and he seems happy, right?"

"He does, but he never said anything about meeting Zoe the night you did your open mic at Caffe Lena, so he's pretty good at keeping things to himself. I distinctly remember how he came back from the bathroom, Greg asked him, 'Everything come out alright,' and he answered, 'Every last drop,' and he didn't say one word about Zoe."

"You got me there, but it wasn't classic Hank. Which tells you he was speechless with love at first sight. Or first song."

"Did he tell you that?"

"No, but he told me about her while we were still on the road, and there was no missing how besotted he was. By the time we got home, they'd exchanged about a billion texts, and once he could retreat to the privacy of his bedroom, they talked on the phone every day."

"You're full of great words. 'Besotted' is a jewel. But do you think they're in it for the long haul? You think Zoe's your future daughter-in-law?"

"Let's give them a year or two before we start listening for wedding bells."

"Here's to them and young love," I said before drinking the last of my second glass of wine.

Pete poured a third one for me and we tried to make up stories we could tell Evie about the grand escapade we weren't having, tales she would know weren't true but might enjoy. We drank until I was too drunk to drive home.

I stayed that night, and the next six. I had a little bit of wrapping up to do at school but otherwise spent the entire banishment from Evie with Pete.

We slept in separate rooms the first two nights, and then he mentioned his family had a sleeping porch when he was growing up in Texas, and I asked if he wanted to try the one there at the lake. I said, "We can both sleep out there and tell Eve Ellen we went camping. We can say we slept in the open air. Technically, it's already true that we're camping because this whole place is a camp. So we won't be lying."

"Except," Pete said, "we'd have to fabricate another location for our campsite, somewhere out in the boonies, and what we did while we were there. She's going to ask us."

"Okay, so we'd have to lie a little."

"What about saying we had a Big Foot sighting? Or even an encounter with one? We could say we had a friendly visit with an enormous, hairy Big Foot. He brought us some fresh fish and we had dinner together. We communicated with hand signals, and when he left, he gave us hugs and grunted affectionately. What do you think?"

I laughed and said, "You're good at this."

"Would an alien abduction be better? You think it would it be more believable to have an alien spacecraft land in the middle of our campsite?"

"Yeah, I think aliens would be good."

"So let's go camping."

I took one of the twin beds in the middle of the porch, in case Pete wanted one next to a window, and he chose the bed that had been mine when I was a kid, the one with a view out toward Evie's old house. And while we were waiting for sleep each night, we worked on our story.

Because Pete was involved, it featured music, a sing-a-long with our alien abductors. To do my part and contribute, I told him I'd written a song that we could teach the aliens.

"It's sort of an *Isla Does Roger Miller* number," I said. Then, realizing that sounded like the title of a porn movie, I added, "Let's pretend I didn't say that. It came out wrong."

Pete just laughed.

"Before we teach my ditty to the extraterrestrials, it needs a third verse and you need to write it because I'm tapped out."

"Sing what you have," he said.

I told him, "That's not going to happen, but I'll read the words to you if you promise you'll come up with the last verse."

"I'll try if you'll sing."

So I got out of bed, went and got my journal from the previous summer, and sang what I'd written about a nitwit going to jail for grabbing a fish at a city aquarium.

When I finished, I said, "I think Monkey needs to come back. Inmate Monkey from the start should reappear before the end. In my expert songwriting opinion."

Before we finally fell asleep, our "Jail Song" was complete, with Pete's closing verse.

Dang everythang
Monkey won again
Playing checkers in this filthy pen

I swear he cheats and he lies through every game
He cheats and it always comes out the same
He gets my dessert
My pie or cake
After dinner
And that's hard to take
'Cause sweet is so hard to find when you're doing time

Oh-oh oh-oh oh oh oh
Every day here is just too long
So listen well, my friend, to the moral of this song
Take a net or don't bet your dessert next time!
I mean, don't go fishing where it's just plain wrong!
No, don't go fishing where it's just plain wrong!

Some mornings we would pick up where we'd left off with our story the night before, over coffee out on the front porch. Sometimes we'd talk about different things. One morning, after he got a text from one of his daughters, Pete asked me, "Did you ever think about having kids?"

My face reacted before I could stop it, and he said, "I'm sorry. I know better than to ask a question like that."

"No," I said. "It's fine. By now I should expect and be prepared for people to ask me about babies. I did want them, and tried to have them, but couldn't make it happen the old-fashioned way and we gave up on the other routes after slogging through the unique hell each one can be."

I told him about seeing Scott with his daughters, and how I'd exploded at Eve Ellen when she brought Annie over. We talked about grief and what a monster it could be, and how it could turn us into monsters. He told me about a time after Lainie died when he'd had enough of a rude cashier at a supermarket.

"I'd forgotten to write the bulk bin number on a bag of peanuts and this cashier was lecturing me about it and wouldn't let it go. He went on and on about how it made his job so much harder and kept everybody in line waiting when somebody forgot to write the bin number. So as I handed him some cash, I said, 'Go fuck yourself.' Then I turned to the people behind me and apologized for making them wait, and I turned the other way and told the poor bagger, 'Pardon my French and keep the change.' I grabbed my groceries and stomped out of the store in a huff."

I laughed and said, "Did your inner Southern gentlemen feel bad afterwards?"

"I think I wished I'd come up with something more original. If you're going to have a hissy fit, be creative. As for Southern, I know many a man and woman in Texas who'd say Texas is Texan, not Southern."

"And what do you say about it?"

"*Whatever.*"

I laughed again and asked him, "Do you think you'll ever move back there?"

"Not a chance."

"That's pretty definitive. Why not?"

"I've lived in California now for longer than I lived in Texas. I left there when I was eighteen. It's not my home anymore."

"Do you feel like a Californian?"

"No. California is where I live, but I can't say I feel like a Californian"

Then kind Pete said, "It must have been really hard for you, seeing your husband with those little girls."

I replied, "Yeah. If I hadn't been so stunned, I might have told *him* to go fuck himself, along with a few more choice words, as I hurled potatoes at him."

"Those choice words would have been what?"

"I hate you for leaving me alone to live with what we went through and going off to make a family with somebody else. I hate you for rising like a phoenix from our ashes. I hope you fall from the sky into a stinking sea of baby poop and pee and never get another whole night of sleep again."

"Do you hate him?"

"No. And I didn't really want to scream at him. Even back when I was at my angriest, early on after we split, the thing I wished for was one more conversation so I could ask him how it happened. So I could understand and sort of tie up our ending. I don't like the word 'closure,' but that's what I've wanted from the beginning."

"You never talked about it?"

"Nope. The night he broke the news that he was leaving, there wasn't any discussion. Just the announcement, followed by silent shock, a few tears, and some sniffles. The next morning, he was sitting in the kitchen eating breakfast and looking at his phone. I got some coffee, sat down, and said, 'Good morning. I guess we talk now.' He looked at me for what felt like a long time, then said, 'I can't do this,' and he stood up, put his dishes in the dishwasher, and left. Other than the bare minimum communication necessary to deal with the divorce legalities and practicalities, we never talked again. So I have a theory about what happened, but I don't really know for sure."

"What's your theory?"

"Well, my mother used to say, if you can't know the truth about something and can't just live with not knowing, then choose to believe the best thing you can believe. Or, to quote her more faithfully, if you can't just live with not knowing, you should work on that and learn to live with it, but in the meantime, choose to believe the most open-minded, optimistic, and respectful thing you can buy. The best I can believe about Scott is that he's a good man with both old and new pain, and when he started having an affair, he was trying to feel better. Then the affair took him to a place he hadn't planned."

Pete replied, "I wouldn't be surprised if that's what it's about a lot of the time, with other couples—somebody looking to feel better, trying to escape discomfort."

"We essentially grew up together, into adulthood anyway, and we knew one another as well as anybody can know another person, so I think I knew him well enough to know he never meant to hurt me and hated doing it. I think he got involved with his running friend as an escape during our fertility nightmare, and he didn't mean for it to turn out the way it did, but then he learned she was pregnant, and he knew how I was going to feel when I found out, so he couldn't bring himself to say anything. I get that. I get how hard it would have been to tell me after everything we'd been through. If I'd gotten pregnant by somebody else, I don't think I would have handled it any better. I wouldn't have been able to tell him because I wouldn't have wanted to see what it did to him."

Pete nodded.

I said, "I sound like I'm trying to convince myself, don't I?"

"I wouldn't say that, no. You sound like someone who wants to believe the best thing you can, like you said, and you're trying to do that. But I'm not convinced you would have ever found yourself having to tell your husband you'd had an affair, so I think you're being generous when you put yourself in his shoes and empathize with him."

"I'd like to believe I wouldn't have cheated on him, but I don't think I'm being generous. We were both in bad shape by the time we gave up on being parents. Then he found out he was going to be a father after all and he wanted to be with his daughters. Of course, he wanted to raise them. If it were me, I'd want that. Maybe he'd fallen in love with their mother, but even if he hadn't, once she was pregnant, there was no way he could have stayed with me. We'd been through too much to make it work. I know people do figure out how to stay together in situations like that, with everybody raising the baby in a blended family network, but we wouldn't have been able to do it. Scott knew that, so he left."

"With unfinished business, without that last conversation."

"Feels that way, but I do understand why he couldn't talk to me," I replied.

Then I asked, "How are you doing—about Lainie?"

"Seeing my kids living their lives again and being happy has helped. For a while there, I was worried about Hank. The first few months, he lit up a joint as soon as he opened his eyes every morning. He'd wake and bake, and never went anywhere without a supply of cannabis edibles. He thought it was cruel that Lainie got cancer after she'd worked so hard to recover from addiction, and his response, ironically, was to self-medicate."

I said, "Addiction?"

Pete nodded again, then explained, "She didn't fit what many people might think of or assume when they think about the opioid epidemic. She always came across as vibrant and focused. She was a respected surf coach, and a really active soccer and surf mom. But she struggled for a long time, finally got clean, quickly relapsed and overdosed, got clean again and had a great year, then got the cancer diagnosis. Hank thought that was so unfair. He and his sisters are good now. I miss their mom, but I've accepted what I can't change. I'm not trying to push reality away anymore, not trying to refuse it, so I feel better too."

"I knew about her breast cancer, but I had no idea about anything else. You've all been through so much."

"I had no idea either, not until she'd graduated from the pain meds her doctor had prescribed to cocktails of whatever she could buy on the street. Xanax, Percocet, Vicodin, Oxycontin, Fentanyl."

"How did it start?"

"The same way I think it does for many people—with the legal prescription from her doctor. Her back was hurt pretty badly when a car clipped her bike and threw her into a curb. The pain was debilitating and painkillers were the only way she could calm it down enough to eat or sleep or do anything at all. So she took them and they became a habit, and she became a statistic in the epidemic."

"Never just that. Never just a number," I said.

"No, never just a number," Pete echoed. "It wasn't for sure her back would ever recover completely. That played a number on her head and roused old demons, which never helps anything. Surfing had been her mental health therapy since she was a teenager, but she couldn't go out and ride waves or even lie on her board and paddle around in the water after the accident. Her back did eventually get better, and she was able to start surfing again, but the depression didn't go away. The demons stayed and she kept using drugs to cope with them."

"I can only imagine how hard all of that would have been. How long did it go on?"

"Six or so years. We didn't tell the kids until we felt confident her sobriety was going to hold and she wasn't going to relapse again. She'd been a functional addict and kept it together so well, nobody knew she had a problem until it was really bad. The kids sensed something was happening with her, but they didn't know what or how serious it was. Then we sat them down, told them the whole story, thinking it was something they could learn from, and a year later we had to tell them she had cancer."

"When we were talking in Philadelphia, you said she was a 'Rita Ballou.' If I understand it right, that song is about a woman who couldn't be caught, wouldn't let any guy catch her, but you caught Lainie. She let you."

"She did," he said. "Then she gave me the big slip. Gave us all the slip and went away. But we're doing fine. At least when it comes to her."

He didn't have to say, "Eve Ellen is a different story."

Instead, he said, "Tell me about the time you and Eve Ellen came back from Canada with four Saint Bernard puppies, and the time you were almost arrested in Iowa or wherever it was. Somewhere in the Midwest."

He'd heard a little bit about a pair of road trips Evie and I had taken and wanted me to tell him more. So I told him about how I'd schemed with Greg to kidnap Evie and take her on a girls' trip to Québec to celebrate her thirtieth birthday, and on the way home, not long after we came back across the border, she spotted a crate stuffed with the Saint Bernard pups abandoned on the side of the interstate. She yelled at me to pull over. And the next thing I knew, we had a car full of canine chaos. The crate wouldn't fit in my backseat or trunk, so we left it and drove the rest of the way with the pups crawling everywhere and chewing everything.

I told Pete, "They had heads as big as basketballs, according to Greg, but more like softballs or a large grapefruit in my memory."

He said, "So it could have been somewhere in between? How about soccer balls?"

"Softballs," I said. "Large grapefruit. That was big enough to be fearsome when all four of them were trying to climb from the backseat into the front and Evie had to keep them off me so I could drive and not kill us all."

Then I told him my version of the cross-country trip we did the summer after our first year in college, when, according to Greg, we were almost jailed for public nudity.

"The rules at my school," I said, "required first-year students to live on campus, in the dorms, and we weren't allowed to bring a car. So when the year was over, I peeled myself away from my college sweetheart and future husband, Scott, and flew home from Oregon. Evie flew home from California. We worked as counselors at a kids' sleepaway camp to earn gas money, then drove back across the country in the dead heat of summer with no air conditioner. We were in my AC-free, flaming orange, hatchback Pinto. Even with the windows wide open, we were roasting, so one day we decided, since we were in the middle of nowhere, a very flat nowhere, and we could see for miles, we would take off our shirts. I had on a black bra that looked like it could be a swimsuit top, and I wasn't worried about anybody seeing me in it, so I whipped off my shirt and tossed it into the backseat, but Evie had pulled off her bra somewhere in Nebraska and vowed she wasn't going to wear one for the rest of the trip, so when she took off her shirt, she was boobs to the breeze. She was riding shotgun and figured she could keep her top in her lap and easily put it back on fast enough if we saw somebody coming. In theory, that was true, and all was well for a while. We were cooler. Then I saw a car in the rearview mirror, so Evie grabbed her shirt and started to put it on, her right arm first, the arm beside the open window."

"Uh oh," Pete said.

"Yep. Out and away it flew, flapping in the wind. Gone. The car behind us, which had been a speck, sped up and turned out to be a highway patrol cruiser. Lights flashed. Swear words flew. I slowed down and pulled over onto the shoulder. Evie couldn't crawl into the back seat to get another top—not with her boobs hanging free and the cop behind us, able to see everything through the Pinto's huge back window—and I was yelling at her to hurry and fasten her seat belt so we didn't get a ticket for that too, so she scrambled to do the belt, then draped paper towels over her chest. When the cop came to my window, I told him what had happened. How we'd been so hot, we thought we might be sick, or we never would have done what we were doing. I tried to look as young and innocent and pure as I could. When I finished, he chuckled, then wrote a ticket for littering and told us to be more careful because the next officer we met might not be as understanding."

But talking about Evie started to feel like we were reminiscing about somebody who had already died, so I had to quit or take a break. I was so afraid it would be Greg who called, and he'd say she was gone.

When I couldn't talk about her anymore, I suggested we take the kayak out on the water and get some exercise. Pete wasn't a kayaker but got the hang of it right away, and for the next few days, we went paddling or for a walk every afternoon, then cooked dinner together and encouraged one another to eat. Cooking one evening, I found myself thinking he moved around the kitchen with the fluid ease and calm of a cat in its native habitat—a cougar or mountain lion—and there was a time when I would have been turned on by that, but I didn't feel anything that night. I couldn't feel physically attracted to Pete or wonder whether he was attracted to me. I couldn't be neurotic or self-conscious.

I couldn't care that he saw me in the same baggy flannel pajamas and old sweater every day. We always took our coffee out to the front porch, and early mornings were still chilly, so I needed the sweater and didn't care that it had a big moth hole on one shoulder. I didn't care that he always swapped his pajama pants for a pair of Levi's and put a denim shirt on over his t-shirt before he joined me outside.

One morning, I decided to clean out the garden beds and he helped. We pulled up the dead vegetable stalks and vines I'd left in the ground the previous autumn, and a new crop of weeds. I hadn't planted anything at either the camp or my new house in Saratoga that spring—it was the first year since college that I hadn't grown at least tomatoes. When we finished with the beds, I told Pete I was thinking about filling them with flowers, and asked if he was game to go to a nursery and do some plant shopping. He said he was, so I showered and dressed. Then we didn't go anywhere. We sat on the dock, ate tuna sandwiches, and shared the one bottle of beer in the fridge for lunch. We were both on a media hiatus, taking a break from reading and watching the news, so it was like we were isolated in a bubble for those six days.

On the seventh morning, over coffee on the porch, Pete said, "You sometimes call Eve Ellen 'Evie.' Is that what most people here call her?"

I replied, "No. Just me. If she had her druthers, everyone would use 'Eve' and lose 'Ellen,' but nobody does. She gave up pushing for that long ago. 'Eve Ellen' is who she's always been to her mother and brothers, and because everyone knew them before they knew her, since her brothers are older and started school before she did, that's who she's always been to everyone else too. She lets me get away with 'Evie' because I've been using it since we met. I picked it up from her father. It was his name for her, which is why she's never liked it—or stopped liking it after he left the family. I think, a part of her likes that I still use it because it reminds her of the good first years with her dad and the relationship they had when she was young."

"To my ear, 'Eve Ellen' is really pretty," Pete said.

"Mine too. It is pretty," I agreed.

"So, are you ready to tell me your racehorse name?"

I smiled, but couldn't muster much enthusiasm, and certainly couldn't go back to the coy way I'd flirtatiously withheld my pony name from him when he first tried to get it out of me. I said, "I am, by my mother's decree and my family's consensus, 'Unabridged.' As in, someone who doesn't do an abridged version of anything. Someone who speaks, feels, worries, reacts, ruminates, exaggerates, commits, cares, loves—"

In a flat drone, I started listing the things my mother said I always did to the nth degree. As I was droning on, my phone rang. It was Greg. He said we should come as soon as we could.

We were back in Saratoga in record time. Evie lasted another twelve hours. She was conscious when we arrived, but in and out after that. She didn't ask about our adventure, and we didn't tell her our camping story. She smiled when we came through the bedroom door, but never spoke.

Even smaller than she had been just the week before, she took up almost no space in the bed, so we were able to circle her with room to spare. Greg and Annie on opposite sides of the bed, Pete and I down at the foot. At first, we all sat upright, with our backs straight and our legs pretzeled, and Pete and I pretty much stayed that way, but Greg and Annie eventually laid down and curled around Evie like a pair of parentheses. When the end came, when our Eve Ellen slipped away, Pete pulled me close and held me. Greg and Annie, with Evie between them, held one another. Together, they held Evie.

THIRTY-NINE

Although she said she didn't want a traditional funeral, Greg wanted the party Evie had requested to start with something like a memorial service, and he wanted to do it right away because he hoped Annie would then go back to France and finish her degree. He said it would be good for her to get back to school. She said she would leave when she was ready. Maybe soon, maybe not.

"Hope springs eternal," he told me. "Let's do it and maybe she'll go."

Dale stepped in to help pull together the catering, rentals, and flowers, and to make sure everything looked beautiful. For the service, she had rows of chairs set up by the lake, close to the dock and facing down its length. And where the dock was wider at the start, with wings extending out to each side, she had a piano on the left wing, and, on the right, a guitar on a stand and a stool. Greg had asked Pete to do two songs, and Hank to accompany him.

Before the music, several people got up and spoke. They shared Evie stories. I couldn't, but Glyn and Dale did. One of Evie's brothers spoke for the family. He went last and delivered a beautiful eulogy. When he finished, Hank went up and sat at the piano, and Pete picked up the guitar and sat down on the stool. The first song was Kris Kristofferson's "A Moment of Forever," and almost from the start, I could hear muffled sounds from people trying not to cry. I looked over at Greg and Annie, and they were holding hands so tightly, Annie's knuckles were white. It was near the end of the second verse that a sob escaped from her. Greg's head was down, his shoulders were drawn forward, and his body was heaving, but he didn't make a sound. I started crying when Pete's voice broke on the words "I know."

Was it wonderful for you
Was it holy as it was for me
Did you feel the hand of destiny
That was guiding us together

You were young enough to dream
I was old enough to learn something new
I'm so glad I got to dance with you
For a moment of forever

Sometimes when you're cryin'
You're happy
Sometimes you're just cryin'
I know, I know

Come whatever happens now
Ain't it nice to know that dreams still come true
I'm so glad that I was close to you
For a moment of forever

Pete made it through the final verse without another break, but many of us had tears streaming down our faces by then. I'm guessing we all cried for Greg, as well as Evie. Pete had introduced the song with, "For Eve Ellen. From her Greg."

When Pete and Hank finished the song, they sat silently for a moment—everyone was silent—then Pete said, "My son and I are going to play some steppin' music now to carry you on up to the lawn. Eve Ellen wanted a party, so please go have something to eat and drink in her honor."

With that, he and Hank began Greg's second song request, John Prine's "I Just Want to Dance with You," and Evie's partygoers began their migration.

I took refuge at the buffet table, helping people fill their plates. And with my face arranged around what I hoped was a convincing smile, I repeated the same few lines and answered the same questions countless times.

Let me help you so you don't have to put down your drink.

Yes, you're right, this Cobb salad was her favorite.

How about some of this Waldorf too?

Just hang onto your wine and I'll load up your plate.

Yes, she loved a party.

Yes, she really did love it up here.

Tom came over, hugged me, and whispered, "I'm sorry, Isla." Then Dale appeared beside us, handed me a glass of wine, and told me I had to have something to eat. Before turning away to leave me in Dale's command, Tom gently squeezed my arm, but he didn't say anything more.

FORTY

Throughout the day, the urn holding Evie's ashes sat on a small table at the far end of the dock. That evening, after everyone else left, Greg, Annie, Evie's father and brothers, Pete, and I went and scattered her on the lake. To be more precise—Evie-precise—we gathered around Greg as he emptied the urn, pouring slowly so the ashes would land lightly on the water's surface and drift with its movement. I don't know about everybody else, but I never thought to check whether it was legal to do that. Or maybe I didn't check because I feared it was illegal and I knew I'd be torn about whether we should go ahead anyway. I still don't know if we broke any laws. It was what Evie wanted, so it's what we did.

Then we went up to the house for several more hours of drinking and telling stories. I'd had my one safe glass of wine earlier, so I stuck to water. I wanted to be sharp enough to get everyone settled in beds when they were ready for sleep.

In the morning, Pete and I were the first to get up. We tried to be quiet as we gathered empty wine and beer bottles, washed and dried dishes, and put the place back together. We were standing at the sink, finishing up, when I told him I wanted him to stay.

I said, "I don't think you should go back to California. Be here with us. With me. We make a good team."

"We do," he replied.

I looked up from the dish I'd been drying to see if I could read on his face whether he would go or stay, and he leaned over and kissed me. It lasted only a moment because we could hear footsteps starting down the stairs, and it was only our mouths that touched because our hands were full, but it was more than a peck. Much more. There's no exaggeration when I say it was far and away the most meaningful, wonderful kiss I'd ever received.

Eve Ellen Minton was engineering until the end. But if engineering is problem solving through applied science and math—or *solution creation* based on analysis and logic, as one online expert informed me—I'd say Evie was more than an engineer. Or that she was an engineer who worked from her heart as much as her head.

If I could talk with her now, if she could come back and have one more conversation with me, I'm afraid there wouldn't be enough time for everything I'd want to ask and tell her. Of course, no amount of time would provide closure because there's no such thing. I'll never get over losing her. But if I could talk with her again, I'd have endless questions about where she is, what it's like, what she does there, how she's doing. I'd update her on Greg and Annie, and assure her they're okay, all things considered. I'd tell her how Pete and I are doing, and how she was the perfect zipper for us.

But maybe she knows.

Thank you, Evie. Thank you.

THE MUSIC

King of the Road (Roger Miller)

Husbands and Wives (Roger Miller)

Dang Me (Roger Miller)

Chug-a-Lug (Roger Miller)

Moon River (Henry Mancini, Johnny Mercer)
Recording by Audrey Hepburn

Ring of Fire (Merle Kilgore, June Carter)
Recording by Johnny Cash

Walkin' in the Sunshine (Roger Miller)

Rita Ballou (Guy Clark)

My Darlin' Hometown (John Prine, Roger Cook)

My Favorite Memory (Merle Haggard)

My Favorite Picture of You (Guy Clark, Gordie Sampson)

Sugar Moon (Cindy Walker, Bob Wills)
Recordings by K.D. Lang (1988) and Willie Nelson (2006)

Waltz Across Texas Tonight (Emmylou Harris, Rodney Crowell)
Recording by Emmylou Harris, Dolly Parton, and Linda Ronstadt

Wake Up Time (Tom Petty)

Walkin' After Midnight (Alan Block, Donn Hecht)
Recording by Patsy Cline

Wildflowers (Tom Petty)
Recordings by Tom Petty (1994) and The Wailin' Jennys (2017)

It Takes All Kinds to Make a World (Roger Miller)

Kansas City Star (Roger Miller)

Samba Pa Ti (Carlos Santana)

You'll Lose A Good Thing (Barbara Lynn, Huey P. Meaux)

Help Me Make It Through the Night (Kris Kristofferson)
Recordings by Kris Kristofferson (1999), Sammi Smith (1970), Elvis Presley (1972), Tammy Wynette (1974), Willie Nelson (1980), and Lady Antebellum (2017)

I Got Rhythm (Ira Gershwin, George Gershwin)
Recording by Ella Fitzgerald

A Moment of Forever (Kris Kristofferson, Danny Timms)
©1994 Jody Ray Publishing (BMI), Jody Ray Publishing obo Knode Music (BMI). All Rights Reserved. Used By Permission.

I Just Want to Dance with You (John Prine, Roger Cook)

ACKNOWLEDGEMENTS

My eternal thanks to you, Cal and Jules, for giving of your time and eyesight to read drafts at various stages. Your feedback improved the final draft and made working on this project hugely more fun.

My boundless thanks to you, Jack, for helping and inspiring me always and in more ways than I have words to describe, and for being my creative compass and battery charger.

Gratitude and ovations to all the songwriters and music makers who have inspired and uplifted me, who have made my good times better and my hard times easier. With a special standing ovation to Yo-Yo Ma for The Bach Project and Songs of Comfort.

Thank you to my mother for filling our home and my head with tunes. When I was young, books and music so outweighed television at our house, it wasn't until after I'd been in school for two or three years, exposed to other kids and their talk about TV shows they loved, that I came to understand televisions weren't empty boxes on all but certain occasions, such as Sunday nights, when, for a short time, our big boxy set would magically fill up with *The Wonderful World of Disney*. TV shows came and went, but music was ever-present under my mother's roof, and she opened my ears and mind to all kinds. She was really something, my mom, and without her *What Do You Do?* wouldn't exist.

ABOUT THE AUTHOR

Rosebud Birdshaw Mapel has written about everything from new technologies to national parks and wildlife for an array of clients. *What Do You Do?* is her third foray into fiction, following two she credits to her alter ego, Buddy Mapel. First, *The Quail Runner*, a mystery set among the mountains, mesas, and river valleys of Northern New Mexico. Then, *The Answer*, a novella in the form of a letter written by a father to his son in an attempt to answer a question he once dodged.

Rosebud, aka Buddy, was born in the Rio Grande Valley and has since lived in a number of states on both the Pacific and Atlantic coasts of the United States.